THE LEGEND OF THE Monkey King

Wu Cheng'en and Ruo Gu

illustrated by Zdenka Krejčová

TREASURE PRESS

Original Chinese text by Wu Cheng'en and Ruo Gu as
Xiyouji gushi ('Stories from the Journey to the West')
Translated from Chinese into Czech and adapted
by Zdenka Heřmanová-Novotná
English version based on the translation by George Theiner
Graphic design by Václav Konečný

Published in Great Britain in 1992 by
Treasure Press
An imprint of Reed International Books Limited
Michelin House
81 Fulham Road
London SW3 6RB

ISBN 1 85051 662 6

Printed in Czechoslovakia by Naše vojsko, Prague
1/23/07/51-01

Contents

Introduction

Stories about the creation of the world have been told in China for thousands of years. One of these legends tells of P'an Ku.

In the very beginning the world was just an egg. One day the eggshell split in two. The top half became the sky and the bottom half became the earth. Out of the egg came P'an Ku. Each day P'an Ku grew taller and each day the sky became higher and the earth thicker. After 18,000 years P'an Ku died and his body broke into many pieces. His head became the sun and moon, his blood became the rivers and the seas, his hair became the forests, his sweat the rain, his breath the wind, his voice thunder and his fleas became animals and people.

Of all the animals which were important to the ancient Chinese, none was more important than the twelve beasts of the Chinese calendar, first established in 2637 BC. In this calendar one creature represented each year in a twelve-year cycle. If a person was born in the year of a particular animal, they shared some of the characteristics of that animal and the animal also influenced their destiny. The animals of the Chinese calendar are the rat, ox, tiger, hare, dragon, snake, horse, sheep, monkey, rooster, dog and pig. The year 2000 will be the year of the dragon. The year 2004 will be the next year of the monkey.

The stories in this book are about a monkey, and not just any monkey — they tell of the deeds of a very special monkey. Like the creator of the world, P'an Ku, Monkey was also hatched from an egg on top of the magic Mountain of Many Flowers. Out he sprang and at once set off to explore the world. Like many other mythical beasts, Monkey has special powers which ordinary monkeys do not have. Soon he is the king of the monkeys, but this is not enough for him. Monkey wants more, much more. In fact, he wants everything. Most of all, he wants to live forever and he sets off on an exciting journey in search of immortality.

Right from the start, Monkey has none of the noble qualities that we would expect of a traditional hero. Monkey is arrogant, boastful, selfish, greedy and violent. He is a liar, a cheat and a thief and he never feels remorse for any of his crimes, only annoyance when things don't go his way. He is also very clever and with the help of his special magic power can outwit anyone who opposes him.

As well as his magic powers Monkey decides he needs a special weapon and he visits the Dragon King of the Eastern Sea. Here he behaves very rudely and bullies the Dragon King into handing over a magic cudgel which only Monkey can lift and which changes size at his command. The Dragon King and his brothers are so angry at Monkey's behaviour that they complain about him to the Jade Emperor himself.

Most people would be afraid of the anger of so great and powerful a person as His Holiness the Jade Emperor, but not Monkey. He demands an important post in Heaven and is put in charge first of the imperial stables and then the Peach Orchard belonging to the Empress. But Monkey is far from grateful and he behaves so badly and is so boastful and arrogant that soon complaints about him are pouring in from all sides. The Jade Emperor decides it is time to arrest Monkey and punish him, but by now Monkey's powers are so great that none of the Emperor's warriors can subdue him.

He is finally caught through a trick more powerful than one of his own and is taken before the Supreme Buddha himself for judgement. Even now he has not learned his lesson. Faced with the all-powerful Buddha he is not in the least humble or repentant. He continues his arrogant boasting and finally insults the Buddha so much that Buddha imprisons him. At last Monkey has met his match and he is banished to a prison cell.

Luckily, throughout all his wrongdoing, the Star of Long Life and Kuan-yin, the Goddess of Compassion, have tried to prevent him from making some of his worst mistakes and have then come along afterwards to try to put things right again — usually to no avail. Even when he is in prison Kuan-yin does not forget him. She persuades Buddha to give Monkey a second chance by giving him a dangerous and difficult task to perform.

When Monkey is let out of prison he is so delighted that he promises to do anything, but he has no intention of keeping his word. It is only when Kuan-yin places him under a strong magic spell that Monkey falls in line. He is sent to protect the monk Tripitaka and his two servants on their journey to collect holy scriptures which will be of great benefit to the whole world.

They make an odd set of travelling companions. Tripitaka is an ordinary mortal without any magic powers to protect him. He is honest, innocent, helpless and a man of peace and goodwill. From the start of their journey the monk is shocked by Monkey's wicked and violent ways. Monkey is equally scornful of Tripitaka's lack of fighting spirit and the way he trusts everyone they meet. The party of travellers have many adventures on their journey and Kuan-yin's faith in Monkey is repaid time after time. As they stumble into one trap after another, are attacked and robbed, it is always Monkey who saves them and protects them from the worst disasters. Although he continues his tricks as a thief and a cheat, he also learns about loyalty to his master and to be brave in the defence of others and helpful to those who cannot help themselves.

At the end of Monkey's adventures he has done something to help the whole world, not just himself. Although his character is still not totally admirable, he is a little more of a real hero than when he started out.

The Birth of the Stone Monkey

Long, long ago when the legendary Creator, P'an Ku, first divided the earth and the sky, the world was made up of four continents, and in one of these was the land of Ao-lai. It was bounded on all sides by the sea and out of the sea there rose the Mountain of Many Flowers, which was famous far and wide. On the top of this mountain was a magic rock. One day this rock burst apart and out fell a round stone egg. Fertilised by the wind, the egg came to life and hatched into a monkey, who was named Stone Monkey. The monkey possessed all five senses and four limbs. He quickly learned to climb and walk, and he made a deep bow to the four quarters of the earth.

The monkey bounded over the hills, feeding on grasses and roots, drinking from the mountain streams, gathering mountain flowers, and looking for fruits. The baboons and all the other monkeys were his relatives; the wolves, tigers, panthers and deer were his friends. At night he made his bed under the rock cliffs, by day he wandered over the hills and into the caves. He had no idea of time, and so one winter followed another, year succeeded year.

One very hot morning the monkeys took shelter from the sun in the shade of a pinewood. They climbed the trees and scrambled among the branches, picked flowers and looked for fruit, played marbles and tag, made hollows in the sand and built sandcastles. They chased dragonflies and caught grasshoppers, occasionally looking up at the sky and bowing to the gods. Then they started tearing down tendrils of ivy, making grass cushions, grooming each other's fur, clipping their nails, pulling and pushing and jostling and pinching. When they had frolicked to their hearts' content in the shade of the pine trees, they went to bathe in a mountain stream. The water came rushing down from the rocks like a rolling wave, and broke into a fine spray.

"Where does this stream come from?" the monkeys asked. "As we have nothing to do this morning, why don't we go upstream and find its source? That ought to be fun."

Whooping for joy, they took their young by the paws and, calling out merrily to each other, set out on their journey, clambering up the hillside until they reached a waterfall whose waters came tumbling from far above them.

"How splendid! How splendid!" cried the monkeys, clapping their paws enthusiastically. "It comes from somewhere deep inside the mountain and flows all the way to the ocean. If any of us were bold enough to get through to the very source and back again without ruffing a hair of his body, we would make him our king!"

They repeated their challenge three times, and suddenly the Stone Monkey leapt forward, crying: "I will go!"

He narrowed his eyes and prepared to jump. Then with a mighty leap he vanished behind the waterfall. After a while he opened his eyes and, looking round, saw no water, but a great bridge glittering in front of him. Monkey stretched himself. Taking a closer look at the bridge he realised it was made of polished iron. The water under it flowed in cascades from a hole in the rock and swirled under the arches. Monkey climbed up on the bridge, leant over the edge and, looking even more closely, was astonished to see a beautiful house.

He jumped down from the bridge, and saw a stone plaque with an inscription in large letters: "This Water Curtain Cave on the magic Mountain of Many Flowers leads to Heaven".

Monkey was beside himself with excitement. He turned round quickly, closed his eyes, and crouched in readiness for a jump. He flew back through the waterfall like an arrow and, gasping for breath, cried: "A miracle, it's a miracle!"

All the monkeys crowded round him, showering him with questions: "What is it like on the other side? Is the water very deep?"

"There is no water there at all," the Stone Monkey explained. "There is only an iron bridge and behind it a beautiful house! Heaven must have intended it for us."

"What kind of a house?" asked the monkeys eagerly.

"The water flows out of a hole in the rock, swirls under the bridge and conceals the entrance. There are flowers and trees on either side of the bridge, and a stone chamber behind the entrance with stone couches, stone tables, stone chairs, dishes and cups, a stone cauldron and a stone oven. In the middle of this chamber there is a stone tablet with the inscription: 'This Water Curtain Cave on the magic Mountain of Many Flowers leads to Heaven'. It would make a perfect home for us. There is room for hundreds, even thousands of monkeys, young and old. Let's all go there straightaway. We shall be well sheltered from every kind of weather."

The monkeys were overjoyed. "Lead the way!" they cried.

The Stone Monkey again closed his eyes, crouched, and cried: "Follow me!" He jumped through the waterfall in one bound. The bolder monkeys followed him at once, but the more timid ones only stretched out their necks and then drew them back again, scratched behind their ears and rubbed their cheeks. Then they too plucked up courage and, with a loud screech, threw themselves forward. In a flash they were over the bridge and immediately started to fight each other for the couches and the oven, seizing dishes

and plates and carrying them from one place to another. They got up to every kind of mischief, and were never still for an instant, until they were all completely worn out.

The Stone Monkey placed himself at the head of the throng and said: "Gentlemen! A monkey's word is as good as his bond. You swore that if anyone succeeded in getting through the waterfall and back again, you would make him your king. I have done that, and, what is more, I have found you a pleasant home in which you can bring up your families. Why then do you not bow to me as your king?"

Hearing this, the monkeys all bowed low before him. Then they stood in a line according to age and again bowed and hailed their new king.

Thus the Stone Monkey won the throne of the Monkey Kingdom. He forbade them to use his old name and invented the new title of "Handsome Monkey King". He chose his courtiers and ministers from among the baboons, chimpanzees and monkeys, and wandered about with them by day over the Mountain of Many Flowers, returning for the night to the Water Curtain Cave. They lived in perfect harmony, and did not mingle with any other beasts or birds. The Monkey King ruled everything and his subjects were happy and contented.

Several hundred years passed by with the Monkey King enjoying these innocent pleasures. Then one day, when all the monkeys were feasting, he was suddenly overcome with sorrow and tears came into his eyes. The monkeys gathered round him at once and asked what was making him so sad.

"This is a merry occasion," replied the Monkey King, "but I was suddenly overcome by a fear of the future, and that is why I am unhappy."

"Your Majesty is very hard to please," said the monkeys, laughing. "Day after day we hold fine feasts on sacred mountains, in ancient caves and on legendary islands. We are not ruled by the Unicorn or the Phoenix, nor any human king. Such freedom is an immense blessing. So why should you feel so sad and apprehensive?"

"True," replied the Monkey King, "we are not bound by human laws, or governed by the world of the beast or the bird. But there will come a time when we shall grow old and weak, and ultimately die. I must find out if it is possible for me to live

forever among the gods rather than be born again on this earth."

Hearing this, the monkeys covered their faces with their paws and wept pitifully. Sorrow spread throughout the Monkey Kingdom.

Suddenly, from among the monkey throng, a big, broad-chested monkey sprang out, crying in a loud voice: "Your Majesty, if you fear for the future, then that means that a desire for the everlasting life called immortality has been kindled within your heart. In the world there are three kinds of creatures that are not subject to the King of Death."

"Which are they?" asked the Monkey King.

"Buddhas, Immortals, and Sages," said the monkey. "They are not bound by the laws of birth and death, being as eternal as Heaven and Earth, the hills and the rivers."

"But where am I to look for them?" the Monkey King enquired.

"Here in this world of ours, in the caves of the sacred mountains."

The Monkey King was delighted to hear this.

"Tomorrow," he said, "I shall leave you, go down the mountain and across the sea.

If need be I shall travel to the end of the world to find these Immortals. From them I will learn the art of eternal youth and everlasting life, and thus escape the clutches of the King of Death."

The monkeys clapped their paws and shouted their approval: "Splendid! Splendid! Tomorrow we will scour the mountains and gather fruits and berries to hold a great farewell banquet."

The next day they went out to gather peaches and rare fruits, lilies and orchids, and many other flowers and herbs which they laid out carefully on the stone tables. Then they brought delicious meats and fine wines. They sat the Monkey King at the head of the table and took their places according to their age. All day long they paid homage to their ruler with fruit and flowers.

Next day the Monkey King rose early and ordered the monkeys to make him a raft of dry pine trunks. He also asked them to find him a tall bamboo for a pole, and to prepare some food and fruit for the journey. Then he stepped onto the raft and pushed off with all his might, letting the wind carry him across the sea in the direction of the Southern Continent. Luck was with him, for a strong south-east wind blew him towards the north-western shores which are the frontier of the Southern

Continent. Coming close to land, the Monkey King tested the water with his pole. Finding it shallow, he left the raft and waded ashore. On the beach there were people fishing, shooting ducks, collecting oysters and draining salt from the sea.

The Monkey King pulled faces and performed strange antics as he approached them. This frightened the people so much that they dropped their baskets and nets and scattered in great haste. One was not quick enough, however, and the Monkey King caught him, took his clothes and put them on in the way he had seen people do. With a rolling gait he travelled through towns and villages, listening to the people in the market-places in order to learn the ways and language of humans. Day and night he thought only of the Immortals from whom he might learn how to be young forever and thus achieve immortality or everlasting life.

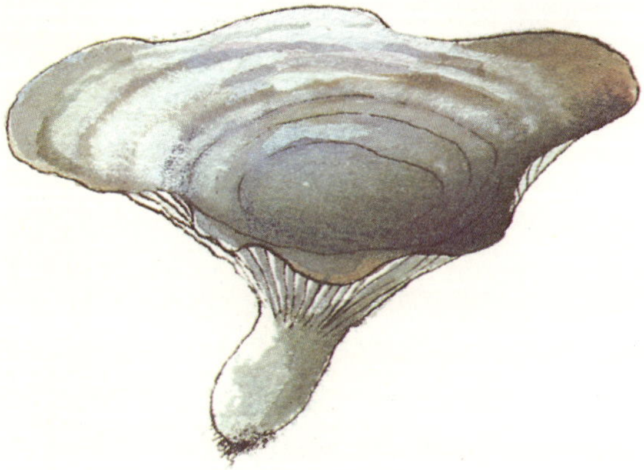

The Monkey King Looks for a Teacher

The Monkey King searched for the Immortals without success. For eight or nine years, he travelled across the Southern Continent, moving from town to town and village to village, until he found himself on the shores of the Western Ocean. He felt sure that beyond this ocean he would find an Immortal; so, he made himself a new raft and again let himself be carried by the waves, until he reached the Western Continent. Going ashore he continued his search. Soon he saw a high mountain covered with deep, mysterious-looking woods. The Monkey King was not at all afraid of wolves, tigers or panthers, and so he climbed to the very top of the mountain and looked round.

In the distance he could see a woodcutter cutting brushwood. He sprang forward into the forest and approached the man, telling him he was looking for an Immortal who would be his master. He discovered that an honoured Immortal lived near by.

"His name is Patriarch Subodhi," said the woodcutter. "You'll find him at the Holy Terrace Mountain, in a cave called the Cave of the Three Stars and the Crescent Moon. He has had countless disciples, and even now he has thirty or forty of them. Just follow this path south for about two miles and you will get there in no time at all."

The Monkey King thanked the man and said goodbye. Emerging from the wood, he took the path leading to the south. Having climbed uphill for about two miles he found the cave the woodcutter had told him about. But the door was locked, everything was quiet, and there was nothing to show that anyone lived there. The Monkey King looked around and, on top of the cliff above him, he saw a stone tablet about eight feet wide. On it was carved an inscription in large letters which said, "Cave of the Three Stars and the Crescent Moon on the Holy Terrace Mountain".

He gazed at the door for a long time, not daring to knock. Then he jumped up into a pine tree and began to eat the cones. Before long he heard the door creak and then saw it open. A beautiful boy came out of the cave. He could see at once that the boy was no ordinary mortal.

"Who is making a nuisance of himself out here?" the boy shouted.

The Monkey King leapt down from the tree, and said with a bow: "I am a disciple who has come to learn immortality.

I should not dream of making a nuisance of myself."

"So you want to learn immortality?" asked the boy, smiling.

"Yes, that's right," said the Monkey King.

"Our master has just finished resting and is about to teach. Before starting the lesson, however, he told me to open the door, as there was someone outside waiting to become a disciple and that I was to welcome him. Did he mean you?"

"Of course he did," laughed the Monkey King.

"Then you must follow me," said the boy.

The Monkey King brushed the dust off himself and followed the boy into the cave. Huge chambers and halls opened out before them as they went deeper and deeper into the earth; he saw pearl-studded bowers, jewelled halls, many arcades and private rooms. At last they came to a platform of green jade, upon which was seated the Patriarch Subodhi. Thirty more Immortals stood on either side of him.

The Monkey King bowed low, knocking his head three times upon the ground.

"Oh, Master!" he cried. "Your pupil has come to pay his deepest respects!"

"Where do you come from?" asked the Patriarch. "First tell me your name, and then pay your respects once more."

"I come from the land of Ao-lai, from the Water Curtain Cave on the Mountain of Many Flowers."

"Out with him!" shouted the Patriarch Subodhi. "He is nothing but a cunning liar and is not interested in learning."

The Monkey King beat his forehead against the ground.

"Humble disciple that I am, I speak

nothing but the truth, Master. I have not told you a single lie."

"The land of Ao-lai lies beyond two oceans and the whole of the Southern Continent. How could you have got here?"

"I floated over the seas and oceans and wandered over the continents for ten years before I reached you."

"Very well, I suppose it is possible if it took you that long," said the Patriarch. "What is your name?"

"I have no name to speak of. When someone abuses me, I am not annoyed. If someone hits me, I am not angry, I even bow to him in return. All my life I never had a special name."

"I don't mean a nickname," said the Patriarch. "What were your parents called?"

"I have neither a father nor a mother," said the Monkey King.

"Did you grow on a tree then, that you have neither a father nor a mother?"

"No, not on a tree. I grew out of a stone. All I remember is that there was a magic stone on the Mountain of Many Flowers. One day it burst open and I came out of it."

"That means he was born out of a union of Heaven and Earth," thought the Patriarch Subodhi, but all he said was: "Show me how you walk."

The Monkey King straightened himself, gave a little jump and, swaggering mightily, walked up and down in front of the Patriarch.

"You have a body as ugly as a monkey's. I shall give you the surname of Sun, meaning Monkey."

"How splendid! Now at last I know what my surname is! Thank you, dear Master, a thousand times. And now that I have a surname, perhaps you would be kind enough to give me a first name as well, to make it all sound better."

"I give my disciples names according to the twelve virtues. You are a disciple of the tenth order."

"What are the twelve virtues?" asked the Monkey King.

"The twelve virtues are Generosity, Greatness, Liveliness, Prudence, Wisdom, Sincerity, Naturalness, Moderation, Benevolence, Understanding, Perfection and Knowledge. Yours is Understanding and I therefore give you the name of Wu-k'ung which means He Who Understands Emptiness."

"Excellent!" rejoiced the Monkey King. "As from today I am called Sun Wu-k'ung, He Who Understands Emptiness."

He was delighted with his new name and hopped about happily in front of the Patriarch, bowing deeply all the time to show his gratitude. The Patriarch Subodhi then ordered his disciples to take the Monkey King out by the other door and show him how to sweep the floor, how to reply to questions, how to conduct himself and how to enter and depart. The disciples took the Monkey King out and taught him everything.

When they had finished, the Monkey King bowed deeply to them and went out into the passage to find himself a place to sleep. Next day he joined the other disciples in learning good manners and correct speech. He learned to write, listened to the teaching of the holy scriptures and burned incense. The days passed, each one just like the last. In his spare time he swept the floor and dug the garden, grew flowers and tended the trees, gathered and burned brushwood and brought water. He had everything he needed. Before he knew it, some seven or eight years had passed. One day the Patriarch Subodhi sat himself on his throne and, calling all the Immortals to him, began to lecture them.

The Monkey King listened intently and was so pleased with what he heard that he began to scratch behind his ears and rub his cheeks in delight. His eyes danced with mischief and he could not keep his hands

and feet still. The Patriarch noticed this and rebuked him: "Why do you not listen to my lecture instead of jumping about like a fool?"

"Your disciple is listening most carefully," the Monkey King apologised, "but just now, Master, I was overcome with joy, and that is why, without knowing it, I started to jump and dance about. Please forgive me if I annoyed you."

"What kind of wisdom do you still hope to learn from me?" demanded the Patriarch.

"I leave that to you, esteemed Master," replied the Monkey King modestly. "I shall be happy to learn anything you will teach me."

"There are three hundred and sixty schools of wisdom," said the Patriarch Subodhi. "Each of them leads to salvation. Which do you want to study?"

"Whichever you think best, Master. I shall gladly follow your advice," said the Monkey King, humbly.

The Patriarch suggested several different skills, but to the Monkey King none of them seemed good enough; they all lead only to a longer life, not to immortality. At last the Patriarch lost his patience. He hissed angrily, stepped down from his platform and, picking up a ruler, struck at the Monkey King's head.

"You wretched monkey!" he cried. "You won't learn this, you won't learn that, what do you want to learn?" And he hit him three times over the head. Then, dismissing the other disciples, he folded his hands behind his back and strode out, banging the door behind him. The other pupils were very upset by this and turned indignantly on the Monkey King, but he did not mind and just kept on smiling as though nothing had happened.

The Monkey King believed that he had succeeded in solving the Patriarch's secret signs, and for that reason he was feeling very pleased with himself. That was why he did not argue with anyone, but suffered their abuse in silence. By striking him three times, folding his hands behind his back and slamming the door, Monkey thought the Master had indicated that he wanted him to come in by the back door at the third watch of the night to receive instruction on how to become immortal.

The Monkey King Learns Magic Changes

For the rest of that day the Monkey King frolicked with the other disciples in front of the cave. He kept looking up at the sky, impatiently awaiting the night. As soon as it grew dark he lay down to sleep with the others, closed his eyes and, breathing evenly, pretended to be asleep. There was no night-watchman in the mountains to call the hours, and so the Monkey King had no idea of the time. Instead, he counted how many times he breathed in and out, and when it seemed to him that it must be about midnight he got up very quietly, opened the front door and went out. Going round to the back entrance he found it was only half shut.

"The Master really means to teach me immortality," he said to himself joyfully. "That is why he has left the door open."

He pushed the door open quietly, crept in, and went up to the Master's bed. The Patriarch was sleeping curled up, with his face to the wall, and the Monkey King didn't dare wake him. He knelt by the side of the bed and waited. Presently the Patriarch woke, stretched his legs, and murmured to himself: "Ah me, how hard it is! The world's ways are difficult to understand. Never pour the Elixir of Life as if it were an ordinary liquid. He who entrusts the secret of the dark forces to unworthy ears is making his jaws do unnecessary work and talks his tongue dry to no purpose."

"Master," said the Monkey King softly, "your disciple has for some time now been kneeling by your bed."

Subodhi recognised the voice and, throwing aside the covers, sat up in bed and cried: "What is it you seek here, Monkey? Get back to bed!"

"Esteemed Master, did you not hint yesterday when you punished me with the ruler that I was to come to you at midnight by the back door and that you would reveal to me the secret of immortality?"

The Patriarch was delighted to hear this, realising that Monkey must after all be a natural product of Heaven and Earth, for otherwise he could not possibly have understood the secret signs.

"There is no one to overhear us, I am quite alone," the Monkey King went on quietly. "Take pity upon me, Master, and tell me the secret of eternal life. I shall never forget your kindness."

"You understood the secret signs, and

so it seems it is your destiny. I am glad. Come closer and listen carefully; I shall reveal to you the secret of immortality."

The Monkey King beat his head upon the floor to show his gratitude. He knelt in front of the bed, and gave all his attention to the Patriarch, who gave him the secret formula. Overjoyed, the Monkey King carefully memorised the formula, thanked the Patriarch profusely and left by the back door. Looking round he saw a pale light in the eastern sky and a golden glow in the west. He went back to the front door, opened it cautiously, and returned to his bed. Making a rustling noise with his covers, he cried: "Get up, all of you, it is daylight already!"

All the others were still fast asleep, and they had no idea of the Monkey King's good fortune. He, for his part, could do no work that day, as he was too excited by his secret knowledge. When dusk came again he went to bed at once.

Three years went swiftly by. The Patriarch Subodhi again ascended his jewelled throne and lectured his disciples. Suddenly he interrupted his discourse and asked: "Where is my disciple Sun, He Who Understands Emptiness?"

"Here!" said the Monkey King, who was kneeling in the first row.

"What new knowledge have you gained in these past few years?"

"I have learned to understand Nature, and my powers have been strengthened," replied the Monkey King.

"You must now learn how to ward off the Three Calamities."

The Monkey King gave a deep sigh and said: "Revered Master, there must be some mistake. I have heard that if you reach the highest degree of learning, you become as eternal as Heaven itself, protected from both fire and water, and immune from every kind of disease. That being so, how can one be in danger of the Three Calamities?"

"After five hundred years Heaven will send down lightning," said the Patriarch, "and you must beware of it and avoid it in time. After another five hundred years Heaven will send down a fire which will not be an ordinary kind of fire, nor a heavenly fire, but a magic one. It will consume your heart, then your brain, and then it will turn your insides into ashes and your limbs into dust. All you have sought in your thousand years will come to nothing. Should you survive this, when another five hundred years have passed, Heaven will send down a wind which will be neither the west wind nor the east wind, neither the north wind nor the south wind, neither the warm wind of autumn nor the breeze which shakes the crowns of the trees, but a mighty typhoon. First it will penetrate your brain and your bowels; it will dry up your flesh and bones, and your body will crumble away. These are the three calamities you must learn to avoid."

The Monkey King was horrified and his hair stood on end as he listened. Quickly he bowed low before the Patriarch and, beating his forehead on the floor, he pleaded: "Esteemed Master, have pity upon me and teach me how to avoid these calamities. I shall never forget your kindness."

"That would be quite easy to do," said the Patriarch Subodhi. "That is if you were

like everyone else. As it is, it cannot be done."

"But I have a round head pointing up to Heaven and my feet touch the Earth; I have a brain and all the vital organs, as well as four limbs. In what way, then, am I different from the human race?" demanded the Monkey King.

"True, you do resemble men in many ways, but you lack their high cheek bones."

(Monkeys have hollow, sunken cheeks and a pointed nose.)

The Monkey King put a hand to his cheek and laughed.

"Do not be unjust, revered Master. Though I lack high cheek bones I have a cheek pouch which makes up for everything."

"Very well then," said the Patriarch. "Which series of magic changes do you wish to learn, the Polar Star series which involves thirty-two kinds of change, or the Great Bear series which involves seventy-two?"

"I would like to learn as much as possible, therefore I had better choose the series which has seventy-two magic changes," decided the Monkey King.

"Come closer then," said the Patriarch, "and I shall teach you the words."

He leaned over towards the Monkey King and whispered in his ear. The Monkey King was very quick-witted and often a mere hint was sufficient for him to understand a great deal. As soon as he had learned the words he started practising and did not stop until he had mastered all the seventy-two changes.

One day the Patriarch was sitting in front of the cave with his disciples, enjoying the quiet beauty of evening, when he

thought of the Monkey King and said: "Well, Sun Wu-k'ung, what progress have you made?'

"Thanks to your immeasurable kindness I have managed to learn everything perfectly," replied the Monkey King. "I can even fly in the clouds."

"Show me," said the Patriarch.

The Monkey King put his feet together, gave a mighty leap and, turning two somersaults, jumped high into the air. He caught hold of a cloud and was soon back on the ground again. Altogether he flew less than a mile. He touched down right in front of the Patriarch, crossed his arms on his chest, and asked with pride: "Well, how did you like my cloud-flying?"

"You call that cloud-flying?" replied the Patriarch, laughing. "Cloud-crawling would be a fitter term, I should say. There is an old saying, 'An Immortal leaves the Northern Sea in the morning, and that same evening lands in Ts'ang-wu.' You have taken that time to fly less than a mile. You have a lot to learn before you can become a real cloud-flier."

"What does the saying mean?" asked the Monkey King.

"It means that a real cloud-flier can start in the morning from the Northern Sea, cross the Eastern, Western and Southern Seas, and land again in the evening at Ts'ang-wu, on the evergreen mountain of Ling, the seat of the spirits in the Northern Sea. To cross all four seas in a day, that is real cloud-flying."

"That must be very difficult," said the Monkey King dejectedly.

"Nothing in the world is difficult," replied the Patriarch. "It is only our fears which make things seem so."

The Monkey King bowed low and said: "Please, be so kind as to teach me how to become a real cloud-flier. I shall never forget your kindness as long as I live."

"All the Immortals stamp their foot

upon the ground before taking off," the Patriarch explained. "You did not do that. I have also noticed that you use a double somersault. I shall teach you a better way, with your feet together and your arms outstretched."

The Monkey King bowed again to show his gratitude. Then the Patriarch told him the magic words and said: "Make the magic sign, recite the words, clench your fists, and push yourself off with your feet. You will then travel hundreds of miles in one leap."

Hearing this, the other pupils giggled, saying: "Isn't Monkey lucky! If he learns this trick, he will be able to work as a postman, delivering dispatches, reports and circulars. He will always be able to earn a living."

It was growing dark now, and the Master and his pupils returned to the cave. All night long Monkey practised his jump until he finally mastered it.

The days went by and the Monkey King was happy, travelling in space like a bird and delighting in the beauty of his new life. One day, at the time when spring gives way to summer, the disciples were doing their exercises in the shade of the pine trees. One of them asked Monkey: "How did you persuade our Master to show you how to avoid the Three Calamities? Have you learned all there is to learn?"

"My dear brothers," replied Monkey, "I wish to have no secrets from you. I am very indebted to our Master for his precious words of advice, but I have also worked very hard day and night to learn it all."

"This is as good an opportunity as any," said one of the pupils. "Why don't you show us something of your art?"

Monkey did not have to be asked twice, so eager was he to show off his skill.

"Tell me what I am to change into," he asked.

"Change yourself into a pine tree!"

Monkey made a magic sign, recited a spell, shook himself, and changed into a pine tree. The disciples clapped in admiration and started laughing uproariously.

"Look at Monkey! How clever he is!" they all shouted.

The noise they made disturbed the Patriarch Subodhi in his meditation. He appeared suddenly in the doorway and shook his staff at them.

"What is all this noise?" he demanded.

They all stopped shouting, tidied their dress, and stepped forward. Monkey changed himself back again and, mingling with the others, said: "We were merely doing our lessons out here, esteemed Master. Nobody was making any noise."

"You were screeching like a lot of baboons," the Patriarch cried angrily. "Your behaviour is not in the least like that of people who wish to achieve virtue. The virtuous should always behave with humility and should speak the truth and nothing but the truth. Tell me what you were laughing at so wildly."

"Honoured Master, we would rather not deceive you," confessed the disciples. "Sun Wu-k'ung here changed himself to amuse us. We had asked him to change into a pine tree and he did it so well that we were applauding him and praising his skill. We humbly beseech you to forgive us if in so doing we unwittingly disturbed you."

"Go away, all of you!" shouted the Patriarch. When they had gone, he said: "Sun Wu-k'ung, come here! What made you turn yourself into a pine tree like this? Do you think I took all that trouble with you only to enable you to show off in front of others? If you see that someone else has something worth having, you want it too. And when others see that you have something, they are sure to want it in their turn. If you wish to court misfortune, just teach them all you know. And if you refuse, it will be even worse and your life will be in danger."

Monkey beat his forehead on the ground, humbly begging the Patriarch to forgive him.

"There is nothing to forgive," replied Subodhi. "But you must leave here at once."

Monkey's eyes filled with tears.

"Where am I to go, my dear Master?" he asked.

"Back to where you came from," the Patriarch told him.

"I come from the Water Curtain Cave on the Mountain of Many Flowers in the land of Ao-lai."

"Well then, return there quickly and you will be saved. If you stay here, you are finished."

Monkey knew that he had behaved badly, but he did not wish to go back to Ao-lai.

"Revered Master, you must know that I have been away for nearly twenty years. Though I should dearly love to see my old friends again, I am unwilling to leave you until I have repaid you for your immeasurable kindness."

"Kindness indeed! All I ask is that you should not get me into any kind of trouble or bring misfortune upon my head."

Seeing there was nothing to be done, the Monkey King bowed low to him for the last time and said goodbye to his fellow pupils.

"When you leave here I am sure you will come to no good," said the Patriarch. "Remember that whatever scrape you get into, I forbid you to say that you are my pupil. If you as much as breathe a word, I shall learn about it and I shall flay you alive, break your bones, and send your soul to Hell where you will remain for ten thousand years."

"I shall not say a word about you," promised Monkey. "I shall say I learned it all myself."

A Treasure from the Palace of the Dragon King

Monkey said goodbye. Then he stretched himself to his full height, made the magic sign, and in one great leap flew up into the clouds. He returned to the Eastern Continent. Before long he saw the Mountain of Many Flowers and the Water Curtain Cave. Overjoyed, he thought: "Before, I had to struggle with the ocean waves, but now I am floating with the greatest of ease."

He lowered his cloud and landed right on top of the Mountain of Many Flowers. He was making his way forward when all of a sudden he heard a crane calling and monkeys crying. The crane's voice carried high above the clouds, while the sad wailing of the monkeys pierced his heart.

"I have come back, my children!" cried the Monkey King.

From every crevice in the rocks, from the bushes and trees thousands of monkeys, large and small, came running, and flocked round their handsome King.

"After I left you," Monkey told them, "I learned the ways of humans in the Southern Continent. I acquired this dress, put on these shoes, and wandered for eight or nine years about the world, finding no peace and learning no magic. Then I crossed the Western Ocean and reached the Western Continent, and after a long search I finally found an old Patriarch who revealed to me the secret of long life and immortality."

All the monkeys congratulated him.

"What incredible luck!" they cried.

"Little ones," said Monkey, smiling, "I am even better pleased at having been given a religious name."

"And what is your name, Your Majesty?" the monkeys enquired eagerly.

"My surname is now Sun," the Monkey King replied, "and my other name is Wu-k'ung, which means He Who Understands Emptiness."

Hearing this, the monkeys clapped their paws and cheered.

"Our king is Sun the First, we are Sun the Second, and Third, Little Sun, Tiny Sun, the Tiniest Sun, a whole family of Suns, an empire of Suns!"

One by one they came up to toast their king, Sun the First. Rare flowers and fruits were heaped on dishes and trays, and they drank grape and coconut wine.

Now life returned to normal among the monkeys. Every day they feasted and played and listened to the stories of their king's adventures.

One day the Monkey King thought to himself: "If someone takes these games of ours seriously, or if a human king or the king of the birds or beasts learns what we are doing, he will surely accuse us of hatching some plot against him. And if he sends his army to attack us, our bamboo spears and wooden swords will be of little use to us. What we need are real swords and spears. But where are we to get them?"

The monkeys were dismayed.

"Our great king has foresight, but where are we to get the weapons?"

As they were debating this, four old monkeys stepped forward — two red-bottomed ones with long faces and two tail-less monkeys with humps on their backs. They stood at attention and said: "Your Majesty, it is quite an easy matter to get hold of real weapons."

"What makes you think so?" the Monkey King asked.

"To the east of our mountain," the monkeys said, "there is a huge lake. That is the frontier of Ao-lai. On the other side is another kingdom and in its towns there are many soldiers. They must have large numbers of blacksmiths, silversmiths and goldsmiths. If Your Majesty went there and bought some weapons or had them made for us, we could train with real arms and would be able to defend our mountain, so that our monkey kingdom would thrive in peace and prosperity."

The Monkey King was pleased to hear this.

"Go ahead and play while I see what can be done," he said.

So the Monkey King soared up into the clouds, and in a flash he found himself on the other side of the lake. Here indeed there was a city surrounded by walls and a moat; a city with wide streets and markets. The alleyways were full of houses, while the streets were thronged with people scurrying like ants under the sunny skies.

"They're sure to have plenty of weapons here," thought Sun Wu-k'ung, "but why should I buy them when I can get them by magic?"

He lifted his paws, recited a spell and, stretching himself on the ground, breathed in the dust and then blew it out with such force that a whirlwind seemed to strike the city. Sand and stones hurtled through the air. The inhabitants were terrified; they quickly closed all the windows and doors, and no one dared venture into the streets. Even the king's retinue scattered in fear. Sun Wu-k'ung lowered his cloud, rushed through the main gate of the city and made straight for the arsenal. He threw open all the doors, behind which lay vast quantities of arms: knives, lances, swords, axes, cudgels, scythes, flails, whips, bows and crossbows, spears and other weapons. The Monkey King was overjoyed, but he wondered how he was to carry all these arms back with him. He decided to use his magic to produce a swarm of monkeys who would help him with the task. Plucking out a hair, he put it in his mouth, chewed it and then spat it out, reciting a spell as he did so. At once the hair changed into thousands of little monkeys. They fought each other for possession of the weapons, the stronger ones snatching as many as six or seven, the weaker ones two or three. Before long the arsenal was completely bare. The Monkey King remounted his cloud and summoned a gale which carried him and all the little monkeys back to his cave.

The monkeys, young and old, were playing in front of the cave when they heard the noise of a mighty wind. Looking up they saw a swarm of little monkeys raining down from the sky. This frightened them so much that they all took to their heels and hid. The Monkey King lowered his cloud, dispersed the mist and the clouds, shook himself and put back the hair he had used. At that instant all the little monkeys disappeared and the weapons fell to the ground.

"Come and get your arms!" cried the Monkey King.

When the monkeys saw that it was none other than their ruler who was standing on the hillside, they all came rushing out of hiding, bowed and asked what had happened. Sun Wu-k'ung told them how he had raised a wind and acquired the weapons. The monkeys expressed their gratitude and grabbed at the knives and swords, the axes and spears, the bows and crossbows. They shrieked and shouted the whole day long.

Next day they turned out for arms practice. The Monkey King called the roll and found there were over forty-seven thousand of them. The noise and bustle alarmed all the wild beasts in the mountains — the snakes and reptiles, wolves, tigers, panthers, stags, deer, hyenas, foxes, jackals, badgers, lions, elephants, orang-utans, bears, wild boar, bison, antelopes, rhinoceroses and mountain hares. All these animals had their demon kings who dwelt in seventy-two different caves.

The kings all came to pay homage to the Monkey King, recognising him as their sovereign. From that time on, they paid him regular visits at every season of the year, some of them taking up training in the monkey army, others bringing money. The Mountain of Many Flowers became as strong as a steel fortress and as rich as a city of gold. Some of the demon kings presented golden drums, silk banners and standards, helmets and coats of mail. The whole mountain became a beehive of activity — troops in arms marched and drilled everywhere.

The Monkey King was highly satisfied with all this, yet one day he told his subjects: "You now know how to handle bows and arrows, you can all do the drill, but my sword is heavy and I do not like it. What is to be done?"

The four old monkeys again came forward and, bowing low before him, said: "Your Majesty is an Immortal, that is why ordinary earthly weapons are unsuitable for you. Permit us to ask you a question, Majesty: can you swim under water?"

"Since I have received wisdom, I can perform any one of seventy-two magic changes. I am quite at home in the clouds, I can find my way up to Heaven. If I desire to penetrate to the centre of the Earth I know how. I cast no shadow when I walk on the Sun or Moon, and nothing can stop me if I wish to pass through stone or gold; I will not drown in water, nor be burned by fire. There is no place I cannot go."

"The water that flows under our iron bridge comes from the palace of the Dragon King of the Eastern Sea," said the monkeys. "If Your Majesty has such magic powers as to be able to descend to the bottom of the sea, why not pay the Dragon King a visit and ask him for a weapon. No doubt something to suit Your Majesty could be found there."

"Very good," replied the Monkey King, who was pleased with this suggestion. "I shall go there at once."

The gallant Monkey King went to the bridge-head, recited a spell against the dangers of the water, and jumped into the waves. Pushing them aside he swam straight to the bottom of the Eastern Sea. There he came across a Yaksha, who was keeping watch in those waters. The Yaksha barred his way, saying: "Hullo there, spirit! Who are you that you come pushing through the water in this fashion? Reveal your identity so that I may announce you."

"I am Sun Wu-k'ung, the lord and master of the Mountain of Many Flowers. I am a near neighbour of your Dragon King. How is it that you do not know me?"

Hearing this, the Yaksha quickly made his way to the crystal palace to report the Monkey King's arrival. The Dragon King at once rose and, accompanied by his dragon sons and grandsons, his shrimp soldiers and crab generals, he came out to welcome his unexpected visitor.

"Come in, noble Immortal, come in!"

He took the Monkey King inside the palace and gave him a seat of honour by his side. When they had taken tea, the Dragon King asked: "When did you receive wisdom and what magic arts have you mastered?"

"Ever since I was born," replied the Monkey King, "I have led a virtuous life and have trained myself to achieve immortality. Recently I have taught my subjects the art of war so that we should be in a position to defend our home. I myself, however, have no weapon, and I have heard that you, my noble neighbour, have magic weapons in the pearl halls of your green jade palace. I have therefore come to request one of them for myself."

The Dragon King could not very well refuse this request, and he ordered a trout bailiff to bring a huge dagger.

"I do not know how to use a dagger," said the Monkey King. "Please find me something else."

The Dragon King then ordered a white-bait captain to go with a strong eel and bring a nine-pronged fork. Sun Wu-k'ung picked it up, swung it in the air, and laid it aside again, saying: "No, this is much too light and awkward. Please find me something else."

"Noble Immortal," said the Dragon King, "you perhaps failed to notice that this fork weighs three thousand six hundred pounds."

"It's much too light and awkward," repeated Monkey.

The Dragon King could not understand this, and he ordered a bream steward to go with a carp general and bring a huge spear weighing seven thousand two hundred pounds. The Monkey King weighed it in his hand, made a few thrusts with it in the air, and put it down again, saying: "It is still too light, much too light."

The Dragon King was seized with fear.

"Noble father, this spear is the finest weapon we have in the palace. With the best will in the world I cannot offer you anything else."

"An old proverb says, 'Never fear that you shall not find treasures in the palace of the Dragon King'," said Monkey, laughing. "Go and have a proper look — if you have any weapon that I can use, I shall pay you well."

"Upon my soul, I have nothing else," said the Dragon King.

While they were talking, the Dragon Queen Mother and her daughter came out from the back rooms of the palace, and said: "Your Majesty, this Immortal is truly an exceptional person. In our ocean treasury we have the magic iron with which the bottom of the Celestial River was levelled. For some days now it has been glowing with a light more dazzling than the morning sun. Is that not a sign that it should be brought out and given to our immortal guest?"

"That is the iron with which the Great Yü measured the depth of the seas and rivers when he subdued the waters," said the Dragon King. "It's nothing but a piece of magic iron. What possible use could it be to him?"

"Never mind about that," said the Queen Mother. "Just give it to him and see

what he makes of it. Why should we care, as long as we get rid of him?"

The Dragon King did as she told him, and mentioned the iron to his guest.

"Bring it by all means," said the Monkey King. "I'll take a look at it."

"But nobody can move it," protested the Dragon King. "You'll have to go yourself."

"Where is it? Show me the way."

The Dragon King led him to the ocean treasury. From far off they could see a brilliant golden glow.

"That light is given off by the magic iron," said the Dragon King.

Monkey rolled up his sleeves and approached the magic iron. It was smooth and round and about twenty feet long. The Monkey seized it in both hands.

"It's just the thing I need, if only it were a little thinner and shorter!"

No sooner were the words out of his mouth than the iron grew thinner and shorter by several feet.

Sun Wu-k'ung turned it round in his hands and said: "It ought to be a little shorter still."

And again the iron became shorter, which pleased Monkey very much. He brought it out into the daylight and found that it was, in fact, an iron bar with a golden ring at either end. Next to one of the rings was the following inscription: "Golden Wishing Cudgel with Rings. Weight thirteen thousand five hundred pounds".

"Splendid!" thought the Monkey King. "This little object evidently changes according to one's wish."

He was toying with the magic iron and he thought: "What a fine thing it would be if it were a little smaller."

By the time they had left the sea treasury, the iron cudgel was less than two feet long. Monkey, pleased with his new weapon, began waving it in the air and running about the crystal palace like a madman. The Dragon King shivered with fright, and the Dragon Princes trembled all over. The tortoises and turtles drew in their heads, the fishes, crabs and crayfish hid theirs in the sand. Finally the Monkey King, his new treasure in his hand, sat down next to the Dragon King.

"Thank you very much, honoured neighbour, for your great kindness," he said, smiling.

"Don't mention it, I'm not worthy of your gratitude," murmured the frightened Dragon King.

"This piece of iron is really useful," said the Monkey King, "but I should like to ask you one more favour."

"What is it, esteemed Immortal?"

"Before I had this cudgel I could go about dressed in whatever pleased me. Now, however, I require some suitable clothing to go with it. If you happen to have a coat of mail here, kindly give it to me and I shall pay you well for it."

"I am terribly sorry, but we have nothing of that sort here."

"Do you not know the old proverb which says, 'One guest should not trouble two hosts'?" said the Monkey King. "I shall not budge unless you give me what I require."

"Great Immortal, perhaps you could try elsewhere in the sea. I'm sure you'd find something suitable."

"It is always better to sit in one spot than run all over the place," replied the Monkey King. "I insist that you bring me a coat of mail."

"But I really haven't got one," said the Dragon King. "If I had, I should have given it to you long before this."

"All right, then, I'll try my new weapon out on you, and we shall soon see whether you have something or not."

"Oh, great Immortal, do not strike me, do not strike!" cried the Dragon King in terror. "Perhaps one of my brothers might have something you can use."

"Where do your brothers live?" asked the Monkey King.

"My brothers are the Dragon Kings of the Southern, Northern and Western Seas."

"I don't feel like going that far," said the Monkey King. "A bird in the hand is worth two in the bush. It doesn't matter where you get my coat of mail from, but I must have it at once."

"Please do not trouble yourself, great Immortal. We have here some iron drums and golden bells. Whenever there is anything urgent to be discussed, we strike the drums and ring the bells, and my brothers come immediately."

So a turtle general rang the bells and a crocodile brigadier sounded the drums.

The sound of the bells and the drums carried to the Dragon Kings of the other three seas, and they quickly arrived.

"What has happened, brother, that you have had the drums struck and the bells rung?" asked the Dragon King of the Southern Sea.

"What indeed, brothers," sighed the Dragon King. "A while ago an Immortal from the Mountain of Many Flowers came

to me as a neighbour and asked me for a weapon. I gave him a steel fork. This he found too small. I gave him a huge spear, and that again seemed to him too light. With his own hands he lifted up the magic iron from the bottom of the Celestial River. Now he is sitting in my palace, demanding that I give him a coat of mail. I have nothing like that here at all, which is why I had the drums sounded and the bells rung to call you, my wise brothers. If you have a coat of mail, please bring it and help me to get rid of him."

The Dragon King of the Southern Sea was furious.

"Let's call in our armies and attack him!" he cried.

"It can't be done," replied the Dragon King. "You'll never touch him. A single blow from that magic iron would kill you. Even if he just scratched you with it, you would be marked for life."

"We'd better not provoke him then," advised the Dragon King of the Western Sea. "Let's give him his coat of mail and be rid of him. Then we can go and complain to Heaven, and Heaven will punish him."

"Yes, that's the way to do it," agreed the Dragon King of the Northern Sea. "I have a pair of cloud-walking shoes made out of lotus fibre."

"And I have a coat of mail made of yellow gold," said the Dragon King of the Western Sea.

"And I'll give him a cap made of red gold, decorated with phoenix feathers," said the Dragon King of the Southern Sea.

The Dragon King was delighted, and he took them to the Monkey King, to whom they gave their gifts.

The Monkey King placed the gold cap on his head, put on the gold coat of mail and the cloud-walking shoes and, grasping his wishing cudgel, he strode out of the palace.

"You dirty scoundrels!" he called out as he passed the four dragons.

The Dragon Kings were furious, and they immediately wrote a complaint which they sent to Heaven.

The Monkey King Crosses His Name off the Death List

The Monkey King again pushed aside the waters, emerged on the surface and swam up to the iron bridge. The four old monkeys had brought all the little ones to the bridge and they were all waiting for him. Suddenly Sun Wu-k'ung rose out of the waves, his body completely dry and shining like gold, and he came towards them along the bridge. Astounded by the sight of him, all the monkeys knelt down, saying: "How noble you look, Your Majesty! What splendour!"

Smiling happily, the Monkey King ascended his throne and laid his iron cudgel at his feet. Suspecting nothing, the monkeys rushed forward and tried to lift it, but it was as if a dragonfly had tried to shake an iron tree — they could not budge it.

"How heavy it is! How can you carry it, Your Majesty?"

Sun Wu-k'ung stood up, stretched out his hand, and lifted the rod high into the air.

"Each object has its master," he said. "This treasure lay hidden in the ocean treasury for who knows how many thousands of years and only today did it start to shine. The Dragon King thought it was just a piece of iron; he told me that the bottom of the Celestial River had been levelled with it. His subjects could not move it, and I had to fetch it myself. When I saw it for the first time it was twenty feet long. I picked it up and thought I would prefer it to be smaller — and at once it diminished in size. Again I ordered it to become smaller, and again it did so. Then I looked at it against the light of the sky and I found it had this written on it: "Golden Wishing Cudgel with Rings. Weight thirteen thousand five hundred pounds'. Stand aside and I shall show you what it can do."

He placed the cudgel in the palm of his hand and cried: "Smaller, smaller, smaller!" The cudgel dwindled in size until it became no larger than a needle, and the Monkey King put it behind his ear. The monkeys clapped their paws in delight and demanded that he show them some more tricks.

The Monkey King took out the needle and put it in his palm again, saying: "Larger, larger, larger!" The cudgel grew. He found this game extremely amusing. Running out of the cave he jumped up on the bridge, clutched his cudgel and began to perform magic. He bowed from the waist and cried: "Tall!" At once he grew a hundred thousand feet tall, his head on a level with the mountain peaks, the ridges showing green at his waist. His eyes flashed lightning, his mouth was red as blood, his teeth were like daggers and swords. The cudgel in his hand reached up to the thirty-third floor of Heaven and down to the eighteenth pit of Hell. All the tigers, panthers, wolves and other beasts, all the evil spirits and the demon kings from the seventy-two caves paid homage to him in terror, trembling so much that their souls flew out of their bodies. Before

long, however, the Monkey King called off the magic, turned the cudgel into a needle again and, putting it behind his ear, returned to the cave. The demon kings were dumbfounded, one and all, and they came to pay homage to him.

All the flags were run up and the bronze drums sounded, and the monkeys gave a banquet at which they served the finest foods, filling the cups with wine and coconut milk. They feasted for several days, and then drilled in arms again. The Monkey King promoted the four old monkeys, making field marshals out of the two red-bottomed, horse-faced ones and generals out of the two with humps on their backs. The four of them were responsible for keeping order in the camp, meting out punishment and distributing rewards. The Monkey King was free to do as he pleased, and he flew about on clouds every day, crossing all the four seas and thousands of mountains. He displayed his skill at arms and everywhere he went he sought out heroes and adventurers, performing magic tricks and making countless wise friends. It was at this time that he became friendly with six demons — the king of demons called Strong Buffalo, the king of demons known as Hydra, the bird Roc, the king of lions, the king of maggots, and the king of wolves.

All seven pledged brotherhood, and they met every day to discuss many things, to drink and play stringed instruments, to sing and dance. In the mornings they would set out on their wanderings and return at dusk. Journeys up to ten thousand miles were mere strolls for the Monkey King. He had only to bow from the waist and he was eight hundred miles away; he shook his head and at once he travelled three thousand miles.

One day he ordered the four old monkeys to prepare a banquet. He invited his six brothers, had cattle and horses killed, and offered sacrifices to both Heaven and Earth. All the demons and spirits were carried away with the singing and dancing, the food and the drink. When at last the Monkey King had seen his guests off, he generously rewarded his officers, lay down in the shadow of a pine tree and fell asleep at once. The monkeys, led by all the marshals and generals, surrounded him and no one dared to speak for fear of waking him.

In his sleep he saw two men approaching him with a document bearing his name. Giving him no time to say anything, they threw a noose round his soul and dragged him off towards a city. Lifting his head he saw a plaque on the city gate with the inscription "World of Darkness". "Why," he cried, "this is the abode of the King of Death! What am I doing here?"

The two men told him: "Your days in the world of the living are over. We two have received orders to bring you here."

"But I have done with all that," said the Monkey King angrily. "I am not compounded of the Five Elements, and Death has no sway over me. Are you really so stupid and so insolent as to arrest me?"

The two men took no notice whatever, pulling at the rope and dragging the Monkey King towards the centre of the city. His patience ended, he took the needle from behind his ear, enlarged it, and beat the two messengers to a pulp. Then he cast off the noose, freed his hands, swung his cudgel in the air, and walked on into the city. He frightened all the buffalo-headed and horse-faced demons so much that they ran helter-skelter trying to hide from him. Evil spirits and demons crowded into the Palace of Darkness, shouting in confusion: "Oh, King of Death, alas! Outside there is a furry-faced thunder-god and he is fighting his way in."

The Judges of Death from all the ten palaces were overcome with fear. They rushed out into the city square to see for themselves. Seeing the Monkey's ferocious apperance they lined up quickly and called out to him: "What is your name, noble Immortal?"

"How is it that you have sent for me since you don't even know who I am?" demanded the Monkey King.

"We should never have dared to do such a thing," said the kings. "The messengers must have made some mistake."

"I am Sun Wu-k'ung, master of the Water Curtain Cave on the Mountain of Many Flowers, an Immortal conceived by Heaven. Who might you be?"

The ten judges bowed low before him.

"We are the Judges of Death from the ten palaces of His Majesty the King of Death."

"How is it that you judges, who mete out rewards and punishments, do not know what is right and proper? I, Sun Wu-k'ung, have received wisdom and shall enjoy the same age as the Heaven and the Earth. I have been elevated over Heaven, Hell and the world of humans, having freed myself from the bonds of the Five Elements. How dare you send your messengers to bring me here?"

"Please do not be angry with us, great Immortal," the Judges of Death begged him. "There are so many people bearing the same name in the world — our messengers must have mistaken you for someone else."

"Don't talk such rubbish!" cried the Monkey King. "I want to see your lists of the living and the dead."

So the Judges of Death invited the Monkey King into the palace to inspect the lists. Grasping his cudgel firmly in his hand, he entered the Palace of Darkness, and took a seat in the very middle. The judges ordered the official in charge of the records to bring the ledgers. The official returned with five or six ledgers divided into ten different files, and he began going through them quickly. He failed to find Sun Wu-k'ung's name in the list of furry, thick-skinned or feathered creatures, nor was it to be found in that of insects or fishes. He tried the file headed monkeys, but again without success; the Monkey King resembled a human being and was therefore not listed under monkeys. Yet he was not entered under humans either. He resembled a thick-skinned creature but had no permanent home. He looked like a four-legged animal, but was not subject to the unicorn. And not being subject to the phoenix, he could not be classed as a bird. But then, in a special section, which he examined himself, the Monkey King found his name under the number 1350. His name was given in full, with the note: "Stone Monkey, conceived by Heaven, life span of 342 years, a peaceful end."

"I don't remember what my age is anyway," said the Monkey King. "My name must be crossed out. Give me a brush!"

The official was so frightened that he handed him a brush, having first dipped it in heavy ink. Sun Wu-k'ung took the brush and crossed out not only his own name but also those of all the monkeys listed under Sun. Then he threw the ledger aside, saying: "There, that's done it! Now you've no more right over us."

With his magic cudgel in his hand, he made his way out of the underworld, and not one of the ten judges dared stop him. They went at once to the Blue Skies Palace to consult the King of Death and agreed to lodge a complaint against the Monkey King in Heaven.

The Monkey King fought his way out of the city, but his foot caught in some grass and he stumbled and fell. He awoke with a start and found it had all been just a dream. While he was still stretching himself and rubbing his eyes, he heard the voices of the monkey generals: "Your Majesty, you drank so much wine that you slept all night, and even now you are drowsy with sleep."

"Never mind that," said Sun Wu-k'ung. "In my dream I saw two men who tried to drag me off. When they'd got me as far as the gates of the World of Darkness I realised what they were up to. Making use of my magic powers I made the ten Judges of Death show me the lists of the living and the dead and I crossed off all our names. Now those scoundrels have no more power over us."

All the monkeys bowed to show their gratitude. Since that time many mountain monkeys have never grown old because their names cannot be found in the registers of the King of Death.

When the Monkey King had finished telling them about his dream, the four old monkeys went off and told all the demon kings who came to congratulate Sun Wu-k'ung. Several days later his six pledge-brothers arrived, and when they learned that the King of Death no longer had their names, their joy knew no bounds.

The Monkey King is Appointed Groom of the Celestial Stables

One day the most august ruler of Heaven, the supreme sovereign of the celestial spheres, His Holiness the Jade Emperor, ascended his diamond-studded Throne of Providence in the golden halls of the Palace of Supreme Wisdom. He had just called in all his spiritual and military advisers for their morning conference when an official stepped forward and announced that the Dragon King of the Eastern Sea was asking for an audience. The Jade Emperor had him shown in, whereupon the Dragon King advanced to the throne and bowed low before the Emperor. Next to him stood a celestial page, who handed the Jade Emperor a written complaint describing the Monkey King's behaviour in the Dragon King's underwater palace. The Jade Emperor read the document and said: "Let the Dragon King return to his sea. I will send officers to arrest the Monkey King."

The Dragon King bowed low to show his gratitude and departed.

One of the celestial messengers, the ancient Sage Ke, stepped forward next, saying: "The First Judge of Death is here, bringing greetings from the King of Death."

A celestial jade girl handed the Emperor another document, describing the Monkey King's behaviour in the underworld. The Jade Emperor read it through and said: "Let the Judge of Death return to the underworld. I will send officers to arrest the Monkey King."

The Judge of Death bowed his head to show his gratitude and departed.

The Jade Emperor then consulted his ministers, asking them: "When was this magic monkey born and how did he achieve wisdom?"

The ministers Thousand Eye and Sharp Ear at once stepped forward and said: "He is a stone monkey, conceived by Heaven three hundred years ago. We ignored him then, but he, in some way and at some time unknown to us, managed to achieve Immortality. He learned to catch dragons and tame tigers, and succeeded in getting his name crossed off the list of mortals."

"Which of you deities is willing to descend to Earth and deal with Monkey?" the Jade Emperor asked.

The Star of Long Life stepped forward. Kneeling in front of the Emperor, he said: "Highest and Holiest! All creatures in the world of animals, the world of humans

and in Heaven who are possessed of five senses and four limbs can achieve Immortality. This Monkey has been conceived by the Heaven and Earth, created by the Sun and Moon. His feet tread the earth and his head touches the stars, he drinks the dew and eats the morning light. Now that he has discovered the secret of Immortality, learned to catch dragons and tame tigers, in what way does he differ from humans? I therefore beseech Your Holiness in your greatness as the Creator of the World, to grant Monkey your gracious pardon, call him up to Heaven, have his name entered in the celestial register, and entrust him with some minor office. This would solve everything. If he obeys the order he can later be rewarded and promoted; if he tries to resist it, we shall take him prisoner. This way we shall not have to resort to military action and our ranks will be increased by another Immortal."

The Jade Emperor was pleased with this suggestion.

"Let the will of my wise subject be done," he said and instructed the Star dealing with spiritual matters to draw up a formal pardon, sending the Star of Long Life to deliver it to the Monkey King.

The Star took the Emperor's document and, leaving by the southern gate, he mounted a magic cloud and was at once taken to the Water Curtain Cave.

"I am a messenger from Heaven," he

told the monkeys, "and I bring orders from the Jade Emperor, calling your king to the Upper Realm. Go quickly and announce me to him!"

The monkeys passed this message along from one to the other, right to the middle of the cave.

"Your Majesty, there is an old man outside who says he is a messenger from Heaven. He has a large document in his hand and claims it is an order for you to accompany him."

Hearing this, the Monkey King rejoiced.

"I have been meaning to visit Heaven. This messenger could not have come at a better time. Show him in at once!"

Quickly he tidied his dress, straightened his cap, and went to meet the messenger. The Star of Long Life came in, faced the south, and said: "I am the Star of Long Life from the west. I have come upon the orders of His Holiness the Jade Emperor, who invites you up to Heaven and wishes to confer a celestial appointment on you."

"A thousand thanks, noble Star, for your trouble," said the Monkey King, and he ordered the monkeys to prepare a banquet.

But the Star of Long Life declined, saying: "I have now handed over the Emperor's orders and dare not linger. I therefore ask Your Majesty to accompany me up to Heaven. Once you have been appointed there will be plenty of opportunity for chatter."

"Thank you for your great kindness," said Monkey. "Let us set off at once."

He called in the four older monkeys and

told them: "See to it that the young ones are given careful training while I am away. I'm going to take a look around Heaven and then I'll come back for the rest of you and we can all settle there."

The four old monkeys bowed to show their agreement. The Monkey King and the Star of Long Life mounted a cloud and soared up to Heaven.

Sun Wu-k'ung was far better at cloud-soaring than any celestial spirit and he soon left his companion far behind, reaching the southern gate of Heaven long before him. He was just about to descend from his cloud and enter when the celestial King of Growth and the Guardians of Heaven stopped him. Armed with spears, daggers and swords, they ranged themselves in the gateway and would not let him pass.

"What a cheat that old Star is!" said the Monkey King to himself. "Why has he invited me up to Heaven if he sends these ruffians to bar my way?"

He was about to attack the Guardians when fortunately the Star of Long Life arrived at the gate. As soon as he caught sight of him, the Monkey King turned to him angrily, crying: "You old impostor, how dare you deceive me like this? You said the Jade Emperor had invited me up to Heaven. Why then are these men standing in my way and why do they refuse to let me in?"

"Don't be angry, Your Majesty," said the Star of Long Life, smiling. "You have never been inside the celestial halls and your name has not yet been recorded in Heaven. The Guardians do not know you, therefore they were quite right in preventing you from coming in. As soon as His Holiness the Jade Emperor has received you, your name will be entered in the official register and you will receive an appointment. Then you will be free to come and go as you please and no one will dare molest you."

"If that's how things are, you can keep your Heaven. I want no part of it," said Monkey.

"No, no, you must come with me," replied the Star of Long Life, taking him by the paw to make sure that he did not run away.

They approached the Gate of Heaven.

"Guardians of the Gate," cried the Star of Long Life, "captains great and

small, make way! This Immortal from the Earth comes at the invitation of the Jade Emperor."

The Guardians stood aside, and the Monkey King regained his confidence. Slowly he walked by the side of the Star of Long Life as they entered the gate. They went as far as the Hall of Magic Clouds. Without waiting for permission, they presented themselves to the Jade Emperor. The Star of Long Life bowed low, but the Monkey King stood next to him like a pillar of stone, showing not the least sign of humility. He was waiting to hear what the Star of Long Life had to say.

"I beg to report that, according to the orders given to me by Your Holiness, I have brought the rebellious Immortal up to Heaven," the Star of Long Life announced.

The Jade Emperor peeped out from behind the curtain of his throne.

"Which of the present company is he?" he asked.

The Monkey King bowed slightly and answered the question with a curt: "It's me."

All the celestial dignitaries went pale with shock.

"What an ill-mannered monkey! Why don't you bow low and say your name in the proper way? 'It's me', indeed! The death sentence is too soft a punishment for such insolence."

However, the Jade Emperor in his mercy told them: "Sun Wu-k'ung is a mere Earth-dweller. He has only recently learned human ways and as yet knows nothing of court etiquette. He shall be forgiven this once."

All the celestial dignitaries thanked the Emperor for his great clemency. The Monkey King came before him and bowed. The Jade Emperor then ordered the officials to examine the lists and find out whether there was any vacancy for Sun Wu-k'ung. The Star dealing with military matters stepped up and said: "There is no vacant office in any of the celestial halls or palaces. The only post that needs to be filled is that of permanent supervisor in the celestial stables."

"Very well," decided the Jade Emperor, "let him become a celestial groom."

Again all the dignitaries thanked him, and again the Monkey King bowed. Full of joy, he followed one of the deities who showed him the stables and, having installed him in office, returned to the palace. The Monkey King at once called the superintendent, the stewards and the grooms to him to find out what his office meant. There were some thousand horses in the stables. The Monkey King inspected the lists and checked the number of horses. The stewards looked after the fodder, the grooms brushed and washed the horses, chopped hay and brought water. The superintendent and his deputy were responsible for the smooth running of the stables. The Monkey-Groom was busy day and night. Things were not so bad during the day, but at night he had to sit up and guard the horses. Those which slept for a long time he drove out to pasture, those which ran away had to be brought back to their stalls. When the celestial horses saw the Monkey King they pricked up their ears and pawed the ground. They seemed to thrive under his care. Before he realised it, a fortnight had passed by.

One morning when the grooms had a little time to themselves they gave a banquet to celebrate Monkey's appointment. When the feast was at its height, he suddenly paused in the act of drinking and asked: "What kind of office was I actually charged with when I was appointed a groom?"

"That is simply your official rank," they replied.

"Where in the list of important posts does this rank belong?"

"It doesn't appear in any list," was the reply.

"Oh, I suppose that means it is a very high sort of rank," said the Monkey King.

"On the contrary," laughed the others, "it isn't even mentioned in the official lists."

"Well, and what does *that* mean?" the Monkey King asked again.

"That means that it's such a low rank that it cannot be put in any list. Officials like that can only be trusted to mind the horses. You have no doubt had a busy time of it since coming here, and the horses have put on quite a lot of weight as a result of your efforts. But you wait and see, you'll get no thanks for your trouble. Yet if the horses lost weight instead, you'd be held responsible. And if by any chance one of them happened to fall ill or get hurt, you'd be fined or punished."

Flames leapt in the Monkey King's heart when he heard this. Gritting his teeth with rage he shouted: "What an insult! They've had the cheek to swindle me, the King of the Mountain of Many Flowers and patriarch of the Sun family. Giving me horses to look after! Why, they've put me among the lowest of the low. But I'm not going to stand for it. I shall not stay here another minute."

Bang! With a crash he overturned the banqueting table, took his treasure from behind his ear and, wielding it furiously, fought his way out of the celestial stables and to the southern gate. The Guardians of Heaven knew he had been appointed celestial groom, and therefore they dared not stand in his way. He mounted his cloud and flew through the gate like an arrow.

Soon the Monkey King lowered his cloud and landed on the Mountain of Many Flowers. From afar he could see his generals and the demon kings drilling the monkeys in arms.

"Little ones," he cried, "your Sun has returned!"

The monkeys beat their foreheads on the ground and led him inside the cave to a throne ornamented with precious stones. A great banquet was prepared in the next hall.

"Congratulations, Your Majesty," the monkeys called out to him. "After ten

years in Heaven you must be covered with glory."

"Ten years?" The Monkey King was puzzled. "But I've only been away a fortnight."

"In Heaven you can't tell the passage of time," they replied. "One day there is equal to a year on the Earth. What kind of rank did they give Your Majesty?"

"I am ashamed to speak of it," he said, shaking his head sorrowfully. "It was absolutely disgraceful. The Jade Emperor simply has no idea how to make use of capable people. He made me a groom and said I was to look after his horses. My rank was not even mentioned in the official lists. I, of course, knew nothing of this when I accepted the appointment and for a time I really did mind the horses. It was only today that I thought of asking the others and learned how shabbily I'd been treated. I was so furious that I overturned the banqueting table, gave up my office, and ran away."

"Well done, Your Majesty!" cried the monkeys. "You are the king of this blessed land and this rich cave. You have all you require here. Why be a servant?"

Someone suggested that they pour out the wine and dispel their sovereign's gloom. They were in the middle of their feast when one of the monkeys announced that the Unicorn demon kings were outside and wished to speak to His Majesty.

"Let them enter," said Monkey.

The demons came in, bowing low before him.

"What brings you here?" the Monkey King asked graciously.

"We have known for a long time that

Your Majesty is surrounding himself with wise lords and heroes, but until now we have had no opportunity of presenting our compliments. However, today, when Your Majesty has received a celestial appointment and returned home in triumph, we have brought this earth-coloured robe as a token of our great admiration. Furthermore we hope that you will not refuse us, unworthy though we are, but will take us into your service. We wish to serve you all our lives."

The Monkey King was delighted. He at once put on the new robe, and all the monkeys lined up to pay homage to their ruler. The Unicorn demon kings were appointed Supreme Commanders of the Vanguard. They thanked the Monkey King and asked him what position he had held during his long sojourn in Heaven.

"The Jade Emperor has no appreciation of talent. He made me a groom in the celestial stables."

"Your Majesty has such great magic powers," said the Unicorns. "Why should you look after their horses? The Great Sage, Equal to Heaven, that would be a fitting rank for you."

The Monkey King found this title very much to his liking and kept repeating it aloud. Then he ordered the four generals to provide banners with the inscription "Great Sage, Equal to Heaven" in large letters. He also informed his subjects that he wished to be addressed only in this way, forbidding the use of the title "Your Majesty". Instructions about this were to be sent at once to the demon kings in all the caves.

The Great Sage Defeats the Heavenly King Li

When the Jade Emperor held his court next day, a messenger showed in the Superintendent of the Stables and his deputy. They knelt on the steps leading up to the throne and announced that the new groom, Sun Wu-k'ung, had marched out of the palace because the appointment he had received did not suit him. They had hardly finished telling their story when the King of Growth came with the Guardians of Heaven, to state that the celestial groom, Sun Wu-k'ung, had, for reasons unknown, left Heaven by the southern gate.

The Jade Emperor ordered the commanders of the first and second regiment to return to their units, muster their troops, and arrest the criminal. The Heavenly King Li and his son, Third Crown Prince Natha, stepped forward from the throng of assembled courtiers and volunteered to go and capture the Monkey King themselves. The Jade Emperor was delighted and, on the spot, he appointed King Li Marshal of the Expedition for the Subduing of Evil Spirits, telling him to go to muster his forces and descend to Earth.

King Li and Crown Prince Natha beat their foreheads on the ground to show their gratitude, and returned to their palaces. They immediately raised three armies, sending their commanders and the Spirit of Enlightenment ahead as their vanguard. General Fish Belly was in charge of the forces that brought up the rear, while the General of the Yakshas urged the troops on. Soon they had passed through the southern gate of Heaven and arrived at the Mountain of Many Flowers. They set up camp on a plain just below the mountain and despatched the Spirit of Enlightenment to provoke the first battle. He put on his armour and, brandishing his axe which gleamed in the rays of the sun, he made his way to the Water Curtain Cave. In front of the cave he found a great many demons and monsters — wolves, tigers, and panthers — waving their swords, flourishing spears and shouting.

"Accursed creatures," cried the Spirit of Enlightenment, "go and tell the Celestial Groom that I, a general from Heaven, have come to arrest him upon the orders of the Jade Emperor. Tell him to submit without delay, or you will all pay with your lives!"

The demons were terrified and rushed into the cave.

"Woe is us! We are ruined!"

"Why should we be ruined?" asked the Monkey King calmly.

"There's a heavenly general at the gate. He called the Great Sage by his official title in Heaven and says he has been ordered by the Jade Emperor to arrest you. If you don't submit at once, he says we shall all pay with our lives."

"Bring me my armour!" cried Monkey.

He put on his dark gold helmet, his light gold coat of mail, and his cloud-walking shoes. Then, seizing his magic cudgel, he led the monkeys out of the gate and prepared them for battle.

"Accursed monkey! Do you not know me?" cried the Spirit of Enlightenment in a mighty voice.

"What kind of scurvy spirit are you?" asked the Monkey King. "I have never seen you in my life. Tell me your name at once."

"Do not provoke me, you vile ape!" shouted the Spirit of Enlightenment. "How dare you pretend not to know me? I am the heavenly general, Spirit of Enlightenment, chief of the vanguard of the Supreme Heavenly Commander, King Li. I have come to arrest you upon the orders of the Jade Emperor himself. Discard your finery and submit to the will of Heaven, or I shall make a slaughter house of your mountain! If you so much as breathe half a word, I shall cut you to pieces!"

This enraged the Monkey King, who replied: "You worthless, scurvy spirit! Stop your bragging and posturing! I ought to

strike you dead with my cudgel, but if I did so you could not take my message back to Heaven. I shall therefore spare your life. Return at once and tell the Jade Emperor that he does not know how to make use of talent. I, Sun Wu-k'ung, am endowed with great magic powers, yet he would have made me mind his horses. Just look at the inscription on my banner! If the Emperor grants me an office in keeping with that title, I shall withdraw my troops and leave him in peace. However, if he delays, I shall march up to his palace and drive him from his dragon throne."

The Spirit of Enlightenment looked up and saw the banner hoisted above the gate with the words "Great Sage, Equal to Heaven" written on it.

"What an insolent monkey you are," said the Spirit of Enlightenment, smiling icily. "So ignorant, and yet you dare to brag like this. A monkey, yet you think yourself equal to Heaven! First I'll give you a taste of this axe of mine!"

With these words the Spirit of Enlightenment struck at the Monkey King's head. But Sun Wu-k'ung remained unruffled and merely lifted his magic cudgel. A battle followed, but it was soon over, for the Spirit could not withstand the Monkey's onslaught. Sun Wu-k'ung aimed a blow at his head, and the Spirit tried to parry it with his axe. The axe split in two, and the Spirit was forced to run for his life.

"What a weakling!" the Monkey King laughed derisively. "Now that I have let you go, at least tell your people all about it."

The Spirit of Enlightenment returned to the camp. On his way he met King Li and, kneeling before him, panted: "That groom really does possess magic powers. I have been unable to do anything with him and come to ask your pardon."

"You scoundrel, you only spoil my appetite for battle. Take him away and cut off his head!" raged the king.

The Crown Prince Natha stepped forward just then, saying: "Royal father, do not be angry. Forgive the Spirit of Enlightenment and let me go and find out how matters really stand."

King Li calmed down slightly and ordered the Spirit of Enlightenment to go back to camp and await his punishment.

In the meantime Crown Prince Natha put on his armour and set out for the Water Curtain Cave. The Monkey King was just dismissing his army when he saw Natha approaching.

"Whose little boy might you be?" the Monkey King asked. "And what are you doing on my territory?"

"Wretched monkey," shouted Natha, "don't tell me you don't recognise me! I am Natha, the third Crown Prince of the Heavenly King Li. I have come upon the orders of the Jade Emperor to take you prisoner."

"Little prince," laughed the Monkey King, "you have not yet lost your milk-teeth. How dare you speak to me like this?

I shall spare your life and shall not even beat you as you so richly deserve. Just look at what is written on my banner and kindly tell the Jade Emperor that if he will give me *that* rank, he need not send any more armies, for I shall submit of my own accord. If he does not do as I ask, I shall come and destroy that palace of his!"

Natha raised his head and there, true enough, he saw the inscription "Great Sage, Equal to Heaven". What magic powers could such a monkey have, he wondered, that he dared claim such a title.

"You can't frighten me so easily," he cried. "I'll give you a taste of my sword."

"Strike as often as you please," replied the Monkey King, laughing. "I shall not even flinch."

Natha was beside himself with rage.

"Change!" he roared. At once he changed into a creature with three heads and six arms. In each of his hands he held a different weapon — a sword and a dagger, an axe for cutting off the heads of demons, a rope to bind them, a cudgel, and a ball of fire. He sputtered with rage, grunted and snorted, and attacked the Monkey King straightaway.

"Would you believe it, this milksop knows a trick or two," said Monkey to himself slightly uneasily. Then he said, "Calm yourself, little boy, and kindly watch while I show you what *I* can do." Quickly he recited a spell so that he, like Natha, assumed three heads and six arms. Shaking his magic cudgel, he changed it into three, each of which he grasped with two hands, parrying Natha's furious assaults. A savage battle followed, that shook the ground and rocked the hills. Both Natha and Sun Wu-k'ung displayed their magic powers, and closed with each

other about thirty times. The Crown Prince changed his six weapons into hundreds and then thousands of weapons, the Monkey King changed his six cudgels into hundreds and then thousands of cudgels. Their weapons flashed through the air like raindrops; they flew like falling stars. Still victory did not favour either Natha or Sun Wu-k'ung. But the Monkey King had his wits about him — making use of the confusion he plucked out one of his hairs and changed it into his own shape. Armed with a cudgel, the new Monkey also attacked Natha. The Prince turned round, and Sun Wu-k'ung leapt up behind his back and smote him on the left shoulder. Natha was just getting ready to cast a spell when he heard the swish of the cudgel. It was too late to dodge the blow; the Monkey King hit him with all his might. Whimpering with pain, Natha fled the scene of the battle. He changed back to his original form and returned to the camp.

King Li had been watching the battle from the camp and was just about to go to his son's assistance when the Crown Prince appeared before him, trembling all over.

"Royal father, that groom is indeed adept at magic tricks. I was quite unable to vanquish him, none of my magic art was of any use. In the end he wounded me in the shoulder."

King Li went pale with shock.

"With what magic did the scoundrel defeat you?" he asked.

"Outside the cave he has put up a banner with the inscription "Great Sage,

Equal to Heaven". He keeps bragging and wants the Jade Emperor to grant him such a title, otherwise he says he will come and destroy the Palace of Supreme Wisdom."

"If that is the case," replied King Li, "there is no use in our fighting him. Let's go back and report to the Emperor. Then we shall bring out reinforcements, encircle him, and see whether he can withstand us again."

The Crown Prince was in great pain and unable to resume the fight. So he accompanied his father back to Heaven, where they made their report to the Jade Emperor.

The Monkey King Disrupts the Peach Banquet

After his victory, the Monkey King returned to the Mountain of Many Flowers. His six brothers and the demon kings from all the seventy-two caves came along to congratulate him. The celebrations in the Water Curtain Cave went on without cease.

Meanwhile, King Li and the third Crown Prince Natha and their generals had gone back to Heaven, to the Palace of Supreme Wisdom. They had to admit that Sun Wu-k'ung had great magic powers and that they had failed to subdue him as a result. They therefore begged the Jade Emperor to give them reinforcements so that they could destroy the Monkey King.

"Do you mean to tell me you want reinforcements to deal with a single monkey?" the Jade Emperor asked in disbelief. "What magic can a creature like that possess?"

The Crown Prince went down on his knees in front of the Emperor.

"Spare the lives of your unworthy subjects, Your Holiness," he pleaded. "That Monkey wields an iron cudgel, which first defeated the Spirit of Enlightenment and then injured my shoulder. In front of his cave he has put up a banner with the inscription 'Great Sage, Equal to Heaven'. He demands that you acknowledge this title, in which case he says he will yield to you and give no more trouble; if you do not yield, he threatens to attack Heaven and destroy your own palace."

"How dare he?" said the Emperor, unable to believe his ears. "Call all my generals at once and have him removed."

At that moment the general, Star of Long Life, again stepped forward and spoke up on behalf of Monkey, saying he was sure the threats were mere idle boasts and were not meant seriously. He asked the Emperor to pardon Sun Wu-k'ung once more and to bestow on him the title of Great Sage, Equal to Heaven without, of course, giving him any official post or salary. The Star urged the Emperor to do as he suggested, for it was possible that not even a larger army would succeed in quelling the Monkey King and there would be unnecessary bloodshed.

"But I don't see how I am to give someone a title without the job that goes with it," said the Jade Emperor.

"Your Holiness would simply name him 'Great Sage, Equal to Heaven' and make the appointment public, but he will not be entrusted with any post, nor given a salary. He will live in some remote part of Heaven and will thus be out of harm's way and peace will continue to reign in Heaven as well as on Earth. There will be peace and quiet throughout the Universe."

"Very well," said the Emperor, and he had the pardon written, sending the Star of Long Life to take it to the Monkey King.

The Star of Long Life left Heaven by the southern gate, travelled to the Water Curtain Cave, and looked round. The place had changed greatly since he had last seen it. The clash of arms could be heard everywhere; every sort of demon and devil was running hither and thither, brandishing spears and swords, daggers and forks. They all looked most fierce and bloodthirsty. As soon as they caught sight of the Star of Long Life they rushed towards him.

"Call your commander!" the Star demanded. "And announce me at once to your Sage. I am a messenger sent by the Jade Emperor to invite your master to Heaven."

The demons ran to the Monkey King and reported: "There is an old man outside who claims to be a heavenly messenger and says he is to take you back to Heaven with him."

"That must be the general, Star of Long Life, who was here once before. He has come just at the right time," said the Monkey King. "Last time they failed to give me a position that was worthy of me, but at least I have been to Heaven and know what it's like there. Now I am sure they will offer me something more to my liking."

He ordered the chieftains to raise the banners, sound the drums and mount the royal guard in the visitor's honour. He himself donned his full armour, complete with helmet and coat of mail, and over

the coat he put a dark yellow robe. Then he put on his cloud-walking shoes and, followed by the other monkeys, hurried out of the cave.

"Come in, esteemed Star," he called, bowing low before the heavenly messenger. "Do forgive me for not coming out at once to greet you."

The Star of Long Life quickly went inside the cave and addressed the Monkey King in a solemn voice: "The officials of the Imperial Stables have informed his Holiness the Jade Emperor that the Great Sage was offended because the office of Celestial Groom was not prominent enough for him, and he therefore left Heaven. The Jade Emperor, however, rejected this, saying: 'All the heavenly officials proceed from less important to more important appointments, so there is no reason why he should consider any appointment unworthy of him.' The Emperor then sent the King Li and the third Crown Prince Natha down to Earth in order to punish the Great Sage. They little knew what magic powers the Sage possessed. Having suffered a defeat they reported to Heaven that the Great Sage had put up a banner and claims to be an equal to Heaven. The generals were angered by this. I alone dared to speak up on the Great Sage's behalf, putting myself in danger of punishment in the hope that I should be able to prevent further bloodshed. I therefore beseech the Great Sage to come with me and accept his official appointment."

"Thank you very much," said the Monkey King, smiling. "You have been most kind, last time as well as today. But tell me, is there such an office as that of the Great Sage, Equal to Heaven, in the upper regions?"

"I have arranged for you to have it," said the Star of Long Life respectfully. "I would never have dared to come for you if it had been otherwise. If anything goes wrong, I shall shoulder the responsibility."

The Monkey King was overjoyed. He invited the Star of Long Life to a banquet, but he refused; so they both mounted a cloud which took them up to the southern gate of Heaven. They made for the Hall of Magic Clouds, all the porters and guards bowing to them by way of greeting. The Star of Long Life went in to announce their arrival. The Jade Emperor at once asked the Monkey King to enter.

"I give you the rank of Great Sage, Equal to Heaven. It is one of the highest offices, and I therefore strictly forbid you to indulge in any unsuitable behaviour."

The Monkey King bowed low and gave thanks for the honour that had been shown him. The Jade Emperor then ordered the celestial architect to build a palace to house the Office of the Great Sage, Equal to Heaven; it was to stand to the right of the Peach Orchard and to consist of two departments: the Department of Peace and Quiet and the Department of Spiritual Calm. In each of them there would be officials and secretaries to serve the Great Sage. Finally the Emperor charged five Stars with the task of telling him about his job. The Emperor gave Monkey two bottles of his favourite wine and ten golden blossoms which helped to calm the spirit and strengthen the will, so that Sun Wu-k'ung should be prevented from

doing any more mischief while in Heaven.

The Monkey King really believed he was being set up in office. That same day he accompanied the five Stars to his new palace, opened the bottles and treated them all to wine. The Stars then retired to their chambers, and the Monkey King began to delight in his new way of life.

He was only a monkey and knew nothing of official matters or ranks and salaries. He was quite content to have his name entered among those of the celestial officials. His servants from both the departments waited on him from morning till night, he had three meals a day and slept all night, serene and untroubled and free as a bird. In his leisure moments he wandered about the palace making new friends. Although he addressed the members of the Holy Trinity as "Venerable", and the four Emperors as "Majesty", he treated all the others — the Planets and Lunar Quarters, the Heavenly Kings, Spirits of Hours and Days, and the common Stars — as absolutely his equals. One day he went to the east, the next day to the west, flying in the clouds without anyone knowing where he had gone.

One morning, when the Jade Emperor was holding court, the Sage of Genuineness stepped forward and made a complaint against the Monkey King. He said that "The Great Sage" spent his time wandering aimlessly about Heaven, making friends with all the Stars, and treating even the highest of them as his equals.

"I fear, Your Holiness, that he will commit some folly unless we give him something to occupy his time," the Sage said.

The Jade Emperor immediately sent for the Monkey King. Sun Wu-k'ung hurried in, full of glee.

"What reward or promotion am I to receive that Your Holiness should have sent for me?" he asked.

"I hear that you have nothing in particular to do," replied the Emperor, "and I have therefore decided to give you some

work. I want you to take over the supervision of the Peach Orchard. Keep both your eyes open and take really good care of it."

The Monkey King was greatly flattered. Thanking the Emperor for his kindness, he bowed low and respectfully took his leave. Full of impatience he rushed to inspect the Peach Orchard. There the God of Earth stopped him and asked him what he wanted.

"The Jade Emperor has asked me to take over the supervision of the Peach Orchard," Sun Wu-k'ung said proudly. "I have therefore come to have a look at it."

The God of Earth bowed and quickly called the gardeners who were hoeing the ground round the trees, carrying water, picking the peaches and sweeping the paths. They all touched their foreheads to the ground in front of the Monkey King and led him inside the orchard. He spent a long time looking round, and then asked how many trees there were in the orchard.

"There are three thousand six hundred peach trees here," the God of Earth explained. "One thousand two hundred of them have flowers and small fruit. They ripen once every three thousand years and those who eat their fruit become sages, their bodies growing healthy and as light as air. In the middle of the orchard are one thousand two hundred trees with blossoms growing in clusters and with sweet fruit which ripens once every six thousand years. Those who eat it can float in the clouds; they live long and do not grow old. The remaining one thousand two hundred trees at the back have purple-veined blossom and fruit with pale yellow stones. These ripen once every nine thousand years. Those who eat their fruit will outlive Heaven and Earth and be as eternal as the Sun and the Moon."

The Monkey King's joy knew no bounds. That very day he counted all the trees to check their number, and inspected all the groves before returning to his palace. From that time on, he only played once a month, on the day of the full moon. He forgot his new friends. One day he noticed that the peaches on the top branches had become ripe, and he decided to try them. However, the God of Earth, the gardeners and his own personal followers were constantly at his side. He had to think of a scheme to rid himself of them.

"Wait for me outside the gate," he said. "I'm going to have a short nap in the orchard."

They did as he asked. The Monkey King took off his court robes and cap, climbed the highest tree, chose the ripest of the peaches and picked them. Settling himself comfortably in the tree-top he ate all he wanted. Then he jumped down again, dressed, put on his cap, and called back his retinue, asking them to accompany him to the palace. Every second or third day after that he invented some excuse to enable him to steal the peaches.

One day Her Majesty the Queen of Heaven decided to hold a Peach Banquet. She gave orders for the jewel-studded banquet hall by the Jade Lake to be opened, and sent the white-robed, the black-robed, the red-robed, the grey-robed, the pink-robed, the yellow-robed and the green-robed fairies with their baskets to pick peaches for the banquet. The seven fairies came to the entrance of the Peach Or-

chard, only to find it guarded by the God of Earth, the gardeners and the Monkey King's officials, who barred their way and refused to let them in.

"We have come upon the orders of Her Majesty the Queen of Heaven to pick peaches for the banquet," they explained.

"Halt, noble beauties," said the God of Earth. "Things have changed this year. The Jade Emperor has put the Great Sage, Equal to Heaven, in charge of the orchard. You must ask his permission before we can let you in."

"And where is the Great Sage to be found?" the fairies asked.

"He is inside the orchard at the moment. He felt a little tired and is having a nap."

"Very well then, let's go and find him, for we have no time to lose."

The God of Earth led them inside the orchard. The Monkey King was nowhere to be found, there was nothing in the orchard but his robe and cap. They searched everywhere, but to no avail. Monkey was gone.

In fact the Monkey King had played for a while in the orchard, eaten a few peaches, and had then changed himself into a little creature only two inches tall and gone to sleep in the thick foliage high up in one of the trees.

"What shall we do if we fail to find the Great Sage?" lamented the fairies. "We cannot go back empty-handed."

"No, you can't do that," agreed one of the palace officials. "Since you say you have been sent by the Queen of Heaven, go ahead and pick as many peaches as you need. We shall tell the Great Sage about it when he returns. He used to travel a great deal, so I expect he has gone off to see some of his friends."

The fairies trotted off and began to pick the peaches. First they picked two basketfuls from the trees in the front, then three from the trees in the middle. When they came to the trees at the back, they found here and there a green peach and a lot of snapped stalks. All the ripe peaches had been eaten by the Monkey King. The fairies stood there for a long time looking round, until at last they discovered a single half-ripe peach on the southern side. The grey-robed fairy reached up and pulled the bough towards her, the red-robed fairy plucked the peach, whereupon the grey-robed fairy let go of the bough. This woke the Monkey King, who happened to be sleeping on this very bough, in his guise of a dwarf. He assumed his proper shape, took his magic cudgel from behind his ear, waved it in the air, and shouted:

"What monster dares to come and steal my peaches?"

The terrified fairies fell upon their knees, crying: "Great Sage, don't be angry with us! We are no monsters but the fairies of Her Majesty the Queen of Heaven, who sent us to pick the magic peaches for her Peach Banquet by the Jade Lake. When we arrived at the orchard we first spoke to the God of Earth. You were nowhere to be found, and we were afraid we would not fulfil Her Majesty's orders if we waited any longer, and so we began to pick the peaches. We beseech you to forgive us, Great Sage."

Hearing this, Sun Wu-k'ung overcame his rage and put on a kindly expression. "Rise from your knees, dear fairies," he said. "Who did you say was being invited to this banquet?"

"The list of the guests is drawn up in accordance with an old custom," the fairies replied. "It includes the Supreme Buddha of the Western Heaven, the Bodhisattvas and the Holy Monks, the Arhats, the Goddess of Mercy from the Far South, the Holy Emperor of Divine Wisdom from the East, the Immortals of the Ten Continents and Three Islands, the God of Profound Darkness from the Far North, as well as the Yellow-horned Sage, Emperor of the Centre. These are the rulers of the five regions. Then there are the Princes of the Five Planets, the Three Virtuous Ones from the eight parts of Paradise, the Emperors of the eight Purgatories, the nine Guardians of the Heavenly Gates, the Spirits of the oceans and hills, the Lords of Darkness from the eight Infernos, the Gods of Fertility, and others. The various Gods, high and low, from all the palaces of Heaven will also be taking part."

"What about me? Have I not been invited?" asked the Monkey King.

"We regret to say we have heard nothing about that," replied the fairies, bowing before him.

"But I am the Great Sage, Equal to Heaven. Surely they must have invited me as a guest of honour," said the Monkey King.

The fairies told him that the banquet was being organised according to ancient rules and they could not say whether it would be possible to make an exception for him.

"Yes, you're right, it's not your fault," he admitted. "Wait here, while I go and see if I have been invited or not."

He lifted up his hands, recited a magic spell and rooted all seven fairies to the spot. They stood there under the peach trees like seven statues, their eyes wide open. The Monkey King mounted a magic cloud and let it carry him out of the orchard and towards the Jade Lake. He had only floated a little distance when he saw a great spirit going past on a coloured cloud. Approaching nearer, he saw that it was the Bare-footed Sage. He at once thought of a trick by means of which he might fool the old Immortal and secretly attend the banquet himself.

"Where are you going, great Immortal?" he asked.

"I'm hurrying to the Peach Banquet, to which Her Majesty the Queen of Heaven has been kind enough to invite me," the Sage replied.

"I see you're not aware that the Jade Emperor has sent me, because of my ability to move quickly in the clouds, to go round to all the guests and inform them that they are to pay their homage at the Palace of Supreme Wisdom before proceeding to the banquet," lied Monkey.

The Sage was a truthful, trusting soul, and it did not occur to him to doubt the Monkey King's words. Even so, he found the news a little strange.

"In past years we always paid homage and gave thanks at the Jade Lake itself. Why is it that this time we are to pay homage at the Palace of Supreme Wisdom and only then go on to the Lake?" he asked.

Nevertheless he turned his coloured cloud in the opposite direction and floated away to the Palace of Supreme Wisdom. The Monkey King recited a spell, shook himself, and changed into the Bare-footed Sage, in whose guise he hurried to the Jade Lake. Soon he had reached the banquet hall, where he halted his cloud and quietly crept in. Everything was ready for the feast, but none of the guests had arrived yet. As he stood there looking round he suddenly became aware of a strong smell of new wine. Turning to the right he saw several celestial vintners making wine. Their assistants were taking away the mashed grapes, servants brought water, kitchen-boys stoked the fire, washed the jars and cleaned the jugs. The finished wine, as clear as jade, gave off a delicious odour. Sun Wu-k'ung's mouth watered. If it had not been for all those people, he would have gone and drunk some at once. As it was he had to resort to magic. Plucking out a few hairs, he put them in his mouth and chewed them up. Then he spat them out and cried "Change!", whereupon the hairs changed into insects whose sting has the effect of sending their victims to sleep. The insects flew up into the vintners' faces and stung each and every one of them. In a moment their heads drooped, their hands fell limp by their sides, their eyes closed drowsily and they slept.

The Monkey King tasted all of the fine, delicious foods and, going into the gallery, helped himself generously to the wine in the jars and jugs. Having eaten and drunk his fill, he found that he was intoxicated.

"This is bad!" he said to himself in dismay. "The guests will be here any minute now. If they find me, the game is up. I had better go back to my own palace and sleep it off."

Stumbling and staggering along, very much the worse for drink, Monkey lost his way. Instead of coming to his own palace, he found himself on the other side of Heaven. Suddenly, he realised where he was.

"Why, this is the Palace of Joy, the home of the Patriarch of the Way. Well, I've always wanted to meet that old man and have never had time. Now that I am here I might as well go and see him."

He tidied his clothes and went in. The palace was completely empty, for the Patriarch of the Way was busy discussing something with the Buddha Torchbearer on the Red Terrace of the three-storey pagoda, and all the servants, officials and generals from both their palaces were there with them, listening to their learned discussion. The Monkey King ran into the laboratory in which the Patriarch mixed his Elixir of Life. There was no one there, either, but the Monkey King saw a fire burning in the furnace. On each side of it stood five gourds, filled to the brim with the elexir.

"This is the treasure of the Immortals," cried the Monkey King gleefully.

Since he had achieved Immortality and solved a large number of secrets he had intended to produce an elixir with which to save his fellow monkeys, but at home he never seemed to have time to do so. He was in luck today — not only had he found the elixir, but the Patriarch of the Way was out and could not prevent him from taking some.

"I must try the elixir myself!" he said, tilting the gourds and drinking all the liquid inside.

When he had drunk it, the effects of the wine wore off completely and he realised the seriousness of his deed.

"This last prank of mine is even worse than all the others. If the Jade Emperor gets to hear of it, I am done for. I must run away as quickly as I can. The best thing to do is to go back to my own kingdom."

He rushed out of the palace, not going the way he had come but making straight for the western gate of Heaven. He made himself invisible and slipped through the gate, unseen by anyone. Then he mounted a cloud and was carried back to the Mountain of Many Flowers. From afar he could see flags and banners fluttering in the breeze and swords and spears glinting in the sun. The chieftains and demon kings were busily drilling in arms.

"Little ones, I have come back again!" cried the Monkey King.

All the animals laid down their arms and knelt before him.

"Welcome, Great Sage. You have been gone for so long and did not even think to come and see how your subjects were getting on."

"It wasn't a long time at all," replied the Monkey King and he went inside the cave. The chieftains bowed low before him, touching their foreheads to the ground, and did everything they could to make him comfortable.

"How have you fared in Heaven all these hundred years, Great Sage?" they asked. "What office did you hold there?"

"A hundred years?" laughed the Monkey King. "But I have only been gone half a year."

"A day in Heaven is a whole year down below," replied the chieftains.

"I enjoyed the favour of the Jade Emperor, who gave me the rank of Great Sage, Equal to Heaven, and an office with two departments, the Department of Peace and Quiet and the Department of Spiritual Calm. I was attended by celestial officials. Then, when the Emperor saw I had no work to do, he entrusted me with the supervision of the Peach Orchard. The Queen of Heaven wanted to give a Peach Banquet today and failed to invite me. Rather than lower myself by claiming an invitation, I went to the banquet hall of my own accord and ate all their dainty dishes and drank all their wine. Somewhat intoxicated, I got lost and by mistake arrived at the palace of the Patriarch of the Way, where I drank all his Elixir of Life. Fearing the anger of the Jade Emperor, I thought it wiser to leave Heaven."

The animals were overjoyed. They held a banquet, serving coconut wine in large stone bowls. The Monkey King took one single sip and made a face, refusing to drink any more.

"The Great Sage has grown accustomed to special foods and wines in Heaven, so that our coconut wine is no longer good enough for him. But an old proverb says, 'There is no water like the water out of your own well'," said the monkeys.

"There are also no people like your own people," said the Monkey King, adding: "Up there at the Jade Lake I drank such wines and such jade nectar as you've never even dreamed of. They have many more bottles in the gallery. I'll go back and bring you a few bottles from Heaven. Each of you will have half a cup and you'll live long and stay healthy."

The monkeys were delighted. Their King ran out of the cave, made himself invisible, jumped on a cloud, and set off for the banqueting hall in Heaven. The water-carriers, kitchen-boys and others had still not come out of their slumber and were snoring loudly. The Monkey King put a bottle under each arm, took a bottle in each hand, and turned the cloud round. The monkeys held a great banquet with the celestial wine. Each of them drank a cupful or two.

Competition in Magic Changes

Kuan-yin, the Goddess of Compassion from Mount Potaloka in the Southern Sea, had been invited by the Queen of Heaven to attend the Peach Banquet. The goddess, who helps people in distress, came to the Jade Lake accompanied by her disciple, the monk Hui-an. The jewel-studded groves were completely empty, the banqueting hall a shambles. All she found were a few heavenly Immortals arguing and running about in great confusion. Kuan-yin greeted them, and was told what had taken place.

"Since there is to be no banquet and no drinking," she said, "we might as well go and see the Jade Emperor."

The Immortals followed her obediently. When they reached the Palace of Supreme Wisdom, they were met by four heavenly generals and the Bare-footed Sage, who told them how angry the Jade Emperor had been and how he had sent an army to capture the Monkey King.

"I wish to speak to the Jade Emperor," the Goddess of Compassion said.

The Jade Emperor was at that moment engaged in conversation with the Patriarch of the Way, while the Queen of Heaven stood by awaiting further orders.

"What is to be done about the Peach Banquet?" asked Kuan-yin when the customary greetings had been exchanged.

"It is our habit to hold this banquet every year," replied the Jade Emperor, "and we all enjoy it very much. This year, however, it's been spoiled by that diabolical monkey. I have invited you all here in vain."

"What monkey are you talking about?" asked Kuan-yin.

"It was born of a stone egg on the Mountain of Many Flowers in the land of Ao-lai," explained the Jade Emperor. "His eyes gave off a golden glow which penetrated as far as the palaces of Heaven. At first we failed to take any notice of him, and he became a demon, having learned to catch dragons and subdue tigers and having crossed his name off the Death List. The Dragon King and the King of Darkness have complained about him. I wanted to have him apprehended, but the Star of Long Life pointed out to me that all creatures in the world of beasts, the world of humans and in Heaven, who are possessed of five senses and four limbs, can become Immortals. I therefore showed him mercy and wished to teach him wisdom, calling him up to Heaven and appointing him a groom in the celestial stables. The accursed monkey considered this appointment beneath him and ran off. I therefore sent King Li and Crown Prince Natha to recapture him. Again I behaved leniently towards him and invited him back, giving him the title of Great Sage, Equal to Heaven. This being an honorary title with no duties attached, he was bored and wandered all over the upper regions. Fearing that he might get up to some mischief I charged him with the supervision of the Peach Orchard. But he again failed to abide by the rules and ate all the large peaches from the trees at the back of the orchard. We did not invite him to the Peach Banquet, because he did not really hold any official position. He thought of a trick, however, and deceived the Barefooted Sage, taking on his shape and going in his place to the banqueting hall where he secretly ate all the choice food and drank all the miraculous wines. As if that weren't enough, he stole the Elixir of Life from the Patriarch of the Way, and took some of the wine home with him to give to all his monkeys. This enraged me so much that I summoned a celestial army and gave orders for both heavenly and earthly nets to be spread round his mountain. Up to this moment, however, I have had no news from the battlefield and so I don't know whether our troops have triumphed or not."

Hearing this, Kuan-yin told her disciple to go at once to the Mountain of Many Flowers and find out how matters stood.

"If fighting is in progress, you can lend the heavenly forces a hand. In any case let me know without delay what the position is."

The monk Hui-an hitched up his robe, seized an iron cudgel and floated away on a cloud. Reaching the Mountain of Many Flowers he found thick heavenly and earthly nets spread all round and heard bells being rung and orders given all over the camp. The mountain was cordoned off in such a way that not even a drop of water could have got by. Hui-an stopped and called out:

"Celestial sentries, be so good as to announce me. I am the second son of the Heavenly King Li, the Crown Prince

Moksha, chief disciple of the Goddess of Compassion, Kuan-yin. I have come to find out what is happening in the battle."

The sentries hastened to announce the Prince's arrival. King Li gave orders for the nets to be lifted and the Prince admitted to the camp. Dawn was breaking in the east when Prince Moksha entered, bowing to the Kings of the Four Quarters and to his father, King Li.

"Where have you come from, my son?" King Li asked him.

"I accompanied the Goddess of Compassion to the Peach Banquet. Finding the banqueting hall empty and plundered and the Jade Lake deserted, the Goddess of Compassion took all the Immortals to see the Jade Emperor. He told us that my father and the other heavenly generals had descended to Earth to punish the rebellious monkey. No news had come from the battlefield all day and no one knew how things were going. The Goddess therefore sent me to find out."

"We got here yesterday and encamped," said King Li. "I at once despatched the Nine Planets to challenge the Monkey King. But that rogue again resorted to his magic tricks and chased the Planets away. I then led the army into battle myself, but once more he forced us back. My hundred thousand men fought him till dusk; he, however, conjured up hundreds and thousands of monkeys and forced my army to retreat. Later when we counted our prisoners we found they were all wolves and tigers and other animals. We had not succeeded in capturing a single monkey. Today we have not yet gone into battle."

He had just finished speaking when

a messenger came in from the camp entrance.

"The Monkey King and all his host of monkeys are challenging us to battle!"

The heavenly kings at once held a council of war. Prince Moksha addressed them, saying: "I have been ordered by the Goddess of Compassion not only to investigate the military situation but also, if necessary, to aid you in your fight. I should therefore like to take a hand in the battle and see for myself what this Great Sage is like."

"My son," replied King Li, "you have been studying with the Goddess for some years now and have, I am sure, mastered every kind of magic. Now you can turn your learning to good advantage."

Moksha girded up his embroidered cloak and, brandishing his iron cudgel in both hands, rushed out of the camp, shouting: "Which of you is the Great Sage, Equal to Heaven?" The Monkey King, holding his wishing cudgel in his hand, replied: "It's me, Sun! And who are you that you come asking for me?"

"I'm the second Crown Prince Moksha, son of the Heavenly King Li. I am a defender of the Faith and the chief disciple of the Goddess of Compassion Kuan-yin. My religious name is Hui-an."

"What are you doing here then, since you should be practising virtue in the Southern Sea?" the Monkey King asked mockingly.

"My mistress has sent me to find out what is happening on the battlefield," said Prince Moksha. "Now that I see what a rebellious rogue you are, I wish to capture you myself."

"How dare you brag like this!" cried the Monkey King angrily. "I shall give you a taste of my cudgel!"

Moksha was not in the least frightened. Grasping his iron cudgel he leapt forward to attack the Monkey King. They fought mercilessly, engaging fifty or sixty times until Moksha's arms were aching and he could no longer parry his opponent's blows, while his own all went wide of their mark. Seeing there was nothing to be done, he fled the battlefield. The Monkey King withdrew his forces and waited outside the main entrance to the cave. From there he saw the celestial soldiers making way for Prince Moksha, who rushed back to the heavenly camp and reported to King Li: "That is a strange sort of monkey indeed. He possesses great magic powers. I could do nothing with him and had to abandon the field."

King Li was dismayed. He immediately wrote an appeal for help and sent the demon king Great Power and Prince Moksha to take it up to Heaven.

They lost no time and went soaring up on a cloud. In a while they had reached the Palace of Supreme Wisdom, where four heavenly messengers announced them to the Jade Emperor in the Hall of Magic Clouds. There they handed over their message.

"Well, what news have you brought?" asked the Goddess of Compassion.

"My royal father told me," replied Moksha, "that they gave battle to the Monkey King yesterday and captured a good many tigers, lions, panthers, elephants and other animals, but not a single monkey. Just as we were discussing what to do, the Monkey King again challenged us to battle. I therefore seized my magic cudgel and fought some fifty or sixty rounds with him but without success, and in the end I had to flee for my life. My father then sent me with the demon king Great Power back to Heaven to ask for help."

Kuan-yin bowed her head and thought deeply.

Meanwhile the Jade Emperor had broken the seal and read the message. When he discovered that the celestial army was asking for help, he said: "Am I really to believe that a single monkey is so powerful he can overcome a hundred thousand heavenly soldiers? King Li is again appealing for help! But what troops am I supposed to send him now?"

The Goddess of Compassion pressed the palms of her hands together and said: "Do not worry, Your Holiness. I know of a god who will certainly be able to deal with this monkey."

"Which god do you have in mind?" the Emperor asked.

"I mean your nephew, the illustrious Immortal and God of Truth Erh-lang," replied Kuan-yin. "He now has his dwelling at the estuary of the Libation River and is in touch with Hell itself, which sends him incense. Not long ago he defeated six ogres. He has with him his six brothers from the Mountain of Plums and one thousand two hundred demons of immense magical powers. He is unwilling to take orders from anyone, but is always ready to give assistance. Your Holiness should ask him to bring his troops. With his help I have no doubt we shall capture the monkey."

So the Jade Emperor had the appeal written and sent the king of demons Great Power as his messenger. The demon king mounted a cloud and was carried to the mouth of the Libation River. In less than half an hour he reached the temple of the god Erh-lang. The guardian demons announced that a messenger had arrived with a message from the Jade Emperor himself. The god Erh-lang and all his brothers came out to meet the messenger. Burning some incense, Erh-lang then read the message, which ran as follows:

"The rebellious Monkey King from the Mountain of Many Flowers, who has taken the name of Great Sage, Equal to Heaven, is playing havoc both on Earth and in Heaven. While dwelling in the upper regions he stole peaches, wine and the Elixir of Life, and upset all our arrangements for the Peach Banquet. We have now sent an army, one hundred thousand men strong, against him, and his mountain has been encircled with eighteen heavenly and earthly nets. So far, however, our efforts have been unsuccessful. I therefore appeal hereby to my noble nephew and his brothers to go to the Mountain of Many Flowers and assist in apprehending this

evil-doer. I shall not fail to show my gratitude by giving them due promotion and rewarding them generously once victory is won."

Erh-lang was well pleased with the Jade Emperor's message. He asked the heavenly messenger to return to Heaven, saying he himself would put on his armour and set off at once to give what assistance he could. Then he called his six brothers together and told them: "The Jade Emperor has just asked us to go and capture the rebellious monkey on the Mountain of Many Flowers. Let's start out together and be victorious."

His six brothers agreed at once. They marshalled their magic forces, armed themselves with bows and arrows and, taking with them their hunting falcons and dogs, unleashed a strong wind and, in a trice, were carried across the Eastern Sea to the Mountain of Many Flowers. There, the dense barrier of the heavenly and earthly nets halted them. Erh-lang called out: "I am the illustrious Immortal and God of Truth Erh-lang and I have come at the request of the Jade Emperor to capture the rebellious monkey. Quickly make way for us and let us in."

The Kings of the Four Quarters and King Li came out of the camp to meet them. The brothers exchanged greetings and asked how the battle was going and if King Li was winning yet.

"I shall have to try my magic changes on him," said Erh-lang, laughing. "Please have the nets drawn tightly here on the ground but leave the space overhead free. That will make things easier for me. If I seem to be losing the fight, don't bother to come to my assistance as my brothers will look after me. And if I defeat the monkey, you need not trouble yourselves with helping me to tie him up, my brothers will do that too. All I ask is that King Li should hold his magic mirror in the air, so that we can see the monster's reflection in it. When I drive him into a tight corner he will doubtless try to hide from us, but the mirror will reveal him."

The heavenly kings posted sentries to all points of the compass and arrayed their troops. Erh-lang and his six brothers went out to give battle, ordering the generals to stand in a semicircle ready for action with the hunting falcons and dogs. The ordinary demons were drawn up behind them in reserve.

Erh-lang and his brothers advanced as far as the Water Curtain Cave, where they found the monkey host awaiting them in coiling dragon formation. A banner with the inscription "Great Sage, Equal to Heaven" had been raised in the middle.

"How dare that cursed monkey call himself an equal to Heaven?" Erh-lang cried in a rage.

"Never mind about that now, we'd better go and start the fight," said his brothers.

As soon as the monkeys caught sight of Erh-lang, they ran to report to the Monkey King. He grasped his magic cudgel, put on his golden armour, cloud-walking shoes and golden cap, and rushed out of the gate, glaring about him. In his magnificent armour the god Erh-lang presented a most impressive sight.

The Monkey King laughed, wielded his magic cudgel, and shouted: "What audacious corporal is this who dares to challenge me?"

"You scoundrel, have you no eyes that you don't recognise me?" cried Erh-lang. "I am the god Erh-lang, nephew of the Jade Emperor. Today he asked me to capture you, you insubordinate monkey groom. Your last hour has come."

"I remember that once upon a time the Jade Emperor's sister descended to the world of mortals and became the wife of some earthly prince. She had a son by him, and this son is said to have split the Peach Mountain with his axe. Are you he? I ought to give you a piece of my mind, but I can't be bothered with you. I'll take pity on you, for a single blow of my cudgel would put an end to you. Go back where you came from, you low-born princeling, and tell the four kings of Heaven to come in your place."

Erh-lang was furious.

"Accursed monkey, enough of your insolence! I'll give you a taste of my sword!"

The Monkey King dodged the blow and, quickly raising his magic cudgel, struck back at his opponent.

They engaged over three hundred times and still the issue remained undecided. Erh-lang exerted all his magic powers and changed himself into a giant a hundred thousand feet tall. In each hand he brandished three magic swords, pointed like the crags at the top of the Blossom Mountain. His face was pale, his hair ginger, and huge boar's tusks projected out of his scowling mouth. He made straight for the Monkey King. He was not to be outdone, however. He grew and grew until he had become just as tall as Erh-lang. His face was equally horrible and he wielded a single cudgel which was as gigantic as the pillar that stands on top of Mount K'un-lun and supports one end of Heaven. He made straight for Erh-lang. The Monkey King's generals were so terrified by the two monsters that they could not even wave their banners. His other chieftains lost all their courage and forgot how to wield their swords. On the battlefield Erh-lang's six brothers ordered the demons to go forward. They let loose their falcons and dogs in the direction of the Water Curtain Cave, and took up their bows and cross-bows. A terrible battle broke out. The monkeys were scattered, some two or three thousand of them being taken prisoner, including the generals. The rest threw away their lances, dropped their shields behind them, cast off their swords and threw away their rifles. They all ran as fast as their feet would carry them, shrieking at the tops of their voices. Some took refuge in the hills, others tried to hide in the cave.

Suddenly, in the heat of battle the Monkey King saw his subjects fleeing. Frightened, he assumed his normal form and took to his heels as well. Erh-lang gave chase, shouting: "Where are you off to? Give yourself up this minute, or I shall kill you!"

But the Monkey King had no more stomach for the fight and fled as fast as his feet would carry him. At the cave entrance he ran into the six brothers, who barred his way.

"Where are you making for, wretched monkey?" they cried.

Trembling all over with terror, the Monkey King quickly changed his cudgel into an embroidery needle and placed it behind his ear. He shook himself and, changing into a sparrow, flew to the crown of a tree. The six brothers were confused by this trick, and they looked everywhere, shouting: "The monkey has got away! The monkey has got away!"

There was no trace of him anywhere.

Erh-lang hurried to join his brothers.

"Where has he got to?" he asked them.

"We had just managed to surround him when he vanished," they replied.

Gazing round with his eagle's eye, Erh-lang suddenly caught sight of the Monkey King sitting in the treetop in his sparrow shape. Erh-lang assumed his normal form, threw away his magic cudgel, laid aside his bow and quiver, shook his body and changed into an eagle. Spreading wide his wings he pounced on the Monkey King. The latter did not wait, however, but flew off. In flight he changed into a seagull and soared up into the sky. Erh-lang shook himself once more and changed into a huge sea hawk. He swept up into the clouds and was just about to attack when the Monkey King plummeted down and, changing himself into a fish, plunged into a stream. Erh-lang rushed to the bank but could see no trace of his enemy.

"That monkey has certainly changed into a fish and hidden in the water," he thought. "I must change myself too if I wish to get him."

He changed into a cormorant and skimmed low over the stream, waiting. The Monkey King was swimming downstream when he noticed a suspicious-looking bird circling overhead. It looked like a blue kite, but its plumage wasn't dark enough. It looked like a heron, but had no tuft on its head. It looked like a stork, but its feet were not red.

"That must be Erh-lang, waiting for me up there!" he thought.

The Monkey King released a few bubbles, turned round briskly and raced away. Erh-lang immediately noticed this.

"That fish releasing bubbles looks like a carp, but its tail isn't red. It looks like a trout, but it has no spots on its scales. It looks like a tench, but there are no stars on its head. It looks like a perch, but there are no bristles on its fin. Why did it turn tail as soon as it saw me? It must be the Monkey King, changed into a fish!"

Swooping down on the strange fish, he

snapped at it with his beak. The Monkey King shot out of the water and changed himself into a water snake, slithering up the bank and hiding in the grass. When Erh-lang missed the fish and saw the snake coming out of the water he immediately recognised the Monkey King. Turning round, he changed himself into a grey crane with a red cap that looked as if it had been embroidered on the top of his head. He stretched his long neck and his beak, like a pair of iron pincers, and struck at the water snake. The Monkey King was quicker, however, and changed into a freckled bustard, standing motionless in the reeds on the bank of the river. This infuriated Erh-lang, for the freckled bustard is the lowest and most despicable of all creatures. Erh-lang assumed his original form and, coming closer, took a cross-bow, aimed, and shot the Monkey King with such force that the bustard rolled over.

The Monkey King went rolling down

the slope. When he was out of sight he changed himself into a wayside chapel of the God of Earth. His wide-grinning mouth was the doorway, his teeth the doorposts, his tongue the guardian god on the altar, his eyes the window frames. But he did not know what to do with his tail, which stuck awkwardly straight up into the air, so he changed it into a flag-pole.

Erh-lang scrambled down the slope. Instead of the freckled bustard he had shot he found only a small chapel. He examined it carefully with his eagle's eyes and then laughed outright when he noticed the flag-pole at the back.

"So this is where the Monkey King has got to! Trying to trick me again, is he? I've seen a great many chapels and shrines, but never one with a flag-pole at the back! The criminal is setting a trap for me, I suppose. Wants to lure me inside and bite me to death. You won't get me inside — I'll smash your windows and kick your doors in instead!"

The Monkey King was horrified.

"He means to butcher me! The doors are my teeth and the windows my eyes. If he kicks in my teeth and smashes my eyes, what shall I do then?"

Waiting no longer he disappeared in the air with a mighty tiger-spring.

Erh-lang searched high and low for him in vain. While he was thus engaged, his six brothers hurried up to him.

"Well, eldest brother, have you caught that monkey?"

"The scoundrel changed himself into a shrine to confuse me," said Erh-lang with a laugh. "I was just getting ready to smash his windows and kick in his doors, but all of a sudden he shook himself and vanished without trace. It's all very peculiar."

His brothers went pale with shock. They helped Erh-lang in his search, but there was no sign of the Monkey King anywhere.

"You stay here, brothers, and keep a look-out," Erh-lang told them. "I'll go up and see if I can find him."

He mounted a cloud and flew up. Before long he came across King Li who was holding the magic mirror in the sky, with Crown Prince Natha at his side.

"Haven't you seen the Monkey King?" Erh-lang asked them.

"He hasn't been here yet," replied King Li. "If he had, I would have seen him in the mirror."

Erh-lang described the capture of the monkeys and his contest in magic changes with the Monkey King.

"In the end he changed into a wayside shrine and, just as I was going to hit him, he disappeared."

Hearing this, King Li flashed his mirror to every side. Then he burst out laughing.

"Make haste, Erh-lang!" he cried. "The Monkey King has made himself invisible, has left the camp, and is making straight for your temple on the Libation River!"

Erh-lang grasped his magic lance and raced away in pursuit. In the meantime the Monkey King had reached Erh-lang's temple and, taking on the god's form, he lowered his cloud and went inside. The guardian demons did not prevent him from going in — on the contrary, they bowed low and, one after the other, touched their foreheads to the ground in homage. The Monkey King stood in the place of honour and watched the incense smoke. Then he examined the pictures adorning the walls, depicting the sacrifice of a bull, a horse and a sheep; and read letters asking for the birth of a son and for speedy recovery from illness. At that moment someone announced that a second god Erh-lang had just arrived. This caused great consternation among the guardians, who could hardly believe their eyes.

"Have you seen a suspicious-looking creature calling itself the Great Sage, Equal to Heaven?" the genuine Erh-lang asked.

"No such creature has been here," they replied, "but inside there is yet another god Erh-lang taking a look round the temple."

Erh-lang rushed inside. Seeing him, the Monkey King changed back into his true form.

"I hope you won't be too upset, Erh-

lang, if I tell you that your temple now carries my name," he said audaciously.

Erh-lang raised his three-pronged, twin-bladed magic lance and aimed a blow at the Monkey King's face. He dodged and took his embroidery needle from behind his ear, making it grow larger as he did so. Then he stepped forward and closed with Erh-lang. Shouting and cursing, they ran out of the temple gate. They fought in the mist and in the clouds until at last they reached the Mountain of Many Flowers, frightening the kings of Four Quarters, who were on guard there with their troops. His six brothers now came to aid Erh-lang and surrounded the Monkey King, hemming him in on every side.

Meanwhile in Heaven the Jade Emperor, Kuan-yin, the Queen of Heaven and all the heavenly dignitaries were wondering why they had not heard from Erh-lang all day. The Goddess of Compassion pressed the palms of her hands together and appealed to the Jade Emperor to go with the Patriarch of the Way to the southern gate of Heaven and see what was happening. The Emperor thought this a very good idea, and they all went together.

The Guardians of the Gate came forward to meet them and opened the gate for them.

Looking out, they could see the heavenly armies stretching the heavenly and earthly nets and keeping guard all round the Mountain of Many Flowers.

The Heavenly King Li and Crown Prince Natha were holding the magic mirror up in the air.

Erh-lang and his six brothers encircled the Monkey King, attacking him fiercely as they pressed in on him.

"That Erh-lang whom I recommended isn't doing at all badly," said Kuan-yin approvingly. "He has cornered Monkey, though he hasn't succeeded in capturing him yet. If I were to give him a little help I'm sure he would manage it."

"How do you intend to help him?" asked the Patriarch of the Way. "What weapon do you mean to use?"

"I'll throw a vase onto his head," replied the Goddess of Compassion. "That won't kill him, but it will make him lose his balance, and Erh-lang will find it easy to catch him."

"Your vase is made of porcelain," objected the Patriarch of the Way. "It would be all right as long as it hit him squarely

on the head. But if it misses or happens to fall on his cudgel, it will surely break. No, you'd better let me help Erh-lang instead."

"And have *you* got a weapon?" the Goddess asked.

"Yes, of course I have," replied the Patriarch of the Way.

Turning up his left sleeve, he drew from it a magic noose.

"This noose is woven out of well-tempered steel and has been anointed with the Elixir of Life, which has given it magic powers. It is capable of producing magic changes, and neither fire nor water can affect it. It can catch any living creature. I call it my Diamond Bracelet or Diamond Noose. It has the further virtue of protecting one from every kind of danger. Let me throw it down on the monkey."

The Patriarch cast his noose all the way from the gate of Heaven to the Mountain of Many Flowers.

The noose hissed through the air and dropped straight on to the Monkey King's head. He was still busily engaged in fighting off Erh-lang and his six brothers, and little did he realise what sort of weapon was snaking towards him from Heaven. The noose hit him on the skull, and he staggered and fell. He was up on his feet again in a trice and fled.

Erh-lang sent his hunting dogs after him.

The dogs snapped at his calves, and the Monkey King fell once more. He lay on the ground, cursing and shouting:

"You wretched beasts, why don't you go back to your own master instead of biting old Sun!"

He writhed and wriggled, but could not get to his feet.

All seven of the brothers flung themselves upon him and held him down. Binding him with a rope, they pierced his collar-bone with a curved knife to prevent him from changing himself again. The Patriarch of the Way drew in his noose and suggested to the Jade Emperor, the Goddess of Compassion, the Queen of Heaven and all the heavenly dignitaries that they should return to the Hall of Magic Clouds.

The kings of the Four Quarters, King Li and the other spirits who had fought against Monkey now laid down their arms and broke up the camp. They all came to congratulate Erh-lang on his victory.

"It was entirely due to the gracious favour of the ruler of Heaven and the magic powers of all the heavenly spirits," replied Erh-lang, disclaiming all credit for the victory.

"Let's not waste time talking, brother," his brothers said. "Now we must deliver that scoundrel up to Heaven so that the Jade Emperor can decide what is to be done with him."

"Dear brothers," said Erh-lang, "your names are not entered in the celestial records and so you cannot appear before the Jade Emperor. Let the heavenly troops carry the monkey up, while I go with the heavenly kings to make my report to the Emperor. You, in the meantime, search the mountain, and when you have cleaned up here, return to the Libation River. I shall claim my reward and then join you for a celebration."

The six brothers bowed to signify their assent.

Erh-lang and all the others mounted a cloud and, chanting songs of victory, they soared up to Heaven.

They soon reached the Palace of Supreme Wisdom, where they sent a quick messenger to the Jade Emperor with a message, which said: "The kings of the Four Quarters and the other celestial spirits have captured the rebellious Monkey, the Great Sage, Equal to Heaven, and are now awaiting further instructions."

The Jade Emperor immediately ordered the king of demons, Great Power, and the heavenly henchmen to take the Monkey King to the place of execution.

Imprisonment under the Mountain of the Five Elements

The heavenly soldiers brought the Monkey King to the place of execution, where they tied him to a pillar. Yet, try as they might they could not kill him. The Monkey King remained unharmed. Not even the Five Dragons succeeded. Then they called upon the gods of thunder and lightning — again without effect. There was nothing the demon king Great Power could do but report to the Jade Emperor that the Monkey King was quite invulnerable.

"Your Holiness, it is hard to see where that rascal could have learned all his tricks. We haven't managed to harm him in the slightest. What are we to do with the fellow?"

The Jade Emperor was equally puzzled.

"The rogue! What are we to do with him?" he said.

"No wonder," remarked the Patriarch of the Way. "After all, he ate the peaches of immortality, drank the heavenly wine, and stole my Elixir of Life. I had five vessels full of boiled and raw elixir, and he polished it all off. I used the Sacred Fire to fuse the elixir, so that is why Monkey's body is now as hard as a diamond, so that nothing can possibly harm him. Bring him to me and I'll put him in the Furnace of the Eight Trigrams. This will dissolve my elixir, and the monkey will be burned to ashes."

The Jade Emperor ordered six henchmen and six men-at-arms to untie Monkey and hand him over to the Patriarch of the Way. Then he called for Erh-lang and gave him his reward: a hundred golden flowers, a hundred bottles of celestial wine, a hundred bottles of the Elixir of Life, precious stones, shining pearls, tapestries, embroideries and other rare objects which he was to share with his six brothers. Erh-lang expressed his thanks to the Jade Emperor and made his way back to his temple on the Libation River.

The Patriarch of the Way went back to the Palace of Joy, untied the Monkey King, and pushed him into the furnace, telling the stokers to get a good fire going. The furnace was divided up into eight parts. The Monkey King wriggled into the one called *sun*, the part which represents wind. Where there is wind, there is no fire. On the other hand, wind raises smoke, and thus the Monkey King's eyes smarted and became red.

Time went by quickly, and soon forty-

nine days had passed. The smelting in the furnace was drawing to an end. One day the Patriarch of the Way opened the furnace to take out the elixir. The Monkey King was rubbing his eyes so hard that tears started to fall from them. He heard the door of the furnace creak and he opened his eyes abruptly. The light caused him so much pain that he could not stand it. He sprang out of the furnace, which toppled to the floor behind him with a great noise. Monkey rushed out of the palace. The stokers and other servants flung themselves upon him, but he fought them all off. The Patriarch of the Way clutched at him and was pushed by the Monkey King so hard that he fell headlong. The Monkey King ran out, taking his magic cudgel from behind his ear and enlarging it as he went. Looking neither to right nor left he ran through Heaven. The Nine Planets were so terrified that they closed all the doors and windows; the kings of the Four Quarters disappeared without trace. Hitting out furiously with his cudgel, the Monkey King battled his way forward, none of the celestial gods daring to stand up to him. Thus he got as far as the Hall of Magic Clouds in the Palace of Supreme Wisdom, which was guarded by the God of Providence. When he saw the Monkey King, the God of Providence barred his way and raised his golden whip, crying: "Wretched monkey, where are you making for? Let's have an end to your mad pranks. While I am here, you shall not go a step farther!"

Monkey was in no mood to stop and

argue. He raised his cudgel and struck out violently. The God of Providence parried the blow with his whip, and the two fought together. The thirty-six thunder gods soon joined the fray, encircling the Monkey King and attacking him with daggers, lances, swords, tridents, whips, maces, cudgels, axes, spears, sickles, and spades. The Monkey King defended himself valiantly, parrying blows from the left and the right, from in front and behind. Then he grew three heads and six arms, waved his cudgel in the air and changed it into three. The three cudgels whirled in the air like a spinning-wheel, preventing the thunder gods from coming too near. They hemmed him in as closely as they dared, making so much noise that they disturbed the Jade Emperor. At his wit's end, he sent the Chess-playing God and the Winged Immortal to the Western Paradise to ask the Supreme Buddha for help.

The two Immortals set off at once and soon reached the sacred spot, the Voice of Thunder Temple on Providence Mountain. They bowed to the four Guardians of the Gate and the eight Bodhisattvas, asking them to announce their arrival. They were immediately shown into the presence of the Supreme Buddha, who was enthroned on a lotus. The Immortals bowed three times and waited respectfully.

"What has happened that the Jade Emperor should have seen fit to send two such esteemed Immortals on so long a journey?" the Buddha asked.

"Some time ago," the two Immortals said, "a monkey was born on the Mountain of Many Flowers. He practised magic, gathered round him a host of monkeys, and created unrest in the world. The Jade Emperor showed mercy towards him and made him a celestial groom. Monkey, however, did not find this post important

enough and ran away from Heaven. The Heavenly King Li and Crown Prince Natha were sent to capture him, but failed. Again Monkey was pardoned and was given the title of Great Sage, Equal to Heaven, although he was not entered in the official lists. Entrusted with the supervision of the Peach Orchard, Monkey stole peaches. One day he came to the Jade Lake and stole wine and choice foods, spoiling the Peach Banquet. He secretly entered the Palace of Joy and, stealing some Elixir of Life from the Patriarch of the Way, again escaped from Heaven. Once more the Jade Emperor sent a heavenly army, one hundred thousand men strong, after him, but to no avail. Then the Goddess of Compassion, Kuan-yin recommended that they send Erh-lang and his six brothers to deal with Monkey. Erh-lang is master of many magical changes. In the end he managed to capture Monkey, the Patriarch of the Way having first snared him in his magic noose. They tied him up and took him to the Jade Emperor, who gave orders for Monkey's execution. But neither knives nor axes, fire nor lightning had any effect on him. Finally the Patriarch of the Way suggested that he would melt Monkey in his furnace. When, after forty-nine days, they opened the furnace, Monkey jumped out unharmed and chased away the heavenly guards. He penetrated as far as the Hall of Magic Clouds in the Palace of Supreme Wisdom where the God of Providence halted him and they started to fight. Then we sent thirty-six thunder gods to subdue him; they have encircled him but cannot grapple with him. Things are becoming very serious indeed, and that is why the Jade Emperor beseeches the Supreme Buddha to come to his aid."

Having listened to the whole list of crimes, the Supreme Buddha told the Bodhisattvas to stay in their sacred places in the temple, allowing nothing to distract them from their meditation, while he himself went to subdue the evil-doer and save the Jade Emperor.

Asking his two disciples, Ananda and Kashyapa, to follow him, Buddha arrived at the gates of Heaven. From a distance they could hear a fearful din as the thirty-six thunder gods attacked Monkey. Buddha ordered them to lay down their arms and return to their palaces, telling the Monkey King to come forward and show what he could do. The thunder gods drew away, and the Monkey King changed back into his true form. Boiling with rage he stepped forward, shouting:

"Who dares to disturb me in the middle of a battle?"

"I am the Supreme Buddha from the Western Paradise. I have received news of your abominable behaviour in Heaven and I wish to know the reason for it."

"Everyone is entitled to a place in the Hall of Magic Clouds, so why do they refuse to let me in?" asked the Monkey King, fuming with rage.

"You poor wretch," said the Supreme Buddha with an icy smile, "you're nothing but a monkey demon. How dare you try to force your way to the Jade Emperor's throne! That is unheard of! Unheard of! In punishment I'll deprive you of your worthless life. Submit at once and stop this rebellious talk, or you shall force me to lift my hand against you and that will mean the end of you."

"Even if the Jade Emperor has been perfecting himself at his job since childhood, that doesn't mean he's got to keep the throne for ever," retorted the Monkey King cheekily. "There is a proverb that says, 'It's your turn to be Emperor today, it will be mine tomorrow.' Let him clear out and leave his palace to me, or I'll go on worrying them like this and they'll never have any peace."

"What can you do, apart from your magic changes and having the benefit of long life? Why do you deserve the celestial throne?" Buddha asked.

"I can do all sorts of things," replied the Monkey King proudly. "I know how to change myself into seventy-two different shapes. I shall never grow old and shall

live forever. I can float in the clouds, and am able to leap a hundred and eight thousand miles in one jump. That's enough to qualify me for the throne of Heaven."

"Let's have a wager," said Buddha. "If you're really as clever as all that, jump off the palm of my right hand. If you succeed, you have won and will no longer have to demand your rights by force. I myself shall ask the Jade Emperor to move in with me in the Western Paradise and leave his heavenly palace to you. If you fail, I'll send you down to Hell as a demon, and you'll have to stay there for ages before you can come and seek any position in Heaven again."

"What a fool this Buddha is!" rejoiced the Monkey King. "I can jump a hundred and eight thousand miles, whereas that palm of his can't be more than a foot wide. Of course I'll manage it!" Aloud he asked: "And will you keep your word?"

"Of course I shall," said Buddha.

He stretched out his right hand, which was no larger than a lotus leaf. The Monkey King put his cudgel behind his ear, stuck out his chest, and jumped up on to the palm of Buddha's hand.

"Here I go!" he called out.

He flashed up like lightning and was gone. Buddha followed him with his wise eye. The Monkey King seemed to be carried along by the wind, hurling forward heedless of everything. Suddenly he came up against five flesh-coloured pillars, their tops shrouded in mist.

"This must be the end of the world," the Monkey King said to himself. "The Buddha is my witness. As soon as I get back I shall ascend the throne of Heaven. Ah, but wait! I must leave some sign of my presence here in case he doesn't want to believe me."

He plucked out a hair, breathed on it and changed it into a dish of Chinese ink and two brushes. Then he wrote in large letters on the middle pillar: "The Great Sage, Equal to Heaven, got as far as this." He threw away the brushes and the dish and, with one single leap, returned to the place he had started from. Standing on Buddha's palm he cried: "Well, here I am! Go and tell the Jade Emperor to hand over his heavenly palace!"

"You revolting ape!" Buddha scolded him. "You never left my hand."

"You're wrong, you know," said the Monkey King. "I flew as far as the end of the world. There I found five flesh-coloured pillars shrouded in mist. I left an inscription on one of them. How about coming with me, so you can see for yourself."

"Why should I go anywhere?" said Buddha. "Look down here."

The Monkey King looked down, and his fiery eyes bulged. On the middle finger of Buddha's right hand he saw written: "The Great Sage, Equal to Heaven, got as far as this."

"This is impossible!" thought the Monkey King in great dismay. "I wrote those words on the pillars that supported the sky. How can they have got onto his finger? Can he perhaps read people's thoughts? No, I don't believe that. I'll go back and look."

Monkey crouched once more and got ready to jump, but Buddha turned his hand palm downwards and pushed him out through the western gate of Heaven. Changing his five fingers into a mountain of metal, wood, water, fire and earth, he piled it on top of the Monkey King. That mountain was then named the Mountain of the Five Elements.

The Goddess of Compassion Looks for a Pious Monk

Having subdued the Monkey King, Buddha returned to the Western Paradise and again took his seat in the Voice of Thunder Temple on Providence Mountain. One day he called together the Buddhist Immortals, Guardians of the gates and Nuns, and said to them: "Since the day I imprisoned the rebellious Monkey and restored peace in Heaven I have not followed the passage of time. Five hundred years must surely have gone by. Autumn is approaching, and with it the Feast of All Souls. I have here a precious vessel with hundreds of rare flowers and hundreds of rare fruits. We must celebrate the feast properly."

All the Immortals pressed the palms of their hands together and bowed. Buddha then handed the rare flowers and fruits to his disciples Ananda and Kashyapa, who shared them out.

Then Buddha again turned to his disciples and said: "I have been studying the ways of mankind in the five continents. They seem to differ a great deal, the inhabitants in some being kind and good-natured, while those in others are evil. I possess three baskets of scriptures known as Tripitaka which, I think, could help us in making them mend their ways."

"What scriptures are these?" asked the disciples, bowing before Buddha.

"One basket contains scriptures which deal with Heaven, the second contains scriptures which deal with the Earth, and the third contains scriptures which save the damned. These three baskets hold thirty-five volumes written on fifteen thousand one hundred and forty-four rolls. I should like one of you virtuous ones to go to China and there seek out a believer who would be willing to cross a thousand steep mountains, swim across ten thousand rivers, and come here to me for the scriptures, which he would then carry back with him to the people of the eastern land of China and put to good use. That would be an untold blessing. Which of you would care to go on this journey?"

The Goddess of Compassion, Kuan-yin, came up to the lotus throne, pressed the palms of her hands together, and said: "Though my capabilities are but very small, I should nevertheless like to go to the eastern land and find someone to go and bring the scriptures back to China."

This pleased the Buddha, who said: "No one else would do as well. It can only be the venerable Kuan-yin with her immeasurable magic powers."

He then ordered Ananda and Kashyapa to bring a richly embroidered silk cassock and a monk's staff with nine rings, telling Kuan-yin that these were to be presented to whoever went to fetch the scriptures. The goddess bowed to show her assent. Buddha then gave her three head bands, saying: "These all look alike, yet each serves a different purpose and each has its own spell. If on your journey you happen to meet a demon with supernatural powers, you must convert him and make him a disciple of the person you choose to go for the scriptures. Should he disobey him, the pilgrim must put one of these bands on his head so that it cuts into his flesh. As soon as the pilgrim recites the appropriate spell, the demon's eyes will swell, his head will give him great pain, and he will be only too pleased to accept our Faith."

Kuan-yin bowed and called her disciple Hui-an, who carried an iron cudgel weighing a thousand pounds, telling him to prepare for the journey. He never left Kuan-yin's side in case they came up against any evil spirits. Kuan-yin tied the cassock into a bundle, which she gave him to carry. She herself took the three head bands and, leaning on the staff, set out on her journey, followed by her disciple. They came to the source of the Sandy River. There, Kuan-yin said to her disciple: "This will be a very difficult river to cross. Our pilgrim will be just an ordinary mortal — how is he to manage it?"

She stopped and was just looking round when the waters were churned up and a hideous monster reared up out of them, staff in hand. Clambering up on to the bank, the monster rushed straight at Kuan-yin.

"Halt!" cried her disciple, holding him back with his cudgel.

"What monk are you, that you have the audacity to stand up to me?"

"I am Hui-an, the second Crown Prince Moksha, son of the Heavenly King Li. At present I am acting as a bodyguard to my mistress on our journey to the eastern land, where we intend to seek someone who will go and fetch the scriptures. What monster are you, that you dare stand in our way?"

"I remember now," replied the monster. "Didn't you study virtue in Kuan-yin's bamboo grove in the Southern Sea? What then are you doing here?"

"Can't you see that it's my mistress who is standing on the bank?"

The monster was dumbfounded. He laid down his weapon and followed Hui-an up to the goddess, bowing low before her.

"Bodhisattva, forgive me my sins, I shall confess everything. I am no monster, but a general from the Jade Emperor's personal retinue. It was my duty to wait on him whenever he rode in his phoenix chariot. Once at a Peach Banquet my hand slipped and I let fall a crystal dish. I was given eight hundred lashes at the Emperor's orders and was then banished in my present horrible shape to the world below. Now he causes me great suffering for I am plagued by hunger. Little did I think that today I should run into the goddess herself."

"It was for your sins that you were banished from Heaven," said Kuan-yin, "and yet you are killing people and thus piling sin upon sin. I have been sent by the Supreme Buddha to find a man who will go and fetch the scriptures. Why don't you accept our Faith, repent your crimes and become the pilgrim's disciple, accompanying him on his quest and paying homage to the Buddha in the Western Paradise? And if the expedition is a success, your crimes will be forgiven and you will be given back your appointment in Heaven. What do you say to this suggestion?"

"I would very much like to repent," replied the monster.

Kuan-yin then placed her hand on top of his head, and he was accepted into the Faith. She gave him the surname of Sha, meaning Sand, after the Sandy River, and a religious name Wu-ching, which means He Who Understands Purity. The Sandy Priest escorted the Goddess of Compassion across the river. He no longer attacked travellers but spent his time in prayer, waiting for the pilgrim who would fetch the scriptures.

Kuan-yin parted with him and, with her disciple at her side, went on towards China. Soon they came to a high mountain. The mountain was wrapped in dangerous mists, which prevented them from going further. They were just about to mount a cloud and fly over, when there was a fierce blast of wind and another hideous-looking monster came charging at them. He made straight for Kuan-yin, striking out at her with an iron rake.

"Stop, foul fiend!" cried Hui-an, fending off the blows. "Look at my cudgel and beware."

"This monk must be out of his wits," cried the monster, laughing. "Look at my rake!"

They stepped towards each other and began to fight furiously.

When the battle was at its height, Kuan-yin, who had been watching from the air,

threw down some lotus flowers which fell just between the rake and the cudgel, frightening the monster.

"What kind of a monk are you, that you dare throw flowers in my eyes?" he shouted.

"Accursed, low-born monster," cried Hui-an, "I'll teach you manners! I am a disciple of the Goddess of Compassion from the Southern Sea. It was my mistress herself who threw down those flowers. Didn't you recognise her, that you speak so disrespectfully?"

"Do you mean the Goddess of Compassion, Kuan-yin, who saves us from the three disasters and the eight calamities?" asked the monster.

"Whom else should I mean?"

The monster threw aside his rake and bowed low.

"Tell me, brother, where is the goddess to be found? Be so kind as to take me to her."

Hui-an pointed up towards the sky. "Can't you see her?" he said.

The monster bowed again, crying in a loud voice: "Forgive me my crimes, goddess! Forgive me my crimes!"

Kuan-yin descended from the clouds.

"How dare you," she said, "you accursed boar or pig demon, stand in my way? Who are you, anyway?"

"I am neither a boar nor a pig, but a heavenly marshal from the Milky Way. One day, when I was drunk, I tried to kiss the Goddess of the Moon. The Jade Emperor ordered that I be given two thousand blows with a stick and banished to the world below. I lost my way and by mistake got inside a sow's belly, and that's why

I look as I do. I live in this mountain. Little did I dream I should come across the goddess today. Do forgive me and save me!"

"You misbehaved in Heaven," Kuan-yin replied, "and you have not reformed your ways even now. You are guilty of fresh crimes, and you even slay your fellow men. For this you deserve double punishment."

"According to you, I should have lived on air, I suppose," said the monster. "There is an old proverb which says, 'Abide by the laws of the world and you'll be flogged to death, abide by the laws of Buddha and you'll starve to death.' Get away with you! I'd much rather catch a nice fat traveller now and again and eat him, no matter if that is a double crime, three crimes, or ten thousand crimes."

"If you repented, you wouldn't have to starve," Kuan-yin pointed out. "After all, there are five kinds of grains in the world which you can feed on and not be a cannibal."

The monster seemed to waken out of a dream.

"I should like to repent very much," he told Kuan-yin, "but I'm afraid that 'He who has sinned against Heaven cannot be saved by prayer'."

"I have been instructed by the Supreme Buddha to go to the eastern land to find a pilgrim who will fetch the scriptures," said Kuan-yin. "You can become a disciple of his and accompany him to the Western Paradise. If you behave yourself on the way, your sins will be forgiven and you will avoid disaster."

"I'll go with pleasure!" the monster cried, nodding his head eagerly. Kuan-yin then placed her hand on top of his head and accepted him into the Faith. On account of his appearance she gave him the name of Pigsy and the religious name of Wu-neng, which means He Who Understands Strength.

Kuan-yin and her disciple took leave of Pigsy and, floating in the sky, continued on their way. From afar they could hear the moaning of a dragon. Kuan-yin came closer and asked him: "What dragon are you, and for what have you been punished?"

"I am the son of the Dragon King of the Western Sea. By mistake I set fire to the palace, and his Pearls of Wisdom were burnt. My father made a complaint against me in Heaven, saying I had tried to start a rebellion. The Jade Emperor hung me up here in the sky, had me given three hundred lashes, and ordered my execution. I beseech you to help me, if you can."

Hearing this, Kuan-yin, with Hui-an at her heels, hurried to the southern gate of Heaven, where they were met by two heavenly generals, who asked them where they were going.

"I must speak to the Jade Emperor at once," replied Kuan-yin.

The generals quickly ushered them in. The Jade Emperor came down from his throne and welcomed them. Kuan-yin bowed low and said: "I have come to ask you to pardon the rebellious dragon I saw hanging in the sky on my way to the eastern land. Give him his life, Your Holiness, and let me, unworthy as I am, have him so that he can carry the pilgrim to the Western Paradise on his back."

The Jade Emperor pardoned the dragon, sending some heavenly generals to untie him and hand him over to the goddess. She had, in the meantime, expressed her

thanks and departed. The dragon could not thank her enough for his delivery, and he stood by, waiting for her orders. Kuan-yin sent him down into a deep valley, where he was to await the arrival of the pilgrim. He was then to change into a white horse and carry the pilgrim on his back to the Western Paradise to show sorrow for his past crimes. The dragon went off and prepared to wait.

Kuan-yin and her disciple then crossed the mountains and continued their eastward journey. They had not gone far, however, when they noticed a golden glow that flooded everything around them, giving off red shafts of light.

"That glow comes from the Mountain of the Five Elements," said Hui-an. "I can see the imprint of the Supreme Buddha's seal."

"That is where the Monkey King is imprisoned, isn't it? The one who upset the Peach Banquet and played havoc in the heavenly palace?" Kuan-yin said.

"That's right, that's the one," agreed Hui-an.

Kuan-yin and her disciple landed on the mountain. The first thing they saw was the magic spell inscribed on the Buddha's seal in six syllables: OM MANI PADME HUM.

Kuan-yin heaved a deep sigh. The sound disturbed the Monkey King, who called from the foot of the mountain: "Who is it up there?"

Kuan-yin at once came down and looked round. She found the Monkey King imprisoned in a stone casket; he was able to speak quite freely, but could not move so much as an inch.

"Do you recognise me, Sun?" she asked.

Monkey peered at her with his fiery eyes and cried, nodding his head: "Of course I do. You are the Goddess of Compassion, Kuan-yin, from the Mountain of Potaloka in the Southern Sea, the saviour who averts disasters. Welcome, Kuan-yin. A day here seems as long as a year. None of my friends ever come to visit me. What has brought *you* to this place?"

"I have come at the orders of the Supreme Buddha, who has sent me to the eastern land to seek a pilgrim who is to go and fetch the scriptures," replied the goddess. "We were passing by and so have stopped to speak to you."

"Buddha deceived me," cried Monkey, "imprisoning me under this mountain for

five hundred years so that I cannot even move. I entreat you," he added, "to come to my aid and release me."

"You have sinned greatly," Kuan-yin said. "If I were to set you free, you'd only get up to more mischief and there would be trouble again."

"Oh, no, I have repented," replied the Monkey King. "Just tell me what to do and I shall devote myself to good works."

Kuan-yin was delighted to hear this.

"If you really have such good intentions, wait while I go to the land of the great T'ang in the east and find my pilgrim. He will come and set you free. You'll become his disciple and embrace our Faith."

"With the greatest of pleasure," agreed the Monkey King quickly.

"I shall therefore give you a religious name," Kuan-yin went on.

"I have one already," Monkey replied. "My name is Wu-k'ung, He Who Understands Emptiness."

"Excellent," said Kuan-yin. "I have already converted two other disciples, and they also have 'wu', meaning 'to understand', in their names. I have no further orders for you at the moment. We must be on our way now."

And so Kuan-yin and Hui-an continued their journey to the east. In less than a day they reached Ch'ang-an, the City of Eternal Peace, which was the capital of the land of T'ang. They left the clouds which had carried them, disguised themselves as shabby wandering monks, and entered the city.

The Monk Tripitaka is Chosen to Fetch the Scriptures

The Goddess of Compassion searched all over the capital of the T'ang Empire, hoping to find the virtuous pilgrim who was to fetch the scriptures, but it was all in vain. She had already spent several days there without meeting anyone of really outstanding virtue. One day, however, she heard that the Emperor T'ai Tsung of the great T'ang dynasty was holding a great Mass at which he would reward virtuous priests. This pleased the goddess very much, and she set out at once with her disciple Hui-an to sell the treasures she had been given by the Supreme Buddha. These treasures were the richly embroidered silk cassock and the monk's staff with nine rings. She also had the three magic head bands, but she had carefully hidden these for future use. Now she was offering only the cassock and the staff for sale. Wandering about the streets of the city was a stupid priest who had failed to get any reward at the Emperor's Mass. In his pocket he had a few coppers, and when he saw the Goddess of Compassion in her disguise of a shabby monk, barefoot and in rags, offering a cassock shining with gold, he came up to her and asked: "How much do you want for the cassock, shabby monk?"

"Five thousand pieces of silver for the cassock, two thousand for the staff," the goddess replied in the voice of a humble wandering holy man.

The stupid priest burst out laughing. "Why, these two shabby monks must be out of their minds! Have you ever seen such fools! They're asking seven thousand in good silver for a couple of worthless articles such as these. Even if that cassock of yours had the power to make one immortal or a living Buddha, it wouldn't be worth that much. Get out of here, you'll never manage to sell your stuff."

Kuan-yin refused to argue with him and went away. They continued their journey until they reached the Eastern Flower Gate. Here they met the First Minister Hsiao Yü, who was just returning from court. Kuan-yin did not get out of the way, on the contrary she stood right in the middle of the road, holding out the cassock. The Minister reined in his horse and looked at the garment, recognising it as a wonderful piece of craftsmanship. He dismounted and greeted Kuan-yin with respect.

"Reverend father," he said, "His Majesty the Emperor of this great T'ang dynasty is a most devout man and is at this moment celebrating a Great Mass of the Continents and Waters. That cassock of yours would be most suitable for the High Priest, Hsüan Tsang. Come with me, and I shall take you to the Emperor himself."

Kuan-yin was delighted, and she followed him slowly through the Eastern Flower Gate to the Court. An attendant announced them and led them straight into the Throne Room. The First Minister and

the two monks stood in front of the throne. The Emperor asked what their business was, and Hsiao Yü bowed and said: "As your unworthy subject passed through the Eastern Flower Gate he ran into these two monks, who were offering for sale a cassock and a staff. It occurred to me that it would be a good idea to obtain this cassock for Hsüan Tsang to wear at the Great Mass. That is why I have brought both the monks here."

The Emperor rejoiced at this and wanted to know the price of the two precious articles. Kuan-yin and her disciple stood still in front of the throne, not even bowing to the Emperor, and they replied: "Five thousand for the cassock, two thousand for the staff."

The Emperor then asked for the cassock to be spread out. He examined it carefully, convincing himself that it was indeed a splendid piece of work.

"Reverend father," he said after a while, "I do not wish to keep anything from you. I am trying to spread virtue and devotion among my people, wishing to encourage happiness and prosperity. In the Transformation of Life Temple I have brought together monks who are studying the scriptures. One of them is an exceptionally devout priest by the name of Hsüan Tsang. I wish to buy these objects for him. What price are you really asking?"

Hearing this, Kuan-yin and her disciple folded their hands and bowed low, saying: "If that monk of yours is as virtuous as you say, we wish to present them to him as a gift and do not ask for money in return." And with these words they vanished.

On the seventh day of the ninth month of the thirteenth year of the Chen-kuan era the High Priest Hsüan Tsang, on the wish of the Emperor, celebrated the Great Mass of the Continents and Waters, praying for

the salvation of all living beings. Long before the ceremony was due to begin, the Emperor, accompanied by his civil and military officials, the Empress, and all their relatives, set out for the temple, which was thronged with the citizens of Ch'ang-an, adults and children, noblemen and commoners, who came to hear the Mass.

That day Kuan-yin told her disciple: "This is the final day of the Great Mass. Let us mix with the crowds and see what the ceremony is like, as well as what type of Buddhism the monk preaches."

They went to the temple. The High Priest Hsüan Tsang stood on a platform from which he read aloud the scriptures. Kuan-yin went up to the platform and cried: "You speak only of some of the teaching of Buddha. Have you no knowledge of the rest of the scriptures?"

Hsüan Tsang came eagerly down from his platform and greeted the goddess.

"Forgive me, reverend father, for not noticing you earlier. The priests here have always taught only part of the scriptures. The rest are quite unknown to us."

"This teaching of yours cannot bring salvation to the dead," Kuan-yin pointed out. "But I know of three baskets, full of the scriptures, known as Tripitaka, which have the power of carrying the souls of the dead up to Heaven. They help those who are in trouble, making them immortal and free of the chains of Earth."

When her conversation was at its most

interesting, one of the officials in charge of the incense ran up to the Emperor, reporting that the High Priest had been interrupted in his sermon by two shabby monks who had dragged him off the platform and were pestering him with some nonsense. The Emperor ordered that the monks be arrested and brought to him. The monks did not bow before the Emperor, nor did they greet him in any way, but simply stood there looking at him and then asked him what he desired. The Emperor recognised them and said: "You are the two monks who brought me the cassock, aren't you."

"Yes, we are," said Kuan-yin, nodding.

"Since you have come to the ceremony, you should listen to the sermon and share in the special food with the other monks, but you have no right to disturb the proceedings, molesting the priest and holding up the Mass."

"Your preacher teaches only about the part of the scriptures which say that the souls of the dead will not be saved and will not go to Heaven," explained Kuan-yin. "I, however, know of three baskets containing the scriptures called Tripitaka, according to which souls are saved, avoid suffering and attain immortality."

The Emperor was delighted to hear this, and asked: "Where are these scriptures of yours?"

"Far away in the west, in India, in the Voice of Thunder Temple, where the Supreme Buddha dwells," said the goddess. "They will put right the gravest injustice and prevent even the worst danger."

The Emperor stopped the ceremony and decided that he would send someone to fetch the scriptures. All those present in the temple were asked if they would dare to go on this journey in obedience to the Emperor's will, travelling far to the west to pay homage to the Supreme Buddha and ask him for the scriptures. The High Priest Hsüan Tsang stepped forward at once and, kneeling in front of the Emperor, said: "I am but a humble monk with no special talent, but I wish to serve my Emperor with my body and soul. Let me be the one to bring him the true scriptures and win eternal peace for the streams and mountains of our land."

The Emperor was delighted. Raising Hsüan Tsang with his royal hand he said: "If the High Priest really wishes to undertake this proof of his loyalty, untroubled by the length of the journey, the wild mountain ranges and fast rivers, I shall make him my bond-brother."

Hsüan Tsang bowed his head to show his gratitude. The Emperor, in his turn, bowed four times to Hsüan Tsang, standing in front of Buddha's statue in the temple, and addressed him as "Holy priest, brother of mine". Hsüan Tsang thanked him for this unexpected honour.

Next morning the Emperor summoned together all his ministers and court officials to witness the writing of a safe pass for Hsüan Tsang, which the Emperor stamped with his own seal. The astrologers then reported that the position of the stars that day was particularly favourable for the beginning of such a long journey. At that moment a servant announced that Hsüan Tsang had arrived and was awaiting the Emperor's orders. The Emperor had him shown in and said: "Brother, this day is a favourable one for the start of your journey. Here is your safe pass. And

I want you to accept this golden bowl to collect alms in."

Hsüan Tsang was well pleased with all this and thanked the Emperor for his kindness. Finally the Emperor asked him if he had a travelling name.

"Being a humble monk I never presumed to take one," Hsüan Tsang replied.

"The scriptures you are going to fetch are said to be called the Tripitaka," said the Emperor. "Therefore why don't you accept the same name and be called Tripitaka?"

Hsüan Tsang again expressed his thanks and made his farewells. Then, wasting no more time, he set out on his journey.

The Monkey King Becomes Tripitaka's Guide

After Tripitaka left the capital of the T'ang Empire, he journeyed for many days until he reached the frontier. In front of him towered the gigantic peak of the Frontier Mountain, to the west of which was the land of the barbarous Tartars. Tripitaka was just about to cross the frontier when he heard a fierce voice calling from the foot of the mountain: "My Master has arrived!"

Tripitaka was frightened and asked some travellers who happened to be passing by what it meant.

"That must be the old monkey who is shut up in a stone casket at the foot of this mountain," they explained.

"What old monkey is that?"

"This mountain used to be called the Mountain of the Five Elements, but when our Emperor marched westward and conquered this territory, it was renamed Frontier Mountain. Years ago we heard the old people tell that in the days of Wang Mang, who overthrew the Western Han dynasty, Heaven placed this mountain here and imprisoned a magic monkey under it. The monkey is not affected either by heat or by cold, it does not eat or drink in the normal way, easing its hunger with iron pills and its thirst with copper-juice. In spite of winter frosts and lack of food it has survived to this day. That cry undoubtedly came from the monkey. There is nothing to fear, reverend father. Let us go and have a look at it."

Tripitaka took the reins of his horse and followed one of the travellers down the mountainside. After a while they came to a stone casket in which there was a monkey. It put out its head and waved its arms about frantically, crying: "Why have you been so long in coming, Master? Welcome, welcome! Release me, and in return I will protect you on your journey to the west."

"What is it you want me to do?" Tripitaka asked, approaching nearer.

"You are the one whom the Chinese Emperor is sending to fetch the scriptures from the west, are you not?" said the Monkey King.

"I am. Why do you ask?"

"I am a Great Sage, Equal to Heaven, who five hundred years ago turned Heaven upside down. For this, the Supreme Buddha imprisoned me under this mountain. A short time ago the Goddess of Compassion, Kuan-yin, passed by here, having been sent by the Buddha to seek a pilgrim in China who would go and bring back the scriptures. I asked her to get me out of here, and she promised that if I reformed, and helped to protect the pilgrim on his way to the west to the Supreme Buddha's temple, I should be saved. Ever since then, from early morning till late at night, I have been waiting impatiently for you to arrive and set me free. I swear that I shall protect you throughout your journey and, as your disciple, obey you in everything."

Monkey's words filled Tripitaka with joy.

"I am very happy indeed that, on the advice of the Goddess of Compassion, you mean to embrace our Faith. But I have no axe or chisel with which to release you."

"Never mind," said Monkey. "All I need is your goodwill — I can manage the rest myself."

"How is that possible?" Tripitaka asked doubtfully.

"On the summit of the mountain is a seal with the Buddha's own letters inscribed on it in gold," the Monkey King explained. "Go up there, break the seal, and I shall be free."

Tripitaka did as instructed. Holding on to long tendrils of creeper, he scrambled up to the top of the mountain, where his eyes were dazzled by the golden glow of a thousand light rays flowing from a square slab of rock, which carried a leather seal with the inscription OM MANI PADME HUM imprinted on it in letters of gold. Tripitaka knelt in front of the rock, paid homage to the inscription and, facing the west, prayed: "I, the sinner Hsüan Tsang, am journeying to fetch the scriptures. If I am to have a disciple, let this seal be broken and the magic monkey be set free so that he can accompany me to the seat of the All-Highest. If it is not my destiny to have a disciple and the monkey is nothing but a malicious demon trying to deceive me and meaning no good to my enterprise, let the seal remain as it is."

Having finished his prayer, Hsüan Tsang bowed once more and carefully removed the seal. Then he went back to Monkey in his stone casket and told him: "I have broken the seal. You can come out now."

"Would you mind standing a little way off, Master," said the Monkey King. "I don't want to frighten you."

Tripitaka went a little way in an easterly direction. When he stopped he heard Monkey calling to him in a loud voice: "Further still! Further still!" He continued down the mountain, and suddenly heard a tremendous roar, as if the mountain were bursting apart and the very earth splitting under his feet. The next moment he saw Monkey standing naked in front of him. Monkey knelt in front of Tripitaka's horse and said: "Here I am, Master!" And he bowed four times to show his gratitude. Then he picked up the packs and put them on the horse's back.

Seeing that the Monkey King was well intentioned and behaved like a true believer, Tripitaka suggested that he would find him a religious name.

"No need to bother, Master, I have one already," the Monkey King pointed out. "My name is Sun Wu-k'ung, He Who Understands Emptiness."

"That's excellent," replied Tripitaka. "The name is fully in keeping with the teachings of our order. As you look like a small wandering monk, I shall give you the nickname of Wanderer."

Sun Wu-k'ung was delighted. He helped Tripitaka mount his horse, and he stumbled on ahead, loaded with the pilgrim's baggage. They soon left the Frontier Mountain behind them. Suddenly a fierce tiger sprang out at them, roaring in a most blood-curdling fashion and lashing its tail. Tripitaka was terrified, but the Monkey King seemed pleased to see the fearsome animal.

"Don't be frightened, Master. He will provide me with something to wear."

Monkey put down his load, took his magic needle from behind his ear, and, facing into the wind, waved it in the air. It changed immediately into a huge iron cudgel.

"I haven't used you in over five hundred years," he said, smiling happily. "Today you're going to help me to get some clothing."

He placed his legs well apart and stood squarely in the tiger's path.

"Accursed monster, stay where you are!" he shouted. The tiger crouched in the dust, not daring to move. Putting all his strength into the blow, the Monkey King cracked its skull, while poor Tripitaka slid trembling off his horse. The Monkey King dragged the tiger aside, saying: "Sit down awhile, master. I want to undress him and put his clothes on myself before we start out again."

"How do you mean to undress him since he has no clothes?" asked Tripitaka in disbelief.

"Don't worry, I'll manage," replied Monkey. The little Wanderer plucked out a hair and breathed on it with his magic breath, changing it into a sharp knife. He slit the tiger's skin and ripped it off in one piece. Cutting off the paws and the head, he then trimmed the skin into a regular square, picked it up and measured it.

"A bit too wide," he muttered to himself. "I shall have to cut it in two." He did so, laying one of the halves aside and winding the other round him. He fastened it with a long vine he pulled up at the roadside, changed his cudgel back into a needle again, and put it behind his ear. Finally he shouldered his baggage and helped Tripitaka remount, and they started off once more.

"What's happened to that cudgel of yours with which you killed the tiger?" Tripitaka asked. "I don't see it anywhere."

"You see, Master, it's like this," explained Monkey, laughing. "I got that cudgel in the palace of the Dragon King of the Eastern Sea. It's called the Wishing Cudgel with Golden Rings. It was with this very cudgel that I played havoc in Heaven. I can make it grow larger or smaller as I please. At present I've changed it into an embroidery needle and put it behind my ear. There it is ready for use whenever I have need of it."

Tripitaka rejoiced to hear this.

"And tell me," he went on, "why did that tiger crouch on the ground as soon as it saw you and why did it allow you to kill it without a struggle?"

"I wish to have no secrets from you, Master," replied Monkey. "Not only tigers but dragons as well dare not stand up to me. I have such magic powers that I can force rivers to change their course and raise tempests on the sea. I know how to make myself so tall that I reach up to Heaven, or so small that you couldn't find me in the fluff of a dandelion. I am capable of many magic changes. I can vanish and reappear at will. There's nothing much to skinning a tiger. When we get into serious trouble, I'll show you what I can really do."

Listening to Monkey, Tripitaka felt all his doubts disappear, and, feeling better, he spurred his horse on.

They had travelled uneventfully for several days when they heard strange noises and saw six men armed with spears, daggers, sharp swords and huge bows come rushing at them.

"Not another step, priest!" they cried. "Hand over your horse and packs and we shall spare your life."

Greatly alarmed, Tripitaka slid off his horse, not daring to breathe a word. The Monkey King quickly came to his aid.

"Take it easy, there's nothing to worry about," he said. "They have merely brought us some more clothes and money for our journey."

"Are you deaf, Sun Wu-k'ung? You heard them order us to hand over the horse and our packs and yet you talk of clothing and money to be got from them."

"Just keep an eye on our things and the horse. I'll go and deal with them."

"Not even the strongest hand can stand up to two fists and two fists have little chance against four hands. How can a little chap like you think of taking on six of them?"

But Monkey had always been known for his courage, and he would not give in. Crossing his arms on his chest he stepped forward and bowed before the robbers, saying: "Gentlemen, why do you stand in the way of poor priests?"

"We are kings of the highways, benevolent lords of mountain and forest. We are famous far and wide, how come you don't know us? Hand over your things quickly and we shall let you go. But if you utter so much as half a word, we'll cut you to pieces and grind your bones to dust."

"I, too, have been a king and lord of the mountains for hundreds of years. Yet I've never heard your names," said the Monkey King.

"Well, listen, and we'll tell you," barked one of the robbers. "The first of us is called Eye of Pleasure; the second, Ear of Wrath; the third, Nose of Delight; the fourth, Tongue of Desire; the fifth, Heart of Longing; and the sixth, Body of Suffering."

"You're nothing but common thieves," laughed the Monkey King. "Kindly realise that we, people of the monasteries, are your lords and masters. How do you dare to block our path! Bring out all your loot at once and divide it up. If you give me an equal share I shall spare your lives."

Monkey's words angered the robbers and they waved their fists in his face, shouting: "Impudent priest! You have nothing and yet you talk of sharing our spoils!"

They brandished their swords, grasped their spears and fell upon Monkey. He stood in their midst quite unconcerned.

"That priest certainly has a hard head," shouted the robbers.

"Help yourselves," cried the Monkey King, laughing. "When your arms get tired, I'll bring out my little needle."

"He must be a former doctor," said the robbers, puzzled. "But as none of us are ill, what is he jabbering about needles for?"

Monkey raised his hand and from behind his ear brought out his embroidery needle. Shaking it in the air he changed it into an iron cudgel.

"Not another step! Now it's my turn to test my cudgel on you!"

The robbers fled in confusion, but Monkey caught up with them, one after the other, and killed all six. Then he stripped off their clothes and seized their loot. Smiling he returned to Tripitaka.

"We can go on now, Master. I have attended to the robbers."

"You are inviting disaster," wailed Tripitaka. "They were bandits and deserved punishment, but they did not deserve to die. You possess magic powers and so could have driven them away without having to kill them. How can a priest take human life?"

"Had I not killed them, Master, they would have killed us," the Monkey King defended himself.

"A priest should rather die than be guilty of violence," said Tripitaka reproachfully. "If I die, I die alone, but you have butchered six men. What have you to say for yourself? If the authorities got to hear of it, you would not escape the consequences even if your father were a magistrate."

"Let me tell you, Master," interrupted Monkey, "that when five hundred years ago I was King of the Monkeys on the Mountain of Many Flowers I took a great many lives. Had I acted as you propose I should certainly never have become the Great Sage, Equal to Heaven."

"It was just because you were making such mischief in the world of mortals and behaving disgracefully in Heaven, that you were so severely punished five hundred years ago. Now you've accepted the Faith, and if you start your old pranks again and destroy life you cannot remain a priest. You will not be able to accompany me on my journey to the west. Shame on you!"

Monkey had never been able to take criticism. Tripitaka went on scolding him, and at last Monkey's patience was exhausted and he snapped: "All right, if you insist on reproaching me all the time, I shall not be a priest and shall not go with you on your journey to the west. You can keep your nonsense — I'm off."

Tripitaka did not reply, and this angered Monkey still further. He shook himself and crying, "All right then, I'm off!", he vanished. Tripitaka looked up quickly, but Monkey was gone. He could just hear the swish of his rapid flight to the east. Thus the noble pilgrim was left on his own. He nodded his head, gave a deep sigh, and sorrow filled his soul. Gathering his baggage together, he lifted it onto the horse's back and, leaning on his staff with one hand and leading the horse by the reins with the other, resumed his westward journey by himself. Before long he met an old woman carrying a cotton robe and embroidered cap. Tripitaka quickly led the horse out of the way to let her pass.

"Where have you come from, reverend father," the old woman asked, "that you are walking all alone like this?"

"I am a messenger sent by the Chinese Emperor to the Supreme Buddha in the west for the scriptures," said Tripitaka.

"The Voice of Thunder Temple in India, which is the seat of the Supreme Buddha, is a hundred and eight thousand miles distant. On your own, with just a horse and no companion or disciple, you can never get there."

"Several days ago I accepted a disciple," replied Tripitaka, "but he was too quick-tempered and stubborn, and when I had occasion to speak to him about it, he was offended and vanished without trace."

"This cotton robe and embroidered cap used to belong to my son," said the old woman. "Alas, he died three days after entering a monastery. I have just been there to mourn him, and I was taking the robe and the cap back with me to have something to remember him by. If you had a disciple, I'd gladly give them to him."

"You are very kind, thank you," said Tripitaka. "But my disciple has run away, and so I cannot accept them."

"Which way did he go?"

"All I heard was a swish, and that came from the east."

"Not far from here to the east I have a little house," the old woman said. "He is sure to pass it. I know a spell called 'Appropriate Words to Calm the Heart'. I shall teach you this spell if you promise not to tell it to anyone. Repeat it quietly so that you remember it. I shall catch up with your disciple and send him back to you. Give him this robe and cap to wear, and if he disobeys you in any way, recite the spell — he'll give no more trouble, nor will he ever leave you again."

Tripitaka listened attentively to all the

old woman told him and bowed his head to show his gratitude. At that moment the old woman changed into a golden glow and disappeared to the east. Tripitaka realised that she must have been the goddess Kuan-yin. Quickly he burned a little incense and bowed devoutly towards the east. Then he put the robe and cap in his pack and sat down by the roadside to practise the spell. He repeated it several times until he had memorised it.

After Monkey had left Tripitaka, he mounted a cloud and flew off towards the east. In his heart he felt, however, that it would be most ungrateful of him to leave Tripitaka for good, since he had released him from his casket under the Mountain of the Five Elements.

"Just because he annoyed me with a few harsh words I can't leave him to go on alone. No, that's quite impossible," he told himself, turning his cloud round the other way and going back.

In a short while he saw Tripitaka sitting dejectedly by the roadside.

"Master," he called out to him, "what are you doing here? Why don't you go on?"

"Where have you been?" asked Tripitaka, lifting his head. "I didn't feel like going on without you, and all this waiting has made me really hungry. You should be ashamed of yourself!"

"If you're hungry, Master, I can go and beg for some alms," offered Monkey.

"That isn't necessary. We still have some provisions in the pack. Bring me a little water in a bowl. We'll eat and then set out again."

Monkey undid the packs. Inside he found a couple of pancakes made of coarse flour. But underneath the pancakes he saw a glittering, gold-embroidered cap and a cotton robe.

"Have you brought these all the way from the eastern Empire?" he asked.

"I used to wear them when I was young," replied Tripitaka, saying the first thing that came into his head. "Whoever wears this cap can recite the scriptures without having to learn them, and whoever wears the robe can perform ceremonies without having to train."

"Oh, Master, let me try them on!" the Monkey King begged.

"They'll be too large for you," said Tripitaka. "But by all means try them on if you wish."

Monkey took off his tiger-skin and slipped into the robe.

It fitted him perfectly.

When Tripitaka saw that he was putting on the cap, he stopped eating and quietly recited the spell.

"Oh, my head! My head!" groaned Monkey.

Tripitaka went on reciting.

Monkey rolled on the ground in agony, trying to wrench the gold head band, that had been sewn into the cap, off his head. Fearing that he would break it, Tripitaka stopped reciting. The pain immediately stopped. Monkey felt his head with his hands.

The cap seemed to have taken root there.

However hard he tried, Monkey could not get rid of it. He took his needle from behind his ear and tried to push the head band up. Tripitaka was afraid that he would really succeed in breaking it, and he began reciting the spell again. Monkey stood on his head with pain, and turned somersaults on the ground. He went purple in the face, his eyes bulged and his body stiffened. Unable to bear the sight of such suffering, Tripitaka broke off once more.

Monkey's head stopped hurting at once.

"It's all your fault!" Monkey accused Tripitaka. "You've put a spell upon me."

"What gave you that idea?" replied Tripitaka. "I was just reciting a Prayer."

"In that case, pray again and we shall soon see," demanded Monkey.

Tripitaka did as he asked, and recited the spell.

Monkey's head immediately began to hurt him.

"Stop it! Stop it!" he cried. "As soon as you start praying, the pain begins. You can't pretend it's none of your doing."

"Are you going to do as you're told from now on?"

"Yes, yes, I will," Monkey promised quickly.

"Are you going to make any more trouble?"

"No, I shouldn't dare."

But though he made these promises, he was, in fact, up to no good.

His needle seemed to be itching in his hand.

He felt a strong inclination to use it on Tripitaka.

Consequently, he waved it in the air and lifted his arm to strike. Tripitaka, horrified, again recited the spell. Monkey fell to the ground, writhing, the cudgel dropping from his hand.

"Enough, Master, enough! I give in," he shouted, unable to move.

"Are you really so treacherous that

you meant to strike me?" said Tripitaka.

"I didn't mean to hit you," protested Monkey. "But tell me, Master, who taught you that spell?"

"I had it from an old woman who passed by here a few minutes ago."

"I see," replied Monkey, furious. "That must have been Kuan-yin. How does she dare to treat me like this? I'll go at once to her home in the Southern Sea and give her a piece of my mind."

"Since she taught me the spell, she must have known what effect it has," said Tripitaka. "If you go, she will surely use it, and that will be the end of you."

The Monkey King saw that Tripitaka was right.

He thought better of it and stayed where he was. Repenting, he knelt in front of Tripitaka, saying: "Master, with this spell you have me completely in your power. I'll go to the west with you and I shall not give you any more trouble, only promise me not to use the spell too often. I will protect you faithfully all the way and never think of running away again."

"Very well then," said Tripitaka. "Help me onto my horse."

Crestfallen as he was, Monkey felt a little relieved. He tidied his dress, patted the horse, collected their luggage, and they set off once more.

In a few days they reached a river that was so wide that not even an eagle could have got across.

Here they tamed the jade dragon.

The dragon changed into a white horse and carried Tripitaka on the rest of their journey.

By the Cloud-Ladder Cave they took Pigsy into their retinue, and by the Sandy River, the Sandy Priest. The Master and his three disciples were of one mind and helped one another in every possible way. Each passing day brought them nearer to their destination.

Pigsy in the Snare of Demons

Tripitaka and his disciples went on their journey every day, resting their tired limbs every night. One day a tall mountain barred their way.

"We must be very careful," said Tripitaka. "The mountain is very high, and there are sure to be tigers about."

They began ascending the mountain, which towered steep and sheer above them. In a green clearing they came across a woodcutter, who called in a loud voice: "Reverend father, halt your steps a while and listen to my warning: there is a horde of wicked demons and evil spirits on this mountain, and they devour people who pass here from east to west."

His words struck terror into Tripitaka's heart. He sat astride his horse, shaking like a leaf and trying to keep himself from falling off. Quickly he turned his head and addressed his disciples: "Have you heard the woodcutter warning us about evil spirits on this mountain? Which of you will dare to go and ask him for details?"

"Don't worry, reverend father," said Monkey. "I'll find out all about it."

Monkey immediately climbed the slope, walking with a rolling gait.

"Greetings," he called out to the woodcutter.

The woodcutter returned his greetings and asked: "What is it you seek here, reverend father?"

"I do not wish to keep anything back from you. We are monks from the Eastern Empire on our way for the scriptures in the Western Paradise," Monkey explained. "The one on horseback is our esteemed Master. He is a little timid, you know. You have been kind enough to warn us about the wicked demons and evil spirits to be found hereabouts. I therefore wish to ask you what demons and spirits these are."

"This mountain is called the Flat Peak Mountain, and before you cross it you will have covered six hundred miles," said the woodcutter. "On it there is a cave called the Lotus Blossom Cave, inhabited by two demons. They have hung up a portrait of a monk they wish to capture. He is called Tripitaka. The demons mean to devour him. You have come a long way, but if any of you have a name beginning with Tri—, you had better turn back."

"Our Master is called Tripitaka," Monkey pointed out.

"Then I am afraid it is all up with you," said the woodcutter sadly.

This did not seem to worry Monkey at all, but it increased his determination to do everything he could to protect Tripitaka. He left the woodcutter and sauntered back down the hillside.

"It's nothing, reverend father," he announced. "Just a handful of spooks. The local people are cowardly, though, and they build up their own importance out of all proportion. With me, you need not fear anything. Let us go on."

Tripitaka was somewhat reassured, and they went on.

"No useful purpose can be served by my telling our Master everything the woodcutter said," Monkey thought. "Tripitaka would certainly be very much upset. After all, there is an old proverb, 'When you fall into a pond, you can never tell how deep it's going to turn out to be.' And what if the demons did succeed in getting him? That would be enough to make me think twice. The best plan would be to test the demons on Pigsy. I'll send him on ahead to fight them, and then we'll see. If he defeats them, he can chalk up one more good deed. If not, and the demons capture him, there should still be time for me to save him. That way I shall at least show what I can do and make a name for myself."

Then it occurred to Monkey that Pigsy was extremely lazy and would not want to go unless he had to. Tripitaka always took his side. It was clearly a situation requiring a great deal of cunning.

So Monkey put on a dismal face, rubbing his eyes until the tears came. He went back to Tripitaka. Pigsy noticed him, and cried: "Sandy, bring the packs down and take our things out. We'll each go our own way."

"What do you mean by that, brother?" asked Sandy, puzzled.

"We'll each go our own way," repeated Pigsy. "You and I will go back and again attack passers-by. We'll sell the white horse and buy our Master a coffin for his last journey. Each of us will take what belongs to him. What's the sense of going on to the West?"

Tripitaka heard Pigsy and said: "You scoundrel! What's that you're raving? We have to go on."

"It's you yourself who's raving," replied Pigsy. "Can't you see that Monkey's crying? A chap like that, who can fly up to Heaven and crawl underground, whom neither axe nor fire can harm, and who can bathe in molten oil. And now he is frowning and tears are running down his cheeks. That means there must be some truly terrible demons in these hills. How are we, weak worms that we are, to carry on?"

"Enough of this stupid talk," Tripitaka reprimanded him. "I'll ask him myself. We shall see what he has to tell us."

Turning to Monkey, Tripitaka said: "Sun Wu-k'ung, if anything is troubling you, why don't you confide in me? Why are you crying? Are you perhaps trying to frighten me?"

"Reverend father," Monkey sobbed, "that woodcutter told me that there are very wicked demons here and that the going is most difficult. Look, you can see for yourself how tall the mountain is and how steep the path. Perhaps we ought to wait and go on some other time."

Tripitaka was quite bowled over by this.

"My dear disciple," he said at last, clutching Monkey by his tiger-skin breeches, "we are more than halfway now. Why do you say such terrible things?"

"It's not that I'm unwilling," Monkey went on, "but I fear that there will be too many demons for me to cope with. There is an old proverb that says, 'Even though you have a piece of cast iron, how many nails do you think you'll forge from it?'"

"You're right, disciple," replied Tripitaka. "It's too great a task for one person alone. In books on the art of war you will find written: 'A small handful stands no chance against great odds.' But there are Pigsy and Sandy. Let them take their orders from you, helping you in every way they can or waiting to be called in case of need. Together the three of you will doubtless succeed in fighting through and leading me over the mountain. In return all three will win glory."

Monkey's plan had been intended to produce just this result. He wiped the tears from his eyes and said: "Reverend father, if we are to get across the mountain, Pigsy must promise me two things. Then we stand three-quarters of a chance of getting through. If, however, he refuses and will not obey, we haven't even half a chance."

"Brother, if you don't feel like going by yourself, you'd better not drag me into this. Let's each go our own way," put in Pigsy.

"No, my disciple," said Tripitaka. "You

must be ruled by your elder brother and do as he tells you."

Pigsy then turned to Monkey, asking him what it was he wanted.

"In the first place, you must look after our Master," replied Monkey, "and in the second, you must go and explore the mountain."

"Now look," protested Pigsy, "if I am to look after Tripitaka, I have to stay with him, but if I am to explore, I must leave him. How am I to do both these things at once, I'd very much like to know."

"Who said you were to do them both at once?" retorted Monkey. "I'll give you your orders every time."

"That's different," said Pigsy, with a frown. "But I don't know how to look after our Master and how to explore the mountain. You must explain to me first. Then I shall be able to do these things."

"Whenever our Master wishes to go and relieve himself, you'll go with him and will watch over him. When he wants to continue the journey, you'll support him. If he feels hungry, you must find him something to eat. If he suffers from lack of food, you'll get a beating. Likewise if he loses weight or becomes an unhealthy colour."

"I can't do all that," cried Pigsy. "Looking after him and supporting him is easy enough. When he rides his horse and I stay by his side, nothing can happen either. But if you start sending me round the villages to look for food, it's all up with me. Here in the west they don't know that I'm a monk on his way for the scriptures.

They'll think I am just a fat old pig which has run away from someone's farmyard. They'll get hold of their brooms and pitchforks, catch me and cut my throat. They'll salt me and keep me for the New Year. That's what will happen, and I can tell you I'm not very keen about it."

"In that case go and explore the mountain," suggested Monkey.

"And how am I to do that?"

"Climb up as far as you can, find out the name of the mountain and how many demons and other evil spirits there are here, and where they live. Once we know all this, we'll find it easier to pass."

"That's child's play. I'll go and explore then."

Foolish Pigsy spread the skirts of his coat, swung his rake over one shoulder, puffed out his chest, and vanished into the depths of the forest. Whistling merrily, he set off up the hillside. Monkey watched him go and could not help laughing.

"Cursed Monkey," Tripitaka scolded him. "There is not the slightest love between you brothers, only malice. You pack him off into the mountains and then make fun of him."

"I wasn't making fun of him," Monkey replied. "But I had good reason for laughing. You'll see that Pigsy won't explore anything. He hasn't the slightest intention of looking for any demons or vampires, but will hide up somewhere and then will come back with some fine story to pull the wool over our eyes."

"How can you know this?" Tripitaka asked indignantly.

"I know Pigsy inside out," Monkey said. "If you don't belive me, I'll go and see what he's doing. I'll be able help him if he falls among demons, and I'll find out just how sincere his intentions are."

"Very well," agreed Tripitaka. "But you mustn't trick him."

Monkey ran quickly up the hill, shook himself, and changed into a gadfly. He could not have chosen a better disguise. Whizz! He fluttered his wings and off he went in pursuit of Pigsy, settling on the bristles behind his ear. Ignorant of his presence, Pigsy strode on for some seven or eight miles. Then he threw down his rake, turned round to face in the direction he had come from and, waving his arms in the air and kicking out with his legs, began to shout abuse.

"You rotten old monk, you stupid groom, you useless Sandy! You're taking things easy, the three of you, and Pigsy is to do all the dirty work. All of us want to fetch the scriptures and win glory, but it's me who has to creep up this mountain for you. When there are demons and evil spirits about, any sensible person would do his utmost to avoid them. And what do you do? You send me out to look for them. It's enough to make you sick. But I know what I'll do — I'll take a nice nap and then I'll go back and invent some story or other. I can always tell them I looked all over the mountain but could find nothing."

Pigsy picked up his rake again and went on. Opposite him, on the other side of the mountain valley, the hillsides were covered with tall green grass. Hurrying over there, he used his rake to make himself a comfortable bed of grass, and he stretched out his limbs with a small sigh of pleasure. Already half-asleep, he murmured: "Ah, how marvellous! Not even Monkey can enjoy such bliss."

Monkey, sitting behind Pigsy's ear in his shape of a gadfly, heard everything. Unable to resist the temptation, he changed himself into a worm-eating insect. He was now neither big nor small and weighed less than two ounces. His jaws were as red as copper, his legs as black as coal.

Monkey fluttered his wings and hovered above Pigsy, who was sleeping on his back and snoring loudly, and gave him a very painful sting on the lip. Pigsy started, leapt to his feet, and yelled: "Help, the demons have got me! Help! They're shooting at me with their crossbows! Oh dear, my mouth is all sore!"

Stretching out his hand, he touched his lips. They were bleeding. He inspected his bloodstained hand and, his teeth chattering with fear, looked fearfully round him. Not a blade of grass moved anywhere.

"There don't seem to be any demons around here. Who could have shot at me with a crossbow?"

Lifting his head suddenly, he saw the insect hovering in the air above him. He gritted his teeth and cried: "You wretch! It's not enough that Monkey has it in for me, you have to hurt me as well. But I know what happened. The insect probably didn't realise I was a living thing and mistook me for a tree-stump. Meaning to gobble up a worm, it stung me instead. I'll hide my face in my hands and I can go back to sleep again."

Pigsy lay down once more and immediately went back to sleep. Again Monkey flew up to him, stinging him in the ear this time. Pigsy jumped up in terror.

"That accursed insect is at it again! It has its nest here somewhere, I expect, with eggs or young, and I have stretched myself out on top of it. That's why it keeps attacking me. What a pity! That's the end of my nap."

He grabbed his rake and ran down the grassy slope to the path. Monkey laughed until he almost cried. Then he changed himself into a gadfly and settled behind Pigsy's ear, not leaving him for a moment. Pigsy made for the forest and walked on for some four or five miles. In a cleft in the rocks he saw four large, flat-topped stones. He put down his rake and bowed low before them.

"The idiot!" Monkey said to himself. "What is he doing, bowing to lifeless stones that can neither speak nor bow in return? He must be mad!"

But Pigsy was not mad. He had named the stones Tripitaka, Monkey and Sandy and was practising his speech.

"When I get back I'll come up to our Master and when he asks me if there are demons hereabouts, I'll say yes. When he asks me what kind of a mountain this is, it makes little odds whether I say it's made out of earth, stuck together with clay, hammered out of tin, cast from copper, cooked with flour, cut out of paper or drawn with a brush. They'll say I am mad anyway. That's what they're always saying about me; so I'll tell them it's a mountain of stone. When they ask me what kind of caves the demons have, I'll say they're also made of stone. When they ask me what kind of doors these caves have, I'll say they have two parts and are reinforced with iron. When they ask me how large the caves are, I'll say they have three storeys. And if they want to know still more and ask me how many nails there are in the door, I'll say I was too busy worrying about other things and had no time to count them. There, that ought to do the trick. Now we'll see what you make of that, you Monkey Groom!"

Having rehearsed his tale, Pigsy started on his return journey, dragging his rake along the ground behind him. He had no idea that Monkey was sitting behind his ear and had heard every word he had said. Seeing that Pigsy was heading back, Monkey flew off, changed back to his own form, and came up to Tripitaka.

"Well, so you are back, Sun Wu-k'ung," said the monk in surprise. "Why hasn't Pigsy arrived yet?"

"Because he is still inventing his stories, that's why," laughed Monkey in reply. "He'll be back in a minute, you'll see."

"Why, his long ears cover both his eyes and he is an old simpleton. How could he make up any stories?" asked Tripitaka. "I expect you have been up to your devilish trick again in order to put him in the wrong."

"Now don't you start taking his side, reverend father," protested Monkey. "I have proofs."

Monkey told Tripitaka how Pigsy had gone to sleep in the long grass, how he had been stung by insects, how he had invented his story about a mountain of stone, a stone cave, the doors reinforced with iron, and the demons. He had hardly finished speaking when Pigsy made his appearance. Fearing that he might forget his tale, he walked with head bent low, repeating it to himself in a whisper.

"Hey there, Pig!" exclaimed Monkey. "What's that you're muttering to yourself?"

Pigsy realised his hour had come. He stepped forward and knelt in front of Tripitaka.

"Well, disciple," said Tripitaka, raising him to his feet, "I am sure you have had an eventful journey."

"Oh yes," agreed Pigsy. "Pilgrims and those who are forced to climb up mountains are the most wretched people in the world."

"Did you come across any demons?" Tripitaka wanted to know.

"Of course I did, whole troops of them," lied Pigsy.

"And how did you get away?"

"They called me Mylord Pigsy and Duke of Pigsyland, they gave me some soup and vegetables and I had to eat it all. Then, to the sound of drums and with banners flying they led me over the mountain."

"I should say you took a nap in the grass and are now telling us something you saw in your dreams," Monkey cut him short.

Pigsy was so terrified that he shrank by two inches.

"Oh, dear me," he thought, "how can he possibly know?"

Monkey jumped forward and shook him.

"Come here, I want to ask you a few questions now."

Pigsy almost fainted, and he trembled all over.

"All right, ask me all you want to, but stop shaking me like this."

"What kind of mountain is this?" Monkey enquired.

"It's made of stone," Pigsy replied.

"What kind of caves are there on it?"

"Stone caves."

"What are the doors like?"

"They have two parts and are reinforced with iron."

"How big are the caves?"

"They're all three-storeyed caves."

"That's enough, I remember it all," Monkey interrupted him. "I was only afraid our Master wouldn't believe me. I have told him everything already."

"You foul-mouthed slanderer!" exclaimed Pigsy. "You haven't been anywhere, so how can you know? What can you tell Tripitaka about me?"

"When I ask you how many nails there are in these doors, you will tell me that you had other things to worry about and didn't have the time to count them. Isn't that right?" Monkey laughed.

Pigsy knelt in front of him.

"You bowed before the stones," Monkey went on, "and pretended that they were the three of us, and you answered their questions. That's right too, isn't it? Then you said: 'That ought to do the trick — now we'll see what you make of that, you Monkey Groom!' Isn't that so?"

Pigsy quickly beat his forehead on the ground.

"Surely, brother, you didn't follow me and listen as I went round the mountain?"

"I have half a mind to thrash you, you good-for-nothing," Monkey scolded him. "I give you a responsible job, sending you out to explore, and you go and take forty winks. If that insect hadn't bitten you, you'd have been snoring away still. And then you have the nerve to invent such lies. Hasn't it occurred to you that by your conduct you have put us in danger? Quickly, stick your behind out, I'm going to give you five blows to make you remember never to do anything like this again."

"That cudgel of his is very big," thought Pigsy in great terror. "Even if he only taps me with it, I'm done for!"

"Why do you lie to us if you're afraid of a hiding?" Monkey shouted at him.

"Brother, leave it this time, I'll never dare to do it again," Pigsy pleaded.

"In that case I'll only give you three blows," said Monkey kindly.

"Oh dear, I can't take even half a blow or it'll be the death of me," wailed Pigsy.

In his desperation he pulled Tripitaka by the sleeve, saying: "Reverend father, please put in a word for me."

"Sun Wu-k'ung always said you were a liar, yet I didn't believe him," said Tripitaka. "Now I see he was right. You indeed deserve a beating. But we have to get across this mountain and there are only a few of us. For that reason I ask you to forgive him, Sun Wu-k'ung, and leave his punishment after we have got across."

"Our Master says I am to forgive you," said Monkey. "Therefore I forgive you. And now you're really going to explore. If you come back telling any more lies, you needn't think I'll be so lenient again."

Foolish Pigsy leapt to his feet and rushed off as if a fire were raging behind him. At every step he suspected that Monkey had changed into something and was following him. Every time he saw anything strange he was sure it was Monkey. When he had gone some seven or eight miles, a tiger came charging down the hill towards him. Pigsy wasn't a bit frightened, but raised his rake and said: "Have you come to see if I am lying, brother? I wouldn't dare any more."

The tiger ran away and Pigsy went on. A mighty wind arose, lashing the trees until their branches touched the ground and hit Pigsy across the face. He only stamped his feet and beat his breast with his fist.

"Come, brother, what is this? Haven't I promised not to tell any more lies? Why then do you change yourself into trees and slap me?"

He went on again, and saw a crow with a white front. It cawed right in his ear.

"Brother, you ought to be ashamed of yourself!" exclaimed Pigsy. "I have promised not to lie, and I mean to keep my promise. Why do you consider it necessary to change into a crow? Trying to tail me again, are you?"

But this time Monkey was not following him at all. Pigsy was getting worked up for nothing, all his suspicions were false. He was convinced that Monkey was everywhere, keeping track of him.

The mountain was called the Flat Peak Mountain, and the cave on it the Lotus Blossom Cave. Two demons lived there, one being called King Gold Horn, the other King Silver Horn. At this moment Gold Horn was sitting on his throne. He said to Silver Horn: "Tell me, how long is it since we last inspected the mountain?"

"About a fortnight, isn't it?" replied Silver Horn.

"Brother, go and inspect it today," Gold Horn urged him.

"Why today of all days?" Silver Horn asked.

"Don't you know? Some time ago I heard that the great T'ang Emperor in the east had sent his pledge-brother, the monk Tripitaka, to the west to pay homage to Buddha. He has with him three disciples: the Monkey Sun Wu-k'ung, Pigsy and Sandy, as well as a white horse. Go and see where they have got to, and catch them for me."

"We can always catch somebody if we feel like a bit of human flesh," replied Silver Horn. "Monks like that are to be had for the asking. Let him go where he pleases."

"Ah, but you don't know that when I was in Heaven the other year, I heard that this Tripitaka did penance for ten generations, and that anyone who tasted of his flesh would live forever."

"Since if we eat his flesh we'll live forever, why should we try to win wisdom, do good deeds and worry ourselves about this, that and the other?" said Silver Horn. "We'll just taste his flesh and that'll be that. I'm going to capture him."

"Don't be so impatient, brother," said Gold Horn, holding him back. "Why this rush? If you go rushing away like this without thinking the matter over first, you'll as likely as not bring back some ordinary monk, who'll not be worth your trouble. I know what Tripitaka looks like — I have been given portraits of him and his disciples. You can take the portraits with you. When you meet a monk, just compare his looks with the portraits."

Gold Horn again told his brother the disciples' names, and Silver Horn took the portraits and left the cave. Choosing thirty imps to go with him, he began to search the mountain.

Pigsy was out of luck. As he walked along, he happened to run straight into the imps, who stopped him and asked: "Who are you and where do you come from?"

Pigsy raised his head, pricked up his ears, and found that he had been questioned by imps. This frightened him very much.

"If I say I am a monk on my way for the scriptures, they are sure to take me prisoner," he thought. "Better tell them I am a traveller."

The imps reported to Silver Horn that they had met a traveller. Of the thirty imps, most had not recognised Pigsy, but a few had. One of these now stepped forward, saying that the traveller looked remarkably like the disciple called Pigsy in one of the portraits. Silver Horn then gave orders for the portraits to be unfolded. When Pigsy saw them, he was horrified.

"No wonder I am not myself lately," he thought. "They have stolen my soul."

The imps pointed their spears at the pictures. Silver Horn got up, pointing with his hand: "The one on the white horse is Tripitaka. The hairy one is Monkey."

"Lord of Darkness," muttered Pigsy, "if they fail to recognise me I'll give you a pig, a fish and a cock in sacrifice."

"The tall, dark one is Sandy," went on the demon. "The one with the long snout and huge ears is Pigsy."

Hearing this, Pigsy hid his snout in his hands.

"Monk, show your face," cried the demon.

"Since my birth I have been afflicted with a disease which makes it impossible for me to keep my head up properly," Pigsy lied.

Silver Horn ordered the imps to stretch his neck with a hook. Terrified, Pigsy quickly looked up.

"I look just like everybody else, what do you expect. You're welcome to see for yourself, if you want to. Why should you have to use a hook?"

Silver Horn at once recognised that it was Pigsy. Drawing his sword, he jumped forward and hit out at him.

Pigsy parried the blow with his rake, saying: "Careful, not so fast, I'll give you a taste of my rake."

"This monk only entered a monastery recently," said Silver Horn, laughing.

"Clever, aren't you," retorted Pigsy. "You're right, as it happens, but how did you know?"

"Judging by the way you wield that rake, you must have been a gardener. I suppose you stole it from your master."

"Of course you can't know what kind of rake this is," replied Pigsy proudly. "This is not an ordinary, common or garden rake. If you don't belive me, I can always convince you by giving you a few cuts with it to remember me by."

The demon, of course, did not stand for such talk.

He grasped his sword decorated with seven stars and hit out once more. Pigsy and he fought, pushing and prodding each other right in the middle of the mountain. They clashed some twenty times, but victory favoured neither one nor the other. Pigsy attacked the demon with great courage. When the demon saw Pigsy coming at him, his ears erect, saliva trickling from his mouth, his rake held in front of him like a shield, he felt a little frightened and called in the imps to help him.

While they had fought one against one, Pigsy had given very good account of himself. But now that the imps rushed at him, one after the other, he felt his strength ebbing away and could no longer keep them all at bay.

He decided to call it a day, and fled from the battlefield.

The path was very rough, Pigsy didn't look where he was going, and suddenly he tripped and went sprawling.

He picked himself up with difficulty and ran on again.

One of the imps, however, flung himself on the ground in front of him, catching hold of his hooves and sending him flying once more.

The other imps caught up with them now and pressed Pigsy to the ground. They tore his bristles, tweaked his ears and pulled his nose and tail. In the end they lifted him bodily and carried him away to the cave.

Danger Lurks in the Lotus Blossom Cave

The imps dragged Pigsy to the cave and announced they had managed to catch one of the pilgrims.

"Bring him to me," said the first demon.

"It's the right one, isn't it?" asked the second.

"You've made a mistake, brother. This one is no good to us."

"Since I am no good to you," put in Pigsy, "how about letting me go again, Your Majesty?"

"Don't do that, brother," said the second demon. "Even if he isn't any good, he belongs to Tripitaka. It's Pigsy. We can soak him in clean water in the pond, rub off his bristles, salt him and dry him in the sun. He'll do in winter as a dessert to go with our wine."

"Aren't I unlucky," thought Pigsy sadly. "I have to go and fall into the hands of demons who like dried meat."

The imps dragged him out of the cave and threw him in the pond.

Meanwhile Tripitaka was sitting on the hillside, feeling very worried. His face was hot and his heart throbbed inside his chest.

"Why isn't Pigsy back yet from his trip round the mountain?" he asked Monkey anxiously.

"You don't know him yet," Monkey replied.

"What do you mean?" asked Tripitaka.

"If there were demons on the mountain, he would not dare to go on but would come rushing back at once, exaggerating as usual. It looks as if there aren't any demons here, and so he has wandered off somewhere."

"If that's so, where can we find him?" Tripitaka was worried. "For miles around there is nothing but desolate mountains, with not a single town or village anywhere."

"Don't worry, reverend father," Monkey reassured him. "Get on your horse again. Pigsy is terribly lazy, and I'm sure he is dawdling along the way. We'll catch up with him if you will only make your horse go a little faster."

Tripitaka mounted his horse. Sandy shouldered their packs and Monkey led them up the hillside.

In the cave the older demon called his younger brother to him and said: "As you have caught Pigsy, it's obvious Tripitaka must be somewhere near by. Go and search the mountain once more so that he doesn't give you the slip."

"Righto," said the younger demon. Hurriedly he counted off fifty imps and together they started searching the mountain from top to bottom. Suddenly they saw in front of them a magic cloud floating in the air and a strange golden glow.

"Tripitaka is here," said the second demon.

"Where?" asked the imps, surprised.

"Good people always have a halo of light around their heads," said the demon. "Evil-doers have a dark cloud floating above them, reaching as far as Heaven. Tripitaka practised virtue for ten whole generations, that's why there is a golden glow above his head."

The imps, however, saw nothing.

"Look, over there," the demon said, pointing.

At that moment Tripitaka felt a chill run down his spine. The demon pointed again, and again Tripitaka's spine tingled. This was repeated three times, and it made Tripitaka extremely worried.

"Why does a chill run down my spine?" he asked his disciples.

"It must be your old stomach ailment troubling you again," suggested Sandy.

"Nonsense!" exclaimed Monkey. "Our Master doubtless feels somewhat afraid of these barren mountains and steep slopes. Have no fear — Monkey with his cudgel will clear the way for you. There's nothing to be worried about."

Monkey wielded his cudgel, swinging it deftly up and down and to the right and to the left in front of Tripitaka's horse in a way that would have done credit even to the masters of the ancient art of war. Tripitaka watched him with an appreciative eye, thinking that indeed he had no equal in the world. Having cleared the way for them, Monkey headed straight on, frightening the imps almost out of their wits as they gazed down at him from the summit.

"I've heard a lot about the Monkey King," whispered the second demon nervously.

"Now I can see for myself that his reputation is not exaggerated."

The imps came forward, asking: "Your Majesty, whom are you praising in this way?"

"The Monkey King truly has great magical powers," the demon told them. "We are not likely to taste Tripitaka's flesh after all."

"If Your Majesty can't deal with him, we shall go and appeal to His Majesty Gold Horn," suggested the imps. "He'll call to arms the entire forces of our kingdom. We'll array ourselves for battle, and together we shall surely take him. He can't get away."

"Haven't you seen his iron cudgel? With it he can vanquish ten thousand men quite easily," the demon said angrily. "We only have some four or five thousand soldiers. What chance would we stand against him?"

"That being so, it really seems as if we shall not have the pleasure of tasting Tripitaka's flesh. We needn't have bothered to capture Pigsy in that case either. What are we to do with him? Return him to his friends?"

"No, I don't think so," replied the demon. "We shall not give him back for nothing. We'll enjoy Tripitaka yet, even though it takes a little time."

"How many years shall we have to wait?"

"It's not a question of years," said the demon. "It seems to me that what is

needed here is a little cunning. It's no good trying to catch Tripitaka by force. If we do that, we shall not as much as smell his flesh. No, we've got to try to get him on our side, then I'll think of some trick, and he'll be ours."

"If Your Majesty has any ideas, we wish to volunteer," cried all the imps eagerly.

"Go back to the camp, but don't say anything to His Majesty my brother as yet," the demon ordered them. "If you disturb him, he'll give the show away and spoil my plans. I can change myself into any shape I choose, just like Monkey, and I mean to capture Tripitaka on my own."

The imps dispersed, and the demon ran down the moutainside and changed himself into an old, lame monk. His legs were cut and bleeding, and he cried desperately for help.

Tripitaka, Sandy and Monkey were walking contentedly along when they heard someone calling.

"This is very strange," said Tripitaka. "Who can be calling for help here in such a deserted spot in the mountains, where there is not a soul and not a dwelling for miles around? I suppose it's someone who has got lost and has been attacked by wolves or tigers."

Tripitaka stopped his horse and cried: "Who is it calling for help? Let him come forward."

The demon struggled out of the bushes and bowed before Tripitaka. When Tripitaka saw it was an old monk, he was deeply moved. Jumping down from his horse he helped the old man to rise to his feet.

The demon groaned as if in pain. Tripitaka noticed the blood on his legs.

"How did you get here, reverend father?" he asked. "And how did you come to hurt yourself?"

The demon did his best to look sad. He had a good story ready: "Reverend father, I am in charge of the sacrifices at a little sanctuary to the west of here."

"Why then aren't you looking after the place and praying in your sanctuary? What are you doing here?" asked Tripitaka.

"A few days ago a benefactor who lives to the south of this mountain invited us to come and sacrifice to the stars and ask them to bring good fortune to his house. Dusk fell as I and my disciple were on our way back. A fierce tiger attacked us in the dark and carried away my disciple. Shaking with fear, I sought a place to hide and stumbled over a heap of stones, injuring my leg. Now I have lost my way. Heaven itself has sent you to me. I beseech you, reverend father, to save my life. When we reach the sanctuary I shall richly reward you."

Tripitaka was completely taken in by the demon.

"Reverend father," he said, "we are both monks, and though we do not profess the same faith, our lives are linked together. Even though our robes are different, we share the same desire for goodness. May my fellow-believers cast me out if I fail to save you! But tell me, how am I to do it since you cannot walk?"

"No, I can't take a single step. I can't even stand up," the demon whined.

"Never mind," said Tripitaka. "I shall give you my horse and walk by your side. You can return the horse when we get to your sanctuary."

"Thank you for your great kindness, reverend father," replied the demon, bowing, "but my leg is injured in the thigh, and I can't ride either."

"True enough," said Tripitaka. "Sandy, put the packs on the horse and carry the reverend father on your back."

Sandy nodded his agreement. The demon turned round quickly and looked at him.

"Reverend father," he told Tripitaka, "I haven't yet fully recovered from my shock after the tiger pounced on us. Now when I see this monk with such a horrid face, I begin to tremble afresh. I am afraid. Don't let him carry me."

"You must carry the reverend father instead, Sun Wu-k'ung," Tripitaka decided.

"Very well," Monkey agreed readily.

The demon had recognised Monkey and wanted to be carried by him. He therefore said no more and waited in silence.

"This old monk must be blind!" thought Sandy, grinning. "I don't seem good enough to him, and he wants Monkey to carry him instead. If he hadn't met our Master, he'd have broken both his legs on these stones."

"You cursed spook," Monkey said to himself with a laugh, "you have the check to provoke me, have you. Make no mistake, though, Sun Wu-k'ung wasn't born yesterday. You may fool Tripitaka with your glib talk, but don't think for a moment that you can fool me as well. Pshaw! I know that you're the demon of this mountain and want to devour our Master. But Tripitaka isn't just anybody, that you can have your way with him. If you try any of your tricks, you'll have old Sun to deal with."

The demon noticed that Monkey was muttering to himself.

"Reverend father," he said at once, "I come from a good family and became a monk many years ago. Now misfortune has struck me and I have fallen into the toils of tigers and wolves. I really am no demon."

"Why don't you pray, if you're afraid of wolves and tigers?" Monkey asked.

Tripitaka overheard what Monkey said.

"Wretched Monkey!" he cried. "You just carry him and keep quiet!"

"The scoundrel really is in luck," thought Monkey. "That Master of ours is such a good soul. If I refuse to carry the demon, he'll reproach me for it. All right, then," he said out loud, "I'm going to carry you."

Monkey hoisted him up on his shoulders and, with Tripitaka and Sandy following behind, set off again in a westerly direction. The mountain path was very uneven and stony, Monkey soon let Tripitaka and Sandy overtake him, following more slowly at their heels.

Before they had gone five miles, Tripitaka and Sandy had disappeared from view into a valley. Monkey lagged behind with his load.

"The older our Master gets, the less sense he has," he said to himself reproachfully. "Such a long way to go. It's enough to tire you out and make you wish to lie down and rest even if you walk empty-handed. And he has to make me cart this demon about! Even if he were a good man, at his age he has one foot in the grave anyway. It would be far more sensible to dump him here — why bother hauling him any further."

He got ready to shake off his passenger, but the demon guessed his intention. He knew the magic art of moving mountains, and now, sitting on Monkey's back, he recited a spell which brought Mount Sumeru through the air, and he plonked it straight on Monkey's shoulders.

Monkey began to jerk his head from side to side, until he had shifted the mountain to his left shoulder.

"I wonder what he's doing, that he's become so heavy all of a sudden," he said to himself. "It's not that I'm afraid of a little burden, as long as it is well balanced, but he seems to be all lopsided."

"One mountain isn't enough," thought the demon.

Again he recited a spell, and he brought over the O-mei Mountain. Monkey again shook his head and shifted the mountain to his right shoulder. Not only did he not fall under the load, he even increased his pace and hurried after Tripitaka. The demon sweated with anxiety, but then he calmed himself, recited another spell, and brought across the T'ai Mountain, which he placed squarely on top of Monkey's head. Monkey's muscles now grew numb, he felt his strength ebbing fast, and he fell down.

The demon, having at last got rid of Monkey, quickly mounted a whirlwind and rushed in pursuit of Tripitaka. Stretching out his arm from the clouds he grabbed at the monk, making Sandy drop his packs in terror. Sandy recovered quickly, however, lifted his staff for the taming of evil spirits, and faced the demon, who drew his seven-star sword and attacked him. Sandy had never been very strong and, seeing he would not be able to withstand the demon, he took to his heels. The demon snatched Sandy's staff from him, seized Sandy with his claw and put him under his left arm. Then he dragged Tripitaka from his horse with his right claw, hung their packs on his toes, opened wide his mouth and picked the horse up by the mane with his teeth. He whipped up his whirlwind again and with a single blast it carried all of them to the Lotus Blossom Cave.

"Hullo, brother," he called in a voice of thunder. "I am back with three captives."

"Show me," said the old demon joyfully.

"Here they are, look," the young demon replied with pride.

"Wise brother, we've made another blunder," was the old demon's disappointed remark.

"But you told me to catch Tripitaka," protested the young demon.

"Yes, but you haven't caught the Monkey King, who possesses magic powers. We have to catch him before we can taste Tripitaka's flesh. Until you do so, you mustn't even touch the others. The Monkey King knows how to change himself into shapes and recite many spells. If we were to devour his Master, he would never forgive us. He'd come charging at our door, and we should have no peace for the rest of our lives."

"How little you know about people, brother," said the young demon, laughing. "The way you speak of him, one would think he has no equal in Heaven or on Earth. I don't think he is so very special, after all."

"Surely you haven't caught him?"

"I have squashed him under three mountains which I moved by magic. That's how I was able to bring Tripitaka and Sandy with the white horse and all their luggage."

"That's excellent!" rejoiced the old demon. "Since we have that rascal safely stowed away, Tripitaka is ours!"

He turned to the imps, shouting:

"Bring us some wine, so that I may toast our second king and drink to his great achievement."

"Before we start drinking, brother, let's tell the imps to fish Pigsy out of the pond and hang him up from a beam," the young demon suggested.

The imps hung Pigsy by his wrists from a beam in the eastern passage. Sandy was hung up in the western passage and Tripitaka in the middle. They tied the white horse to a trough and brought the packs into the cave.

"My wise brother certainly knows a trick or two," said the old demon approvingly. "Catching all three monks like this! But though Monkey is squashed under the mountains, he'll try to get even with us. Only when we have him frying in the pan shall we be able to breathe freely."

"Just make yourself comfortable, dear brother," said the young demon. "If we want to get hold of the Monkey King, neither you nor I need lift our little finger. All we have to do is to send two imps with two of our treasures, with instructions to put him inside."

"Which treasures do you have in mind?" the old demon asked.

"Let them take my red-gold gourd and your pure jade bottle."

The old demon took out his jade bottle.

"Which two imps shall we send on this errand?" he asked.

"Let's send Cleverhead and Skilful."

The imps were called in and given their orders.

"Take these two treasures and go right up to the mountain-top. There you will put them down, bottom up, on the ground and shout 'Monkey Sun!' When he replies, you will suck him inside and stick a label inscribed 'Upon the Orders of the Patriarch of the Way' across the bottle and the gourd. Within an hour and three-quarters Monkey's body will have been eaten away."

The two imps touched their foreheads respectfully to the ground, took the gourd and the bottle, and set off to catch Monkey.

The Monkey King Wins the Demons' Treasures

Monkey was still lying trapped under the mountains. Even in this trouble his thoughts turned to Tripitaka.

"My dear Master," he cried in a mighty voice, "you broke the seal on the Mountain of the Five Elements, setting me free and accepting me into the Faith. Thanks to the instructions of the wise Goddess Kuan-yin, I learned virtue from you, sharing with you all your joys and sorrows, and fulfilling your every wish. Who would have thought that our journey would be marred by a demon, who has heaped this mountain on my back. Woe is us! My poor Master, you at least will die for your noble cause. But what about Sandy, Pigsy and the little dragon changed into a horse?"

Monkey sighed deeply, and tears started to his eyes, running down his cheeks like raindrops.

Monkey's wailing woke the mountain spirits, the gods of the earth and the guardians of the five quarters. They all met together in the abode of the Goldheaded Guardian.

"Whose is the mountain?" he asked.

"Ours," replied the gods of the earth.

"And whom have you got imprisoned under it?"

"We don't know ourselves."

"You don't know?" said the Gold-headed Guardian. "It's the Monkey King, Sun Wu-k'ung, who played havoc in Heaven five hundred years ago. Now he has mended his ways and become a disciple of Tripitaka. Why did you lend the mountains to the demon, for him to imprison Monkey? By doing so you have signed your own death warrants, for when one day he frees himself, he is certain to punish you for it. And even if you managed to get off lightly, the gods of the earth are liable to be thrown from office, the mountain spirits to be sent into exile, and the rest of us will be given a scolding."

The mountain spirits and the gods of the earth grew frightened.

"We had no idea. We heard the demon muttering a spell for the moving of mountains, and so we obeyed. Who could have guessed it was on account of the Monkey King?"

"Have no fear," replied the Goldheaded Guardian. "The scriptures say 'To err is human.' Take my advice and let him out at once. Don't annoy him in any way, or he's sure to attack you."

"Is he without reason? Surely he wouldn't beat us if we set him free," the gods of the earth said in surprise.

"You don't know him. He has a very mighty cudgel," the Goldheaded Guardian told them, "and if it happens to land on you, your days are numbered."

The gods of the earth and the mountain spirits were terrified. They consulted the Goldheaded Guardian and decided to come up above ground and call Monkey.

Monkey was in a very bad way, but his courage had not left him. When he heard them calling, he replied in a loud voice: "What is it?"

"Listen to us, noble Immortal," said a god of the earth. "We have come to lift the mountain off your back so that you can come out. We humbly beseech you to forgive us unworthy minor gods for the neglect and lack of honour we have shown you."

"Remove the mountain and I shall not insist on thrashing you," said Monkey. "I wish to get out at once," he shouted.

The gods felt as if they had been let off. Quickly they recited a spell and moved the mountains back to their original places, thus freeing the Monkey King. He jumped to his feet, shook himself to get rid of the earth which covered his clothes, tidied his dress, and brought out his cudgel from behind his ear. Then he called all the mountain spirits and gods of the earth to him, saying: "All of you stick out your behinds. I shall give two blows to each of you in order to put myself in a better humour."

"The Great Sage promised a while ago to forgive us our errors," the spirits protested. "Why do you break your word as soon as you are out, and wish to beat us?"

"You're a fine lot, I must say! You're not afraid of old Sun, but you fear every worthless demon."

"This demon possesses great powers and knows much magic," they said by way of apology. "If he recites a spell, we must go to his cave whether we wish to or not. One of us is on duty there every day."

This startled the Monkey King.

All of a sudden a reddish glow spread throughout the mountain valley.

"Tell me," Monkey asked, "what is it that gives off this glow? You must know everything in that cave, since you do turns of duty there."

"It must be the rare treasures belonging to the demons," said a god of the earth. "They probably mean to catch you and seal you up in them."

"This is funny," laughed Monkey, greatly amused. "Tell me, how experienced in

magic are these demons who live in this cave?"

"They dabble in alchemy, they like to prepare the Elixir of Life, and they catch monks," the god told him.

"No wonder then that the demon changed himself into an old monk and thus got the better of our Master," thought Monkey, saying: "If that is so, you can all go home, and just remember you deserve a whipping. I'll attend to the demons myself."

The spirits and gods flew up in the air and vanished. Monkey shook himself and changed into an old magician. Before long, two imps appeared. Monkey held out his cudgel but the imps noticed nothing and tripped over it, falling headlong to the ground. It was only when they got back to their feet that they saw Monkey.

"You scum!" they cried. "If only our kings didn't have such great respect for your kind, we should soon teach you a lesson."

"What kind of lesson, my dears?" said Monkey, laughing. "Surely we monks are one big family."

"Why are you hanging about here and tripping us up with your stick?"

"When youngsters such as you meet an old monk, they ought to go down on their knees to welcome him," said Monkey with dignity.

"Our kings require pieces of silver as a gesture of welcome. How is it that you want a bow?" asked the imps. "You must be from some foreign parts. You don't look like a local monk."

"Of course I'm not a local monk," replied Monkey. "I come from the Fabulous Mountain."

"Why, that's the seat of the Blessed on

an island in the sea," said the imps, very much surprised.

"That's right — I, of course, am one of them," replied Monkey.

The imps now felt great joy instead of their former anger. They came up to Monkey, bowing and apologising.

"Holy veteran, please forgive us if we offended you with our rough words, please forgive us our ignorance in not recognising you at once."

"But I am not in the least annoyed," Monkey assured them. "How could you have known me? I only came to your mountain today to see if I could find some good people here willing to follow me. Which of you would like to come with me?"

Both Cleverhead and Skilful offered to go.

Although he knew everything about them, Monkey nevertheless asked them various questions.

"Where are you from?"

"From the Lotus Blossom Cave," the imps replied.

"And where are you making for?"

"Our ruler has ordered us to go and catch Monkey."

"What Monkey?" the Monkey King asked, pretending not to understand.

"Why, Sun Wu-k'ung, of course," the imps told him.

"Is that the one who is on his way for the scriptures with Tripitaka?" Monkey went on.

"Yes, that's the one," the imps said. "Do you know him too?"

"Yes, I know that Monkey. I find him somewhat impudent. I, too, have a bone to

pick with him," said Monkey, enjoying himself thoroughly. "I'll come with you and give you a hand."

"Oh, but that's hardly necessary, reverend father," the imps refused politely. "Our second king knows something about the art of magic, and he brought over three mountains which squashed Monkey, so that he cannot move a finger. Now our king has sent us with his treasures to put Monkey inside them."

"What treasures are these?" asked Monkey.

"I have a red-gold gourd and my friend a pure jade bottle," said Cleverhead.

"How will you get him inside them?" Monkey asked.

"We'll place these treasures, bottom up, on the ground, and call out to Monkey. If he replies, he will be sucked inside. Then we'll seal the necks with a label inscribed 'Upon the Orders of the Patriarch of the Way'. Within an hour and three-quarters he will have vanished."

Hearing this, Monkey felt frightened.

"Oh, horror!" he said to himself. "Didn't the Judges of Death tell me that there are five treasures in the world? Here then are two of them. Who knows what the other three are like?"

He put out his hand and said to the imps: "Show me those treasures of yours, my friends. I'd like to take a look at them."

As if imps could keep a secret! They

both took the treasures from their sleeves and gave them to Monkey.

"Lovely little objects," he said to himself. "Now I could easily give them the slip, but if I did they'd realise I am the Monkey King. No, I certainly can't steal these things from them, that would only harm my reputation. Sun Wu-k'ung does not commit ordinary theft in broad daylight."

He returned the gourd and the bottle to the imps.

"You haven't seen my treasure, though," he told them.

"What treasure do you have, reverend father?" the imps were curious to know. "Please lend it to us poor mortals so we can touch it for luck."

Monkey plucked a hair from his tail, recited a spell, and changed it into a dark red gourd, one foot and seven inches long, with a golden glow. He pretended to take it out from behind his sash.

"Look at my gourd!"

Skilful took it carefully and examined it.

"Reverend father," he said after a while, "this gourd of yours is very large and has a fine shape, but it isn't any use."

"Why do you say that?" Monkey asked.

"You see, we can get as many as a thousand people into each of our treasures," boasted the imps.

"That's nothing," replied Monkey rudely. "I can even get Heaven inside mine."

"What? Do you really mean to say you can put Heaven inside your gourd?" the imps asked.

"Yes, I swear that's the truth, even Heaven," Monkey said.

"That's impossible, you must be lying. Show us how, if you want us to believe you."

"If Heaven annoys me in any way, I shut it up inside my gourd seven or eight times a month," lied Monkey. "If it doesn't, a whole half-year may go by without my doing it."

"You know what, brother," whispered

Skilful in Cleverhead's ear. "Let's exchange our gourd for his."

"If he really can shut Heaven up in it, he won't want to swop," replied Cleverhead. "Ours only takes people."

"Well, if he refuses, let's offer him the jade bottle as well," suggested Skilful.

"To exchange my gourd for theirs and get the jade bottle into the bargain isn't at all bad," rejoiced Monkey. "One treasure for two, that's quite an achievement."

He pulled Skilful by the sleeve and said: "If I show you how to shut Heaven up in the gourd, will you swop?"

"If you really do it, we'll swop at once. If we don't, may lightning strike us on the spot," the imps cried together.

"Very well then, very well," said Monkey. "I'm going to show you how to do it."

Monkey bowed his head, reciting every kind of spell. He called upon the Spirits of Journeys and the guardians of the five quarters to fly at once to the Jade Emperor and tell him that the Monkey King had repented and was now accompanying Tripitaka on his pilgrimage to the west, and that they had come to a high mountain where the monk had met with great danger. Now Monkey wished to take the treasures from the imps and therefore he bowed a thousand times before the Jade Emperor and beseeched him to black out the sky for a few minutes and thus help him to achieve his aim. "If he utters as much as half a word in opposition, you can tell him I shall bring an army right up to the Hall of Magic Clouds."

A Spirit of Journeys accordingly flew through the southern gate of Heaven and made straight for the Hall of Magic Clouds. There he asked for an audience and gave the Jade Emperor Monkey's message.

"That wretched Monkey ought to be more careful of what he says," exclaimed the Jade Emperor angrily. "The other day the Goddess Kuan-yin was here and said she had released him so that he might protect Tripitaka on his journey, and I myself sent all the guardians of the five quarters and the four Judges of Death to watch over them. And now all of a sudden this Monkey takes it into his head that he wishes to shut up Heaven. How can that be done, anyway?"

No sooner had he finished than the third Crown Prince Natha stepped forward from among the throng of courtiers, saying: "Even Heaven can be shut up, Your Holiness."

"Yes, but how?" the Jade Emperor asked distrustfully.

"Kindly give orders for the God of War at the northern gate of Heaven to lend us his black embroidered banners," Natha told him. "These will then be hung out at the southern gate of Heaven and will cover up the Sun, the Moon and the stars. All will be darkness and nobody will be able to see anything. The imps will be deceived by this, and Monkey can easily pretend he has shut Heaven up in the gourd. Thus we shall have helped him to achieve his purpose."

"It shall be done as my wise subject suggests," said the Jade Emperor graciously.

Crown Prince Natha, having been given the Emperor's permission, went at once to the northern gate of Heaven, where he sought out the God of War and told him

the whole story. The God of War handed to Natha all the black banners. At that moment the Spirit of Journeys whispered in Monkey's ear: "Crown Prince Natha is coming to your assistance."

Monkey looked up to find a magic cloud floating above his head. The Crown Prince was coming. Monkey turned round and said to the imps: "Right. Now we shall shut Heaven up in my gourd."

"Do it then, if you mean to do it. Why all this delay?" cried the imps.

"I have been reciting the necessary spell and calling on the gods," replied Monkey.

The imps opened their eyes wide and watched Monkey putting Heaven in his gourd. Monkey threw his false gourd up in the air. The breeze on the summit got hold of it and sent it spinning, taking a long time before it floated back to the ground again. Meanwhile Crown Prince Natha unfurled the banners by the southern gate of Heaven, thus covering up the Sun, the Moon and the stars. Truly, it was as if someone had painted both Heaven and Earth black. Everything, the whole universe, was dark.

"It is only just past noon," cried the imps in astonishment, "and yet it's dark already."

"Well, that's hardly surprising," said Monkey proudly. "Since I have shut Heaven up you can't tell the time and everything is bound to be in darkness."

"But why is it so dark?"

"The Sun, the Moon and the stars are all shut up in my gourd, not a single ray of light can get out, so no wonder it is dark," Monkey mocked them.

"Reverend father, where are you speaking from?" shrieked the imps.

"I am standing right in front of your noses."

"We can only hear your voice, but we can't see your face," said the imps, feeling about in the dark. "Where are we, reverend father?"

"Don't take another step forward, we're standing on the seashore," Monkey made fun of them. "Should you stumble, you'd fall in the water and wouldn't reach the bottom in a whole week."

"That's enough! That's enough!" yelled the imps. "Let Heaven out again. We believe that you have shut it up in your gourd. If this goes on any longer we'll fall in the sea and never see our home again!"

Monkey, seeing that the imps believed him, signalled to Crown Prince Natha to furl up the banners again. The noonday Sun cast its glow over the Earth once more.

"What a miracle!" the imps cried, smiling. "Such a fine treasure. We'd be unworthy sons of our fathers if we failed to exchange for it."

Cleverhead took his gourd, Skilful his jade bottle, and they handed them to Monkey, receiving his false gourd in return. Having acquired their treasures, Monkey decided to annoy them a little: he plucked a hair from his belly, breathed on it with magic breath, and changed it into a copper coin.

"Now, boys," he ordered them, "go and buy a sheet of paper with this copper."

"Whatever for?" the imps wanted to know.

"I wish to draw up an agreement with you," replied Monkey. "I'm afraid that you may think it unfair to exchange your two treasures for shutting up people for my one treasure for shutting up Heaven, and after a time you may come to regret it. We must therefore draw up an agreement as a proof of the exchange."

"But we have no brush and no ink," the imps protested. "We don't need any agreement. We'll take an oath on it instead."

"What on, I'd like to know," said Monkey to himself, laughing.

"Our two treasures for shutting up people in return for your one treasure for shutting up Heaven. And if we ever regret it, may we be plagued with disease for a whole year," swore the imps.

"I'm sure *I* shall not regret it," laughed Monkey. "But if I do, may disease plague me the whole year just like you."

Having taken the oath, Monkey raised his tail, shook himself, leapt right up to the southern gate of Heaven and expressed his thanks to Crown Prince Natha for his help with the banners. The Crown Prince then went back to the palace to report to the Jade Emperor before returning the banners to the God of War.

The Monkey King Tricks the King of Demons

The imps were kept busy for a time with the false gourd, examining it carefully. When at last they looked up, they found that Monkey had vanished without trace.

"Brother," said Skilful, "even Immortals may lie. He exchanged treasures with us, inviting us to follow him and become Immortals, then suddenly he disappears without a farewell."

"He got the better half of the bargain, how dare he run away from us like this?" said Cleverhead indignantly. "Give me that gourd — we'll try to shut Heaven up in it and see what happens."

They threw the gourd up in the air, and it fell to the ground with a crash. Skilful cried out in vexation: "Why will Heaven not be shut up? Was it by any chance the Monkey King, who changed himself into an Immortal and swindled us out of our treasures in return for a false gourd?"

"Don't talk such rubbish!" retorted Cleverhead. "The Monkey King is lying squashed under the three mountains. How could he have got out? Give me that gourd, I'll recite the same spell as he did, and then we'll see what's what."

The second imp now threw the gourd up, reciting: "If he utters so much as half a word in opposition, tell him I'll bring an army right up to the Hall of Magic Clouds."

The words were hardly out of his mouth when the gourd landed with a crash and lay there on the ground in front of them.

"It's no good," cried the imps. "The gourd is false."

Monkey was up in the air above them, listening carefully to what they were saying. He soon saw that they had found out the truth, and he grew afraid that if they played about with the gourd much longer, his trick would be completely revealed. He shook himself and brought back the hair out of which he had made the gourd. The two imps were left with nothing at all.

"Brother, give me the gourd," said Cleverhead.

"But it's you who's got it," replied Skilful. "Oh, Heavens, where did it get to?"

They flung themselves on the ground, looking everywhere, searching like demented creatures in the grass, turning up their sleeves and untying their sashes. But the gourd was nowhere to be found.

"This is a fine kettle of fish!" exclaimed the imps. "When our kings entrusted the treasures to us, they said we were to catch the Monkey King. We haven't got him, and we have lost the treasures. What are we to tell them when we get back? They're sure to cut off our heads for this. What's to be done?"

"Let's go," suggested Skilful timidly.

"Go, that's easily said, but where?" asked Cleverhead.

"Anywhere," said Skilful. "If we return home and confess that we've lost the treasures, our lives will be lost."

"Still, we can't very well run away, can we? I think we had better go back after all," said Cleverhead. "The second king is very fond of you. Let me therefore put the blame on you, and perhaps he will wink an eye and spare our lives. If we don't manage to get round him we're in for it anyway, so we might as well make the attempt. Whatever we do, we mustn't stand here talking and wasting time. Come on!"

Their conference over, the two imps turned round and hurried back to the mountain top. Watching them go, Monkey decided to change himself into a fly, so as to be able to follow them. He changed and flew after the imps.

You will no doubt want to know what he did with the treasures. If he had left them by the wayside or hidden them in the grass, someone might have found them and carried them away. All his trouble would then have been for nothing. Therefore, Monkey kept the treasures with him. Yes, you may well ask, but a fly is no bigger than a bean — so where could he keep them? It wasn't really so very difficult. These treasures were, in fact, much the same as Monkey's cudgel. They could be altered in size according to the skill of their owner, who could make them larger or smaller as he pleased, thus being able to keep them with him all the time.

Monkey flew close behind the imps and before long the imps reached the cave.

Both the demons were lolling about inside, drinking wine. The imps went down on their knees before them, while Monkey perched on the door and listened carefully to what went on.

"Your Majesties," the imps began.

The demons put down their goblets and said: "So you're back already?"

"Yes," whispered the imps.

"Have you caught Sun Wu-k'ung?" the demons wanted to know.

The imps merely beat their foreheads on the ground, not daring to utter a sound. The demons repeated their question, but still the imps said nothing, bowing all the time. When the demons asked a third time, they pressed themselves close to the ground and wailed: "Spare us, miserable wretches that we are! A thousand, ten thousand pardons! We had gone halfway, firmly holding on to the treasures, when we met an Immortal from the Fabulous Mountain. He asked us where we were going, and we told him we were out to catch the Monkey King. When he heard this name mentioned, the Immortal said he, too, had a bone to pick with him, and he offered to help us. We didn't want his help and told him we had treasures which enabled us to catch people. He also had a gourd, and he said he could shut Heaven up in it. We were suddenly possessed by the desire to have it, thinking we could use it to help you. Our treasures were only good for catching people, whereas he could shut Heaven up in his, and so we swopped. First of all we were to exchange his gourd for ours, but then Skilful added our jade bottle as well. How could we have known that sacred objects were not suited to ordinary hands? As soon as we tried to test our gourd, both it and the Immortal vanished without trace. We beseech you ten thousand times to have mercy on your miserable subjects and forgo the death sentence."

"Enough!" shouted the old demon. "Enough! Sun Wu-k'ung changed himself into an Immortal and hoodwinked you. That devilish Monkey is extremely artful and has countless friends and acquaintances. Who knows which spirit set him free, and now he has swindled you out of our treasures."

"Calm yourself, brother," the younger demon tried to pacify him. "That Monkey is very insolent. He has evidently managed to free himself and run away. All right. But why deprive us of our treasures? If I'm not clever enough to capture him, let me not be a demon any more!"

"How do you intend to set about it?" the old demon asked.

"We had five treasures. Monkey has stolen two of them, but we still have three left, haven't we? With the aid of these, I have no doubt that I can get him."

"What do we have left?"

"We still have the seven-star sword and the banana-leaf fan. These two I have with me. We also have the shiny golden rope, which our old mother is keeping for us in the Hidden Dragon Cave on the Dragon Mountain. I think we ought to send two imps to invite our mother to a feast at which we'll eat of Tripitaka's flesh. We will ask her to bring the shiny golden rope for me to bind Monkey."

"Whom shall we send to her?" asked the old demon.

"Certainly not these two clumsy louts," replied his brother, shouting at Cleverhead and Skilful to get out of his sight.

"Aren't we lucky!" cried both the imps, much relieved. "We have not been given a severe whipping. They have forgiven us."

"Let's send my two bodyguards, Mountain Tiger and Sea Dragon," suggested the second demon.

They called these two imps to them, and the imps went down respectfully on their knees. The second demon told them to be cautious and careful, and the imps nodded eagerly.

"And do you know where the old lady lives?" the second demon asked them.

"Yes, we do, we do," the imps nodded again.

"In that case, off you go. When you get there, be as courteous as you can and invite the old lady to come and taste Tripitaka's flesh. And let her bring the golden rope with which we mean to tie up Monkey."

The imps repeated his instructions so as not to forget them, and hastened away, little suspecting that Monkey was there at their heels, listening to every word they said. He spread his wings and perched on Mountain Tiger's shoulder. They went on for some two or three miles. At first, Monkey decided to kill the imps. Then he thought better of it, saying to himself: "Getting rid of them is easy enough. However, that old woman has the shiny rope, and I don't know where to find her. I must find that out first, and only then can I set about them."

Monkey whizzed down from the imp's

shoulder, let them get some hundred paces ahead, and then changed into a little imp. On his head he wore a cap of fox fur, and he hitched up his tiger-skin jacket, tying it with a sash.

"Wait for me, pilgrims!" he called out, rushing after the imps.

"Where are you from?" Sea Dragon asked, turning his head.

"Don't you know one of your own people when you see him?" Monkey replied.

"You're not one of us," said the imp.

"Don't be so silly," protested Monkey. "Just you take a better look at me."

"I don't recognise you. I'm sure we've never seen you before," the imp persisted.

"You're right there," lied Monkey. "We've never met before because I come from a country garrison."

"It's quite true we've never seen anyone from a country garrison before," admitted the imps. "Where are you going?"

"Their Majesties have sent you to their old mother with an invitation to a feast at which Tripitaka is to be eaten. You're to bring back from her the golden rope with which Monkey is to be tied up. Their Majesties suspected that you might dawdle along the way and thus ruin their plans, and they have therefore ordered me to run after you and urge you on to greater speed."

Seeing that Monkey was so well informed, the imps of course did not suspect anything and accepted him without question. They ran on as fast as they could go, covering some eight or nine miles without stopping.

"A little faster still," Monkey hurried them on. "How many miles have we come now?"

"About fifteen or sixteen altogether," the imps replied.

"And how much further is it?"

"We're almost there. The old lady lives in that dark forest ahead of us," the imps told Monkey.

Looking up, he found they had arrived

at a deep forest. So this was where the old witch had her abode, he thought. He stopped and let the imps run on ahead of him. Then he drew his iron cudgel, jumped forward, and struck out at their legs. The poor imps went down like a couple of felled trees, and Monkey finished them off with one more blow. He dragged their bodies away from the path and hid them in the grass. Then he plucked out a hair, breathed on it with magic breath and called "Change!". The hair changed into Mountain Tiger, while he himself assumed the form of Sea Dragon. Then both the false imps headed for the Hidden Dragon Cave, the dwelling of the demon's mother.

Monkey then entered the forest and after a brief search he came across a half-open stone door. Not daring to burst in unexpectedly, he called out: "Open the door, please."

His shout roused the forest fairy who was guarding the door. She opened wide one of its panels, asking where the pilgrims had come from.

"We bring an invitation to the Queen Mother from the Lotus Blossom Cave on the Flat Peak Mountain."

"Come in then," the fairy invited them.

They went in, and Monkey peered around. In the middle of the hall sat an old hag. Monkey did not dare to go any further. He stopped by the door, covering his face with his hands, and began to cry. He wasn't afraid of the old woman. He thought of Tripitaka, remembering all the dangers he had to face on his journey for the scriptures, and tears of bitterness, wrung from his very heart, came flooding out, streaming down his cheeks.

Then he said to himself: "Now I've got this far, there is no sense in standing here like this. I must go and bow low before her. Since I came into the world and started to perform feats of heroism, I have only bowed before three people: before the Buddha of the Western Paradise, the Goddess of Compassion, Kuan-yin, from the Southern Sea, and four times before our Master, when he liberated me from the captivity of the Mountain of the Five Elements. For his sake my head has all but burst with constant worry. I wonder whether a single roll of the scriptures is worth all this trouble? On top of everything else, I am supposed to bow before this old witch. If I don't, though, I'll give the game away. Oh, what a miserable business this is! I have to humble myself only because our Master is in a jam again."

There was indeed nothing for it but to go in, kneel in front of the witch and touch his forehead to the ground.

"Rise, my son," said the witch.

"About time, too!" fumed Monkey silently.

"Where have you come from?" the witch asked him.

"From the Lotus Blossom Cave on the Flat Peak Mountain, upon the orders of both Their Majesties, who have sent me to invite the Queen Mother to join them in feasting upon the flesh of the monk Tripitaka. They also wish me to bring back the shiny golden rope, which they mean to use on the Monkey King, Sun Wu-k'ung."

"It's good to know I have such devoted sons," replied the old witch joyfully, and she at once ordered her litter to be brought out.

"Well, I never!" said Monkey to himself. "Since when do spooks have themselves carried about in litters?"

Two fairies came out of a back room, carrying a litter made out of wisteria. Setting it down by the door, they draped some grey silk curtains over it. The witch got up, hobbled out of the cave and settled herself comfortably in the litter. Several other fairies were standing behind it, carrying combs, make-up boxes, a looking-glass, towels and perfumes.

"Where do you think you're going with all this junk?" the witch shouted at them. "I'm on my way to my sons. Are you afraid no one will look after me there? You'd only make trouble with your sharp tongues. Get back, all of you! Shut the door and keep watch!"

The fairies scuttled back, only the two who carried the litter remaining.

"What are the names of the two messengers who brought the invitation?" the witch wanted to know.

"He is called Mountain Tiger and my name is Sea Dragon," Monkey replied.

"Go on ahead and show us the way," the witch told him.

"This is a nuisance!" thought Monkey. "Instead of capturing her I'm supposed to act as her servant."

But he didn't dare to refuse, and so he hurried along, clearing the way for them and shouting loudly to right and left. They covered some five or six miles before Monkey stopped and sat down on top of a cliff. When the others arrived with the litter, he suggested a short rest.

"I'm sure your shoulders must be aching by now," he said slyly.

Not suspecting a trap, the fairies set down the litter. Standing behind them, Monkey plucked a hair from his chest and changed it into a pancake, which he at once started to eat.

"What is it you've got there, sir?" the fairies asked.

"Oh, that's nothing. I have come a long way to invite your mistress, and if I don't have something to eat, I get terribly hungry. All I have with me is a dry pancake. I'll just finish it and we can go on again."

"Please give us a bite, too," the fairies pleaded.

"Help yourselves," said the cunning Monkey. "We belong to one family, so there's no need to be stand-offish."

The fairies trustingly came up to Monkey and started to share out the pancake. He suddenly produced his cudgel and hit out, striking one over the head and the other across the shoulder. Hearing some commotion, the old witch stuck her head out of the litter. Monkey jumped up to her and bang! he brought his cudgel down on top of her head. When he pulled the body out of the litter he was surprised to find it was not a witch, but a fox with nine tails.

"So that's who you were!" he exclaimed, laughing. "A fine Queen Mother, I must say! If you called yourself queen, old Sun would have to be called the father of all living creatures."

He then rummaged in the litter until he found the golden rope, which he coiled up and put inside his sleeve.

"Those cursed demons are doing nicely," he thought in great glee. "Three of their treasures are now in the hands of Sun Wu-k'ung."

He plucked out a hair and changed it into Sea Dragon, then two more which he changed into the two fairies, changing himself into the witch. He climbed into the litter, the fairies picked it up, and the whole procession moved forward again. Soon they reached the Lotus Blossom Cave. The imps, whom Monkey had produced out of his hairs, shouted for the door to be opened. The guardian imps opened up.

"Is that Mountain Tiger and Sea Dragon?" they asked.

"Yes, we're back," Monkey's hair called out.

"Have you brought the Queen Mother?"

"She is over there, in the litter."

"All right. You wait here, while we announce you," said the doorkeepers. Running inside, they told the demons: "Your Majesties, the Queen Mother has arrived."

Hearing this, the demons at once had the sacrificial table prepared to welcome her.

"That's fine!" rejoiced Monkey. "Now it's my turn to receive homage. While I was transformed into an imp, I had to bow before the old witch. Now I have assumed her form, they will think I'm their mother and will bow to me from every point of the compass. And even if there's nothing much to it, it's nice to have them bowing before me."

Monkey got down from the litter and tidied his dress. The guardian imps at once carried the empty litter to the ceremonial hall, Monkey following slowly behind them. He minced his step and turned and twisted about, just like the old witch herself. All the imps, great and small, had

lined up in a semicircle, and they now knelt before him as a sign of respect. At that moment the sound of drums and pipes filled the hall. Fragrant smoke rose from a huge incense burner. Monkey stopped in the centre of the hall and sat down, facing the south. Both the demons knelt in front of him, touching the ground with their foreheads.

"Mother, your sons bow before you," they said.

"Rise, dear sons," replied Monkey in an affected voice.

Pigsy, who was suspended from a beam in the ceiling, burst out laughing.

"Really, brother," Sandy rebuked him, "you're hanging from a beam and find that a subject for merriment?"

"But I have a good reason, brother," replied Pigsy.

"What is it?"

"Here we were scared stiff that the Queen Mother would turn up and the demons would cook and eat us. Now, instead of the Queen Mother, here is our old friend."

"Our old friend?" repeated Sandy, who didn't understand what he was driving at.

"Why, the Celestial Groom!" laughed Pigsy.

"What makes you think that?"

"When he said 'Rise, dear sons' he leaned forward, and I caught a glimpse of his monkey tail. I am higher up than you, and so I could see it from where I hang."

"All right, keep quiet in that case, and let's hear what he has to say."

"Quite so," agreed Pigsy.

The Monkey King, sitting in state in the centre of the hall, addressed the demons: "And now, dear sons, tell me what made you invite me?"

"Mother," said the older demon, "up to this day we, unworthy sons that we are, have not shown you a proper measure of respect and obedience. This morning we captured the monk Tripitaka from the Eastern Empire, and we do not dare to start on him without your kind permission. That is why we have asked you to come, so that we may show him to you while he is still alive. Then we shall cook him for you, and as soon as you have eaten his flesh you will enjoy eternal life."

"Dear sons," replied Monkey, "I don't feel like Tripitaka's flesh just at the moment. But I have heard that the ears of that Pigsy of his make excellent eating. Please cut them off and prepare them for me to take with my wine."

"Damn you!" yelled Pigsy. "You want them to cut off my ears, do you! But you wait, I'll squeal until your ears tingle!"

Foolish Pigsy, with his heart-rending screams, gave away the secret of Monkey's magic change. To make matters worse, the imps who kept watch in the hills came bursting into the room together with the doorkeepers, and they all shouted: "Your Majesties! A terrible disaster! Sun Wu-k'ung has murdered the Queen Mother and is in disguise here in her place!"

Hearing this, the demons grasped their ornamented swords and struck out at Monkey's head. Monkey shook himself, filled the whole cave with a reddish glare and, before anyone knew what had happened, disappeared. As long as the glare lasted, it formed a red pillar which gave off red steam as it disappeared. The old demon's soul almost left his body in fear, and the imps sucked their fingers and shook their heads, completely bewildered and terrified.

"Brother, let's return Tripitaka, Sandy and Pigsy to the Monkey King, together with the white horse and all their luggage," the old demon said. "I don't want to have any part in this."

"What an idea!" retorted the younger demon. "The trouble I had getting hold of that monk, and you let yourself be frightened by Monkey's tricks and want to return everything. Is this the way for a hero to behave? To cower before the sword and dodge the dagger? Sit down here and have no fear. I know as well as you that Monkey has great magic powers. I have had dealings with him before, but up to now we have never matched forces properly. Let them bring my armour, I want to fight with him. If he doesn't get the better of me in three rounds, Tripitaka will wind up inside our stomachs after all. And if I don't defeat him after three rounds, there will still be time to return Tripitaka."

"My wise brother is right," said the older demon, ordering the imps to bring the armour.

The imps brought it, and the younger demon put it on. Grabbing his sword, he rushed out of the cave.

"Sun Wu-k'ung, where are you?" he shouted.

Monkey was by that time floating in the clouds. Hearing his name, he looked down and saw the second demon.

"Sun Wu-k'ung!" the second demon was shouting. "Return our treasures at once, and the Queen Mother. Then I shall allow that Tripitaka of yours to go and fetch the scriptures."

This angered Monkey, who cried: "Accursed demon! Who do you think I am? At once deliver up our Master, my brothers, our white horse and our packs, as well as some food and money for the journey. If you utter so much as half the word 'No', you had better go and tie yourself up with your own rope, otherwise I shall deal with you myself!"

At these words the second demon leapt into the air and joined Monkey in the clouds, attacking him with his sword. Monkey swung his cudgel and hit the demon in the face. Thus they fought up in the clouds, clashing some thirty times without either of them becoming the victor.

"This cursed demon is protected from my cudgel," thought Monkey. "I have three of his treasures, what's the sense in losing precious time like this. The best thing I can do is to bring out that gourd of theirs and shut him up in it."

Then he at once thought better of it.

"No, that won't do. It's not for nothing that they say, 'Each object has its master'. Should his treasures not obey me, I'd come a cropper. Perhaps I had better tie him up with the golden rope."

Wielding his cudgel in one hand, Monkey pulled out the rope with the other and threw it, catching the demon as if in a lasso. However, the demon knew a spell with which to tighten the rope and another to loosen it. Whenever he wished to tie someone up, he recited the tightening spell, and there was then no escaping from the noose. On the other hand, whenever any of his own people were caught in it, he used the loosening spell, and all was well again. Now he recognised his own treasure and, murmuring the spell, loosened the rope and wriggled out of it. In a flash he had seized the rope himself and thrown it round Monkey. Monkey was just about to make himself very thin and slip out of his bonds, when the demon recited the tightening spell. The rope cut deep into Monkey's flesh, and there was no question of getting rid of it. All he succeeded in doing was to twist the rope round his neck. The demon hauled at the rope, pulling Monkey towards him. He aimed seven or eight blows at the crown of Monkey's head, but nothing happened — his skin did not even turn red.

"Give me back my treasures," the demon said.

"What treasures?" asked Monkey, pretending ignorance.

The demon ran his hands over Monkey's body and soon found the gourd and the jade bottle. Then, dragging Monkey by the rope, he returned to the cave.

"Well, brother, I've got him at last."

"Whom have you got, brother?"

"Why, Sun Wu-k'ung, of course. Come and take a look at him."

When the old demon saw that it really was the Monkey King, his face lit up with a smile.

"Yes, indeed, it is Sun himself! Tie him to a pillar, and let's go and drink to his capture."

The imps tied Monkey to a pillar, while the two demons went off to the back of the hall to drink wine.

Monkey, tethered at the end of a long rope, investigated all round the pillar, bumping into Pigsy and waking him. Pigsy was still hanging from the beam. When he saw Monkey, he burst out laughing: "Not

going to eat my ears now, are you?"

"You fool!" exclaimed Monkey angrily. "Are you hanging quite comfortably? Once I get free, I'll do everything I can to rescue all of you."

"How can you lie like this? You're on your last legs and you talk of rescuing people! We'll all die here together, our Master and us, his disciples. Then we'll see what happens in the underworld."

"Stop blathering!" shouted Monkey. "Just look and see how I slip out of these bonds."

As he talked with Pigsy, the Monkey King was constantly watching the two demons. They were drinking at the back of the hall, with several imps waiting on them, running about with bowls and goblets, and pouring wine out of large jugs. The sentries had relaxed their vigilance a little. Seeing that there was no one near, Monkey took his cudgel from behind his ear, breathed on it with magic breath, cried "Change!" and the cudgel changed into a little steel saw. Clutching the noose which encircled his neck, he cut it with two movements of the saw. Loosening it, he cut through his bonds, plucked out a hair and changed it into a replica of himself, which he tied to the pillar. Then he shook himself to change himself into an imp and stood there waiting.

Pigsy again started to heckle: "There, that's done it! Now you have false goods tied to the pillar!"

The old demon stopped drinking and said: "What's that nuisance of a pig squealing for now?"

Monkey in his new form of an imp, stepped forward, saying: "Pigsy is trying to persuade Monkey to carry out a magic change and escape with him, but Monkey doesn't want to do it and that's why Pigsy is annoyed."

"And I thought that pig was honest," said the old demon. "I never thought it was capable of such deceit. Give him twenty blows on the snout with a stick."

Monkey obediently went to fetch a stick with which to give out the punishment.

"Beat me lightly," Pigsy warned him, "or I'll start shouting again. I know what you're like by now."

"I'm doing all this for you and the others. Why did you have to give me away? The cave is full of imps, and not one of them recognised me. How did you know who I was?"

"Because you changed your head and face, but not your backside. You still have those two red spots there, and that's how I recognised you."

Monkey quickly backed away to the kitchen, put his hand right down into one of the cauldrons and, having blacked his bottom, returned to the hall. This set Pigsy laughing once more.

"Look at that Monkey, he disappears for a minute and back he comes with a blackened behind!"

Monkey stationed himself next to the door to the back room, getting ready to steal the demons' treasures again. Then he thought of something else; he went up to the old demon and said: "Your Majesty, look how that Monkey keeps running about round the pillar. He will soon split our golden rope. Hadn't we better change it for an ordinary strong rope?"

"You're right," nodded the old demon. He untied his sash and handed it to Monkey, who tied the false Monkey to the pillar with it, hiding the golden rope in his sleeve. Then he plucked out a hair, breathed on it and changed it into a replica of the golden rope, which he gave back to the demon. The demon had drunk a lot of wine and it didn't even occur to him to take a good look at the rope. He took it and put it away. Thanks to his magic, Monkey managed to fool the demons with his false rope. Having acquired this treasure, he turned round quickly, ran out of the door, and assumed his true form.

"Hey, demons!" he shouted.

The imp doorkeepers said: "Who are you, that you dare to holler here like this?"

"Go and tell your cursed demon that Monkey Wu Sun-k'ung is waiting for him."

The imps relayed the message word for word. The old demon was terrified by the news.

"We've captured Sun Wu-k'ung," he said. "Who can this Wu Sun-k'ung be, and what is he doing here?"

"What are you worried about, brother?" the younger demon asked. "We have all our treasures — I'll fetch our gourd and catch him in it, and that'll be that."

"Take care, brother," the old demon warned him.

The second demon took the gourd and went out of the cave. The monkey standing there was exactly the same as Sun Wu-k'ung, only perhaps a little smaller, he thought.

"Where are you from?" he asked.

"I'm Sun Wu-k'ung's brother," declared Monkey. "I've just heard that you have captured him, and so I've come to challenge you to a duel."

"Yes, I've captured him. I've got him tied up there inside the cave," said the de-

mon. "So you've come to fight with me. I have not the slightest intention of crossing swords with you, but tell me, have you the guts to answer if I call you?"

"Call me a thousand times, if you wish. I'll answer ten thousand times," replied Monkey calmly.

The demon grasped his gourd and leapt into the air. Turning the gourd upside down he shouted: "Wu Sun-k'ung!"

Monkey didn't dare to answer, thinking: "That would suit you fine, wouldn't it. If I answer, you'll have me inside that gourd."

"Well, why don't you answer when I call you?" the demon enquired.

"Sorry, there's a buzzing in my ears and I can't hear you," Monkey apologised. "Try it again, louder this time."

The demon called again: "Wu Sun-k'ung!"

Monkey, in the clouds a little below him, was thinking: "My real name is Sun Wu-k'ung, I only called myself Wu Sun-k'ung for a jest. Under my genuine name he would be sure to get me inside his gourd, but I don't think it will work with this alias."

He couldn't resist the temptation and answered. Whoosh! and he was inside the gourd. The demon corked it and stuck a label across it. It did not matter a whit, as far as the gourd was concerned, whether the name was genuine or false — as soon as anyone answered, even in the slightest of whispers, he was pulled inside.

It was completely dark inside the gourd. Monkey jerked his head up, but failed to break the walls; they enclosed him so tightly that he could hardly move.

"When I ran into those two imps on the mountain, they told me that anyone shut up in the gourd or the bottle would crumble away in less than two hours," he thought sadly. "Will I suffer this fate now?"

A moment later it occurred to him: "No, it's all right, I shan't crumble away. When I was up to my pranks in Heaven five hundred years ago and the Patriarch of the Way kept the furnace going for forty-nine days with me inside it, he fused my heart until it became like gold, my lungs like silver, my head like copper and my back like iron. I also have fiery eyes, so how could I possibly crumble in less than two hours? Let him carry me away and we shall see what happens."

The young demon hurried back to the cave with the gourd in his hand.

"I've got him, brother," he cried.

"Whom have you got?" asked the old demon.

"Why, Wu Sun-k'ung, of course. I've got him shut up inside my gourd," said the younger demon proudly.

"Sit down, wise brother," the old demon said, feeling very pleased. "You'd better not move that gourd about. Once you can hear it splash inside when you shake it, you can take the cork out."

Monkey heard all this, and he thought anxiously: "I'm as lean as a plank, how can it splash when they shake the gourd? That could only happen if I turned into a liquid. Oh, but I know what! I'll collect a lot of saliva in my mouth instead, and when they shake the gourd the effect will be the same. Then, when they open the gourd I'll get away."

Monkey got ready for this attempt, but the demon was too busy drinking and did not shake the gourd. Sun Wu-k'ung thought of a way to make him do so.

"Oh, merciful Heaven!" he cried. "My legs have completely crumbled!"

Still the demon did not shake the gourd.

"Oh mother!" shouted Monkey once more. "I have nothing left from my waist down!"

"I can hear loud splashing inside the gourd, so the end cannot be very far," the old demon pointed out. "Uncork the gourd and we'll take a look."

As soon as Monkey heard this, he plucked out a hair, cried "Change!" and it became the upper half of his body, which he laid on the bottom of the gourd, changing himself into a beetle and squeezing himself into the neck just below the cork. By the time the second demon had uncorked the gourd and looked inside, Monkey was gone. He turned a somersault and assumed the form of Sea Dragon, the imp who had gone to invite the Queen Mother. Then he placed himself by the side of the two demons. The older one had taken the gourd from his brother and was now peering inside. The upper part of Monkey's body suddenly moved a little, and the demon did not realise that it was a fake.

"Put the cork back, quick!" he shouted. "He hasn't crumbled away properly yet."

The second demon corked the gourd.

"Ho, ho!" Monkey laughed quietly. "Little do they know that old Sun is right here beside them!"

The old demon picked up the wine jug, poured out a cupful and, holding the cup in both hands, passed it to his brother.

"Wise brother, let's drink a toast," he said.

"But we have drunk many a cup already, why should we toast each other now?" the younger demon asked.

"You deserve any number of cups to be drunk in your honour. You have caught Tripitaka, Pigsy and Sandy, and what is more you have tied up Sun Wu-k'ung and trapped Wu Sun-k'ung inside the gourd."

When he heard his elder brother praising him so greatly, he could not of course refuse the drink. As he still held the gourd and it seemed impolite to accept the cup in only one hand, he gave the gourd to Sea Dragon to hold, taking the cup from his brother with both hands. Little did he suspect that Sea Dragon was none other than Monkey himself! Monkey took the gourd from him and held it carefully in the palm of his hand. The younger demon emptied the cup and returned it to his brother, who said: "No, don't return the toast, I'll drink to you again."

Each of them tried to outdo the other in politeness and humility. Monkey did not bat an eyelid but went on holding the gourd carefully and watching the demons exchange cups. In an unguarded moment he quickly pushed the gourd up his sleeve. Plucking out a hair, he changed it into an exact copy of the gourd, which he then held in his hand as though nothing had happened.

The demon kept passing the cup to his brother and accepting it back again; some time later he took the gourd from Monkey, quite unaware that it was not the real one. Both the demons stretched themselves out in their chairs and went on with their drinking. Unnoticed, Monkey slipped out of the cave.

"This demon may be as cunning as a fox, yet it's old Sun who has the gourd," he rejoiced.

The End of the Demons from the Lotus Blossom Cave

Monkey had stolen the demon's treasure and put it inside his sleeve.

"Let the demon try as hard as he likes, he still won't get me," he said, laughing. "He'll be just as successful as if he tried to fish the moon's reflection out of the water. When I get round to catching him, however, it'll be as easy as melting ice in a fire." He hid the gourd carefully in his sleeve and, once outside the cave, put on his real form again and shouted in a mighty voice: "Demon, open the door!"

"Who's making such a rumpus now?" cried the imps.

"Run and tell those accursed demons of yours that K'ung Wu-sun is here!"

"Your Majesties," the imps reported, quite out of breath, "someone calling himself K'ung Wu-sun is outside."

"Brother, this is bad," said the old demon in terror. "We've stirred up a wasps' nest. Sun Wu-k'ung is tied up with the golden rope, Wu Sun-k'ung is inside the gourd, and now out of the blue comes K'ung Wu-sun. That must be a third brother."

"Don't get excited," the younger demon reassured him. "We can get a thousand people inside our gourd. Having just caught Wu Sun-k'ung, I am hardly likely to tremble at the arrival of K'ung Wu-sun. I'm going out to capture him right away."

"Be very careful, though, brother," the old demon warned him.

The second demon grasped the false gourd and once more hurried out of the cave, his chest swelling with confidence and pride.

"Who are you, that you dare to make such a noise?" he cried.

"Don't you recognise me?" Monkey asked. "I am Sun Wu-k'ung's second brother, K'ung Wu-sun."

"Come here!" the demon challenged him. "I don't intend to fight with you. But do you dare to answer me if I call your name?"

"If you call, I shall answer," replied Monkey. "But will *you* answer if I call *your* name?"

"I am going to call you because I have a magic gourd in which I can catch people," the demon said. "What have you got?"

"I also have a gourd," Monkey replied.

"If you really have one, then show it to me."

Monkey took the gourd from his sleeve.

"Look, cursed demon!" he cried, putting it back quickly for fear of having it snatched away.

The sight of the gourd badly frightened the demon.

"Where did he get that?" he wondered. "How is it possible that it's the same as mine? It's also made from the root of the wisteria, it's exactly the same size, and just as rounded. How can they be so alike?"

Then he calmed himself and asked: "Where did you get that gourd, K'ung Wu-sun?"

Monkey had no idea what to say to this, and so he replied by asking where the demon got *his*. The demon did not suspect that Monkey was merely teasing him and thinking he was really interested, he told him the whole story: "When the world was still in its early state of chaos and Heaven was being divided off from the Earth, the Patriarch of the Way made the stones and propped up the sky in order to save the world from collapse. In the spot where the sky did not cover the Earth, at the foot of Mount K'un-lun, he saw a sacred wisteria and, growing on it, a red-gold gourd. This the Patriarch of the Way presented to me, and I have it to this day."

Hearing this, Monkey knew what to reply and he said: "My gourd comes from exactly the same place."

"How can that be?" wondered the demon.

"When Heaven was separated from the Earth," began Monkey, as bold as brass, "a bit of the sky was missing in the north west and a bit of the Earth in the south east. The Patriarch of the Way assumed the form of the Goddess Nü-wa and filled in the sky where there wasn't enough of it.

He went as far as Mount K'un-lun and there he found the wonderful wisteria, with two gourds growing on it. I got the male gourd, and you got the female gourd."

"Who cares whether a gourd is male or female?" the demon sneered. "The important thing is whether it can catch people. Only then is it a real treasure."

"I agree," said Monkey. "Now you start."

This pleased the demon. He leapt into the air and turned his gourd bottom up.

"K'ung Wu-sun!" he cried.

Monkey answered eight or nine times, but naturally, nothing happened. The demon flung the gourd to the ground, stamping his feet and beating his breast in fury.

"Oh, Heavens!" he wailed. "And they say nothing in the world ever changes. Our little treasure is frightened of its mate and refuses to work!"

"Pick up that gourd of yours, it's my turn now," said Monkey calmly.

He made a quick somersault in the air, held his gourd out, bottom up, and aimed it at the demon.

"King Silver Horn!" he shouted.

The demon did not dare to remain quiet. He had no choice but to answer, and the moment he did so he found himself inside the gourd. Thereupon Monkey calmly stuck a label inscribed "Upon the Orders of the Patriarch of the Way" across its neck.

"There, now you can taste a little of your own medicine!" Monkey said to himself gleefully, before flying off with the gourd in his hand. He thought hard, wondering how best to rescue Tripitaka.

He returned to the Lotus Blossom Cave. All the paths in the mountains were rough and uneven, and Monkey was bow-legged, so that as he went, rocking from side to side, he heard a constant plashing and splashing inside the gourd. The demon Silver Horn and his body had been eaten away as soon as he was inside the gourd.

It did not occur to Monkey that it could all be over so soon.

"Well, how are you getting on?" he jeered at the demon. "You let yourself be nicely fooled by old Sun, didn't you? I shan't tear off the label in a week, when nothing's left of you but some juice. Why hurry? I can wait. When I think how easily I got out, I don't feel like looking at you in a thousand years."

Gourd in hand, talking to himself in this fashion, he soon arrived at the door of the cave. There he again shook the gourd, from which there came a great noise of splashing. The imps guarding the door saw Monkey and ran inside, crying: "Your Majesty, a great disaster! K'ung Wu-sun has caught the second king in the gourd and is shaking him about!"

The old demon was beside himself with fear. All his strength left him and he fell to the ground, wailing. Pigsy, hanging from the beam, shouted at him: "Now, none of that, demon! Listen to what Pigsy has to say. The Monkey King Sun Wu-k'ung, Wu Sun-k'ung who came next, and K'ung Wu-sun who arrived last, are all none other than my brother Sun. He has simply changed his name each time. He has come in here, stolen your treasure, and caught your brother. Your brother is done for, and no amount of weeping can help him. You had better release us so that we can join you in prayer for your late brother."

Hearing this, the old demon blazed with fury.

"I thought Pigsy was honest, but now I see he is an insolent cheat. Trying to make fun of me, are you? Imps!" he yelled. "Stop wailing at once, take Pigsy down from the beam, and boil him till he is soft. First we'll have a good meal and then I'll go and revenge myself on the Monkey King."

"Now you've done it!" Sandy scolded his fellow disciple. "I keep telling you that you talk too much. Those who talk too much are always the first to suffer."

Pigsy was shaking like an aspen leaf.

"Your Majesty," said an imp standing beside the demon. "Pigsy won't cook well."

"Oh, Buddha!" cried Pigsy. "This brother is doubtless repaying me for some good deed of mine in a former incarnation. He's quite right — I wouldn't cook at all well."

"Let's skin him first — then we'll manage," suggested another imp.

This scared Pigsy even more.

"No, no! I'll cook very well indeed. I have a tough skin and hard bones, but if you boil me in soup first, I'll turn quite soft."

While they were discussing the problem, one of the guardian imps rushed in from the door.

"K'ung Wu-sun is again shouting at us outside," he shouted.

"That scoundrel thinks he can insult us and get away with it," cried the old demon in great rage. "Hang Pigsy up again and

find out how many treasures we have left."

The caretaker imps reported: "We still have three treasures."

"Which are they?"

"We still have the seven-star sword, the banana-leaf fan and the jade bottle."

"The bottle is no good any more," said the demon. "It works the same way as the gourd; anyone who answers the call is drawn inside. Sun Wu-k'ung has tumbled to this secret, and he has caught my brother in the gourd. Leave the bottle at home, it's useless. Bring me the sword and the fan, quickly."

The caretaker imps at once handed the old demon the two treasures he demanded. King Gold Horn stuck the banana-leaf fan behind his collar, seized the sword in his hand, and ordered three hundred of the imps to arm themselves with rifles, cudgels, chains and daggers. The old demon put on a helmet and a breast-plate, over which he wore a silk robe the colour of flame. The imps fell in and, in battle formation, marched out to attack the Monkey King.

Monkey now knew that the second demon had crumbled away inside the gourd. He screwed the cork down tightly and attached the gourd to his belt. Seizing his magic cudgel, he prepared for a life and death struggle. Meanwhile the imps had unfurled their red flag and came hurtling out at the door. The old demon gave them the orders for battle.

"You insolent, bold Monkey!" he swore at him. "You have destroyed my brother. I loathe you!"

"Accursed demon!" Monkey retorted. "You're asking for it. Here you are mourning the death of one demon, but you calmly hang four such beings as my Master, my fellow disciples, and our white horse from a beam in your cave. Do you expect me to stand by and watch you do this? What kind of behaviour is that? Release them at once and give us some money and provisions for our journey, and I'll spare your miserable life."

The demon would not hear of it. Raising his sword, he struck out at Monkey, who parried the blow with his cudgel. They clashed some twenty times but neither of them was the victor.

Thereupon the demon waved his sword in the air and cried: "This way, imps!"

All three hundred imps crowded round Monkey, hemming him in. He was not in the least dismayed, swinging his cudgel from left to right, warding off blows from behind and parrying thrusts from the front. The imps were good fighters and they harried Monkey more and more, wrapping themselves round him like threads of silk, clutching at his back and tripping his feet. Even Monkey began to find them something of a handful. He plucked out a few hairs from his arm-pit, chewed them up and spat them out again, crying: "Change!" Each of the hairs changed into a monkey. The big ones wielded cudgels, the little ones hit out with their fists, while the smallest of all bit the imps in the thigh. The imps scattered to every side, shouting: "Your Majesty! Woe is us! Monkeys are swarming all over the mountain!"

By means of this magic, Monkey managed to drive off all the imps, and the demon found himself encircled. He ran about in confusion, but there was no way out. He was frightened stiff. Transferring the sword to his left hand, he reached up with his right and brought out the banana-leaf fan from behind his collar. The fan had the power to start a fire anywhere its owner wished. He waved it so violently that a wind was raised and a column of fire sprang up from the ground. The old demon was quite merciless. He waved the fan seven or eight times, until the flames danced wildly, the earth sizzled and the sky blazed. Looking at this great fire, Monkey trembled with fear.

"That's torn it! It's not that anything can happen to me, but I'll have to part with my hair monkeys. How can he start a fire like this so easily?"

He shook himself, and all his hairs except one returned to his body. Out of the remaining hair he made a copy of himself in order to escape the disaster which threatened him. Then he recited a spell against fire, turned a somersault and sought refuge from the leaping flames up in the clouds. He made at once for the Lotus Blossom Cave, intending to rescue Tripitaka and the others. He lowered his cloud outside the cave, where he ran into a group of about a hundred imps. All of them had bruised heads or broken limbs as a result of their fight with the host of monkeys produced by Sun Wu-k'ung. Some of the imps were crying and moaning, others bore their pain in silence. Seeing them there, Monkey was seized by wickedness; he wielded his cudgel again and killed every imp within striking distance. Having removed the imps, he rushed inside the cave. He was on his way to release Tripitaka, but he found that the flames had even reached as far as this, and his arms dropped to his sides in despair.

"That's the end!" he lamented. "The fire has spread from the back door. I shall not be able to save our Master like this."

His hands shaking, he looked carefully all round him. Then he was delighted to discover that what he had taken for flames was merely a golden glow. It came from the transparent jade bottle.

"Lovely treasure!" cried Monkey. "The bottle shone like this when the imps had it with them on the mountain. I took it from them, but then the demon got it back from me. Now it's hidden away here, and yet it still glows."

He seized the bottle and examined it lovingly. Changing his mind, he did not go and set Tripitaka free but ran outside again. As soon as he emerged from the cave, he saw the demon rushing towards him from the south, fan in hand and wielding his sword. Monkey could not dodge in time, and the demon struck at his head. Monkey turned a somersault, leapt into the air, and vanished without trace. The demon saw that there were dead bodies strewn all round the door. They were all his subjects, the imps. He looked up at the sky and sighed.

"Oh, misery! What a disaster."

Shedding bitter tears, the demon Gold Horn shuffled inside the cave. Everything was in its place, but the cave was empty and the demon felt lonely and depressed. He sat down, all by himself, in the middle of the cave. Then he stretched himself out on a stone couch, leaning the sword against one of its edges and putting the fan under his arm. A moment later he was fast asleep. As the proverb says, "When you are happy, you feel light as air, but when the heart is troubled, you try to sleep it off."

Monkey guided his cloud back to the mountain, stopping it just in front of the

summit. He intended to free Tripitaka, so he attached the bottle to his belt and went to spy out the land. The door of the cave was half open. Stealthily he crept inside. The demon was lying curled up on top of the stone couch, snoring loudly. The fan had slipped out from under his arm and partly hid his face. The seven-star sword stood where he had left it, leaning against the couch. Monkey stole up to the demon and with a swift paw he snatched the fan away from him. Turning round quickly, he dashed out of the cave. The handle of the fan had been tangled in the demon's hair, and he awoke with a start. Lifting his head he found that Monkey had stolen his fan. He snatched up his sword and hurried after him. Monkey was well away by this time. He stuck the fan behind his belt and, brandishing his cudgel in both hands, turned to face the demon. They fought some thirty or forty rounds. The sky grew dark. Then the demon could no longer withstand Monkey's assaults, and he fled in a south-westerly direction, seeking refuge in the Hidden Dragon Cave.

Monkey lowered his cloud, ran inside the Lotus Blossom Cave, and untied Tripitaka, Pigsy and Sandy. All three thanked him for having saved them from so great a danger.

"Where have the demons gone?" they asked.

"The second demon is shut up inside the gourd, and I'm sure he has completely crumbled away by now. The old demon has turned tail and is skulking in the Hidden Dragon Cave. As for the imps from this cave, half of their number were slaughtered by the monkeys I produced

out of my hairs. Some of the wounded got away, but I killed them all later. Then I came back here and set you free."

Tripitaka's thanks knew no bounds.

"Thank you, disciple, for everything you have had to undergo on my behalf."

"I have suffered a great deal," replied Monkey, smiling. "But you three also had a bad time of it, hanging like that, tied to a beam. As for me, I almost wore my feet out, running back and forth like an errand-boy. There seemed no end to it. But I managed to steal all the demon's treasures and chase him away."

"Please show us the gourd, brother," requested Pigsy. "The second demon must be quite eaten away by this time."

Monkey first brought out the jade bottle, then the fan and the golden rope. Finally he held out the gourd, saying: "Don't look inside! When they caught me in there,

I spat until there was a splashing sound and they, thinking I had crumbled away, uncorked the gourd, allowing me to escape. I don't want to uncork it yet, lest he trick us too and get away."

Tripitaka and his disciples were overjoyed. They found some rice, noodles and vegetables in the cave, cleaned the cauldron, and prepared some food. Having eaten their fill, they lay down to sleep. The night passed quietly and soon it was morning again.

Let us now take a look at the old demon, who had escaped to the Hidden Dragon Cave. He called together all the fairies and described how Monkey had killed the Queen Mother, trapped his brother in the gourd, slaughtered a whole army of imps and stolen their treasures. All the fairies burst into tears. After a time, when they had ceased wailing, the demon said: "No more weeping now. I still have this seven-star sword. I intend to form an army out of you fairies, assemble you on the Hidden Dragon Mountain, seek out all our relatives, and at all costs avenge my brother's death."

He had hardly finished speaking when the imp doorkeepers announced: "Your Majesty, your maternal uncle is leading an army this way."

The demon quickly changed into white silk mourning clothes, bent low as a sign of respect, and went out to meet the new arrivals. They were led by his mother's younger brother, the seventh King Fox. The sentries in the mountains had reported the death of his sister, whereupon he had raised an army of two hundred imps from his cave and led them out to help the demon king. As soon as he entered, he saw the demon in mourning, and they both started to weep. When they had wept enough, the old demon bowed and told his uncle what had taken place. The seventh King Fox grew very angry and ordered King Gold Horn to discard his mourning clothes, arm himself with his sword, and count the fairies. The two armies joined up, mounted clouds and, driven along by the wind, made for the north east.

"Brother," Monkey called out to Pigsy, "the demon has got together a whole army to help him."

Hearing this, Tripitaka went pale with fear.

"What shall we do, disciples?" he asked anxiously.

"Don't worry," smiled Monkey. "Bring me those treasures of his."

He tied the gourd and the jade bottle to his belt, pushing the golden rope up his sleeve and the banana-leaf fan behind his collar. He brandished his iron cudgel in both hands, and instructed Sandy to stay with Tripitaka in the cave and take care of him. Pigsy picked up his rake, and the two of them went out to meet the foe.

The demons spread out in columns with the seventh King Fox at their head. He had a long beard, eyebrows like steel wires and ears like daggers. On his head he wore a golden helmet. He had on a coat of mail, and wielded a mace.

"You cursed upstart of a monkey," he cried. "How do you dare to commit such felony. You have stolen the treasures, murdered my relatives, and now you make yourself at home in our house. Quickly stick out your heads and accept well-

deserved death, so that I may avenge my sister's family."

"You pack of cut-throats, you are asking for trouble!" Monkey shrieked at them. "You don't know me yet. Don't you run away! I must give you a taste of my cudgel first."

The demon bent low, dodged Monkey's blow, and struck out with his mace. They closed with one another but had not fought more than three or four rounds when the demon found his strength gone and fled the field. Monkey pursued him, and the demon fought again, the seventh King Fox now on the attack. Pigsy noticed this and held him back with his nine-pronged rake. They thrust and parried repeatedly, but victory favoured neither side. Finally the demon shouted a command, and the army of imps fell upon Pigsy and Monkey.

Tripitaka had all this time been sitting inside the Lotus Blossom Cave. Suddenly he heard much noise and shouting, which made the very earth tremble.

"Perhaps you had better go out and see how our brothers are faring," he told Sandy.

Sandy picked up his staff for taming demons and charged out with a hoarse cry. The imps turned and fled. The seventh King Fox, seeing the changed situation, took to his heels. Pigsy caught up with him and struck him across the back with his

rake, until the blood ran in nine places and the King's soul left his body. They quickly stripped his clothes off, and found he was a fox spirit.

Seeing that his uncle was dead, the old demon left Monkey alone and, with sword raised high, turned on Pigsy, who warded him off with his rake. As they struggled, Sandy came running up and beat the demon with his staff. The demon could not stand any more, so he raised a wind, mounted a cloud, and escaped towards the south, with Pigsy and Sandy in hot pursuit. Monkey also leapt up into the clouds, took the jade bottle from his belt, aimed it at the demon, and called out: "King Gold Horn!"

Thinking it was one of his fleeing imps calling him, the demon turned round and answered. Whoosh! and he was inside the bottle. Monkey immediately struck a label inscribed "Upon the Orders of the Patriarch of the Way" across the neck. The seven-star sword fell and lay in the dust. Thus Monkey acquired the last of the demon's treasures.

"Well, brother," said Pigsy, coming towards him, "you have got the demon's sword, but where is the demon himself?"

"He's finished," said Monkey laughing. "I've got him shut up in this bottle."

Sandy and Pigsy were overjoyed. The region was now free of all evil spirits. The three friends returned to the cave and gave the glad tidings to Tripitaka.

"The mountain has been cleansed, the

demons are all dead. You can mount your horse again, Master, and we can continue on our way."

Tripitaka was beside himself with joy. They breakfasted in peace, gathered their luggage together, saddled the white horse, and resumed their westward journey.

As they walked along, they suddenly met a blind musician, who came up to them and, taking Tripitaka's horse by the bridle, said: "Where are you making for, monk? Return my treasures to me."

"This is the end of us!" cried Pigsy. "It's the old demon come for his treasures!"

Monkey took a good look at the newcomer — it was the Patriarch of the Way. Sun Wu-k'ung stepped forward quickly and bowed low before him.

"Where are you bound for, sir?"

The Patriarch of the Way mounted a jade throne, rose high in the air, and stopped in the clouds.

"Sun Wu-k'ung, return my treasures to me," he said.

Monkey soared up into the air after him.

"Which treasures, sir?" he asked.

"I keep the Elixir of Life in the gourd, I use the bottle for water, the sword serves me to command the demons. With the fan I blow up the fire, the rope I use as a belt on my robe. Those two demons were my stokers — one stoked my gold furnace, the other my silver furnace. They stole my treasures and ran away from Heaven. I was unable to find them anywhere. By capturing them you have earned my undying gratitude."

"You're not exactly over-polite, sir," said Monkey boldly. "If your people turn into evil spirits you cannot escape responsibility, you know; I expect you were not masterful enough with them. Had you not turned up here in person, I am sure I would never have returned these treasures to you. Here, take them now."

The Patriarch of the Way accepted all five treasures from him and ascended to Heaven. Tripitaka and his disciples hurriedly continued their journey to the west.

The Fire Mountain Bars the Pilgrims' Way

Tripitaka and his disciples travelled on in complete harmony towards the Western Paradise. Time flew like an arrow; the Sun and the Moon floated across the sky like shuttles on a loom. The hot season passed, and the morning frosts of autumn set in. Then one day they suddenly felt a wave of scorching hot air attack them.

"How is it possible that there should be such heat in the autumn?" Tripitaka asked.

"On our way to the west lies the country of Surya, where the Sun goes down," said Pigsy. "They say it's there that Heaven ends. Every afternoon the King sends out trumpeters to blow their trumpets and sound the drums on the city walls. They produce so much noise that it sounds like the roar of the ocean. It is then that the Sun sets in the Western Sea, burning like fire. As it sets, there is a mighty sizzling, as if red-hot steel were dipped in water. If it weren't for the sound of the trumpets and drums, which drown this noise, all the children in the city would scream their heads off with fear. It's so hot here — we must be approaching the spot where the Sun sets in the sea."

Monkey could not restrain himself from laughter when he heard Pigsy's explanation.

"What nonsense are you talking, you fool? We aren't anywhere near the country of Surya yet. Dawdling along like this we should never get there even if we travelled three whole lifetimes."

"Do you then think, brother, that we are

not in the place where the Sun goes down into the sea?" said Pigsy. "In that case kindly explain why it is so hot here!"

"Perhaps the four seasons have got mixed up and a heat wave has come in autumn," suggested Sandy.

As they were discussing this, they caught sight of a farmhouse by the roadside, its roofs covered with red tiles, the walls built of red brick, the doors painted red. Even the chairs that had been placed outside the front door were red. Tripitaka dismounted and told Monkey to go in and enquire about the cause of the heat.

Monkey hid his cudgel, tidied his clothes, put on a serious expression, and crossed the road. As he was about to enter the farmyard, an old man suddenly came out of the gate. He was dressed in a coarse linen robe of a dirty yellow colour and had a blackish broad-brimmed hat made of bamboo on his head. He was leaning on a bamboo stick which was neither straight nor crooked. On his feet he wore high leather boots which were neither new nor old. His skin was as red as copper, his whiskers were like white tassels. Long eyebrows concealed his jade-green eyes, while gold teeth protruded from his half-open mouth.

Raising his head, the old man was very startled when he saw Monkey. He lifted his stick and cried: "Where have you sprung from, monster? What are you seeking at my doorstep?"

"You have nothing to fear, old man," replied Monkey politely. "I am no monster, but a disciple of the reverend monk Tripitaka from the great T'ang Empire, and we are on our way to the west to fetch the scriptures. When my Master, my fellow-disciples and I reached your country we suddenly felt a great heat. As we don't know what is causing it, nor what your country is called, I have come to ask you for a little information."

The old man recovered his nerve and smiled.

"Reverend father, you must not be surprised by my error," he said. "I am very old and my eyesight is not what it used to be. Thus it happened that I failed to recognise you."

"That's perfectly all right," said Monkey graciously.

"Where is your Master?"

"He is standing over there, on the south side of the road."

"Well, why don't you invite him over here?"

This pleased Monkey very much, and he beckoned to Tripitaka, Pigsy and Sandy to join him. They came, leading the white horse by the bridle and carrying their luggage. All three bowed respectfully to the old man.

When the old man saw Tripitaka's noble face and the strange look of his two disciples, he felt a mixture of joy and fear. Nevertheless, he invited them all in, ordering his servants to bring some tea.

Tripitaka stood up and, with great courtesy, asked about the cause of the mysterious heat, so unusual in autumn.

"We are living on the foothills of the Fire Mountain," the old man explained, "and we know neither spring nor autumn. It is as hot as this all the time."

"In which direction does this Fire Mountain lie? Doesn't it make a journey to the west difficult?" Tripitaka asked.

"You can't travel to the west at all," replied the old man. "The mountain is sixty miles due west of here. For eight hundred miles round it everything is in flames and no grass can grow there. Even if your heads were made of copper and your bodies of iron, you would still melt in the heat."

Hearing this, Tripitaka went quite pale with horror and dared not put any more questions to their host.

A young man was just passing by the house, pushing a small red cart and calling out that he was selling pancakes. He was the old man's next-door neighbour. Monkey plucked out a hair and, changing it into a copper coin, went out to buy a pancake. The young man took the coin, lifted the canvas covering his cart, and took out a hot pancake, which he handed to Monkey. The pancake was too hot to hold, burning the hand like a glowing ember or a red-hot nail that has just been taken out of the forge. Monkey kept moving it from one hand to the other, muttering to himself: "How hot this pancake is! It scorches the skin!"

The young man laughed at the sight of him, saying: "If you're afraid of heat, you had better stay away from this place. Here it's hot all the time."

"This chap doesn't talk any too wisely," said Monkey to himself, adding out loud: "If it's as hot as this with no cold spells in between, there can't be any crops here. Where then do you get your pancakes from?"

"If we wish to have flour for pancakes, we have to ask the God of the Iron Fan," said the young man.

"Ask him for what?"

"For a fan of banana leaves. When he lends it to us, we wave it once to put out the fire, a second time to raise a wind, and a third to bring on the rain. Then we immediately sow and in good time bring in the harvest. Crops do quite well here. But otherwise not a blade of grass will grow."

Having gained this valuable information, Monkey went back inside and gave the pancake to Tripitaka, saying: "There is no need to fear anything, Master. What is to be, will be. Eat this pancake and I'll tell you what's to be done."

Tripitaka accepted the pancake and offered it to their host.

"We haven't yet offered you any refreshment, how could we dare to take something from you," the old man declined courteously.

"Sir, you need not give us either tea or food," said Monkey, smiling. "Tell us, though, where the God of the Iron Fan is to be found."

"Why do you ask?"

"The man who sold me the pancake said that this god has a banana-leaf fan which you may borrow and with one wave put out the fire, with another raise a wind, and with a third bring on the rain. Then, if you plant your crops, they do quite well. I mean to visit this god and ask him for the fan, with which I shall put out the flames on the Fire Mountain. After that you'll be able to have a regular harvest and will live in peace and contentment."

"Have you never heard the old proverb that says, 'Everything in the world has its price?'" the old man tried to dampen Monkey's courage.

"What does he ask for the loan of his fan?" Monkey wanted to know.

"We in this region borrow his fan once

every ten years. In return he wants four pigs, four sheep, a fine robe of flower-patterned silk with a silk lining, rare foods and fruits, geese, chickens and wine, and a purifying bath which we have to prepare for him. All this has to be brought to his cave, where homage must be paid to him."

"And where is this cave of his?" Monkey asked. "What is it called? Is it far away? I want to go and borrow that fan."

"The cave is on the Mountain of Cypress Clouds to the south west of here and it is called the Banana Tree Cave. When we go with the faithful to make offerings there, it takes us over a month, for it is about fourteen hundred and fifty miles distant."

"That's nothing," laughed Monkey. "I'll be back in a jiffy."

"Oh, but wait a little," protested the old man. "You must take a little tea and eat something before you go. I'll also give you some food, and you'll need at least two guides. There are no cities or villages on your way, and the place is full of wolves and tigers. It's a long journey and the dangers are not to be taken lightly."

"No, no, I don't need anything," Monkey laughed again. "Well, I'm off."

With these words he vanished from sight.

"Merciful Heaven!" cried the old man. "He must be one of the Immortals who can fly in the clouds."

The Monkey King Obtains the Magic Fan

In a twinkling Monkey reached the Mountain of Cypress Clouds, lowered his cloud, and started searching for the cave. From the forest came the sound of an axe as a woodcutter felled trees. Monkey went up to him and was told that the God of the Iron Fan was in fact the Princess of the Iron Fan, also known as the Devil Spirit Yaksha, who is the wife of the demon king Strong Buffalo.

"Oh dear, another person who isn't on very good terms with me," Monkey thought. "Long ago I killed a youth called the Red Boy. Then I was told he was the son of this Yaksha. Now I run into his father and mother. A fine chance I have of getting that fan!"

He took his leave of the woodcutter and made his way to the Banana Tree Cave, which lay in a very beautiful spot. The door of the cave was firmly closed. The Monkey King went up to it and called out: "Brother Strong Buffalo, open the door! Open the door!"

The door creaked and opened. A girl appeared, carrying a flower-basket in one hand and a hoe over her shoulder. Monkey greeted her by bowing with folded hands and said: "Be so kind as to announce me to your Princess. I am a monk on his way to the west to fetch the scriptures. We cannot get over the Fire Mountain, and I have therefore come to ask your mistress to lend me her fan."

"Which monastery do you come from and what is your name?" the girl asked. "I have to know if I am to announce you properly."

"I come from the east and my religious name is Sun Wu-k'ung," Monkey told her gravely.

The girl went back to the cave, knelt in front of the Yaksha, and said that the monk Sun Wu-k'ung was outside, having come to borrow her banana-leaf fan so as to be able to cross the Fire Mountain. As soon as she heard Monkey's name mentioned the Yaksha reddened to the roots of her hair, trembling all over with rage. It was as if someone had poured oil on a fire.

"Ah, you cursed ape, now I'll get even with you at last!" she cried.

She ordered her servant-girl to fetch her armour and her swords. Hurriedly she put on her full armour and grasped the two swords of tempered steel before rushing outside.

"Where are you, Sun Wu-k'ung?" she shouted.

The Monkey King stepped forward and bowed low before her.

"Dear sister-in-law, Monkey Sun has come to pay his respects to you."

"Who are you calling sister-in-law?" the Yaksha stormed. "Do you think I'm interested in your respects?"

"His Majesty the demon king Strong Bufallo and I became brothers many years ago. He is my seventh pledge-brother. Today I learned that the Princess is brother Strong Buffalo's wife, and so I took the liberty of calling you my sister-in-law."

"You damned Monkey," the Yaksha swore at him, "since you are my husband's brother, why did you destroy my son?"

"Who may your son be?" Monkey asked, putting on an innocent expression.

"My son was King Red Boy from the Fiery Clouds Cave in the Pine Valley on the Mountain of Sighs. You are the cause of his misfortune and we were never able to settle our account with you. Now you come here of your own accord, tempting providence. You don't think I'll let you get away with it, do you?"

"My sister-in-law is not aware of the real facts of the case," Monkey replied, smiling. "I assure you that your accusations are quite wrong. Thanks to me your son is now Assistant Keeper of the Treasury in the palace of the Goddess Kuan-yin. He has been raised above worldly cares and has become one of the Immortals, like Heaven and Earth, the Sun and the Moon. And you, instead of thanking me for having placed him in this post, are falsely accusing me. That is most unjust."

"Wicked Monkey, you can keep your prattle! Stick out your head, so that I can use my sword on you. If you can bear the pain, I shall lend you my fan. If not, I'll send you straight to the Lord of Darkness."

Monkey crossed his arms on his chest and smiled challengingly.

"Keep your temper, my dear sister-in-law. I'll willingly stick out my head and you can take as many swipes at it as you please. But when you get out of breath, you must lend me that fan."

There was no talking to the Yaksha. She brandished her two swords and swish! swish! struck Monkey on the head some ten times. Monkey did not even bat an eyelid. This frightened the Yaksha and she was about to run away.

"Where are you off to, sister-in-law?" Monkey stopped her. "You must lend me your fan before you go."

"You don't think I lend a treasure like that to anybody who happens to ask for it?"

"All right, if you refuse to lend it to me, I shall give you a taste of my cudgel," replied Monkey.

Monkey held on to the Yaksha with one hand, while with the other he drew his cudgel from behind his ear and lifted it to strike her. The Yaksha wrenched herself free and attacked him with her two swords. Monkey answered with his magic cudgel and a merciless battle was soon in progress on the Mountain of Cypress Clouds. In the grip of an old hatred, both the combatants quite forgot their ties of kinship. The Yaksha withstood him until the evening, but then, having seen for herself the might of Monkey's cudgel and having found it impossible to make any impact on him with her weapons, she realised she would not be able to vanquish him. Suddenly she brought out her banana-leaf fan and waved it in front of him, raising a whirl-

wind which carried Monkey off with such force that nothing in the world could stop him. In an instant he had vanished without trace and the Yaksha returned triumphantly home.

Poor Monkey was tossed and buffeted by the wind. Bending over to the left he was unable to touch the ground, bending over to the right he found nothing which he might catch hold of to stop his flight. He circled in the air like a falling leaf, drifting helplessly like blossoms on water. He remained thus all night long, and only when dawn had come did he land on some unknown mountain. It was some time before he recovered his senses and, looking round, recognised where he was.

"What a shrew!" he sighed. "Why did she have to send me all this way? I must climb down now and ask the God of Mercy what to do — he is sure to tell me how I can get back again."

As he was thinking about his best course of action, Monkey heard the ringing of a bell. Quickly he came down from the mountain top and made for the monastery. The monk guarding the gate recognised him at once and took him inside, where he announced his arrival to the god. Hearing that Sun Wu-k'ung had come, the god hurried down from his throne and went out to meet him.

"Congratulations, congratulations," he said, bowing and leading Monkey inside. "Have you brought the scriptures already?"

"It is too early for congratulations," Monkey replied. "We have not reached the Buddha's dwelling yet."

"In that case, why have you come to see me in these remote parts?" the God of Mercy enquired. Monkey explained that he had been waved there by the Yaksha's fan.

"I see," said the God of Mercy, smiling. "If the Princess of the Iron Fan waves her fan in front of anybody, he is carried eighty-four thousand miles away. It is only fifty thousand miles to the Fire Mountain

— you stopped yourself earlier because you know how to fly in the clouds. An ordinary mortal would not succeed in doing so."

"Oh dear me," wailed Monkey, "this is a very bad business. How is our reverend Master to cross the mountain, with me unable to help him?"

"Calm yourself, Sun Wu-k'ung," said the god. "This, too, has been decided by Fate. This time it is my job to help you."

"Yes, but how?" Monkey asked.

"Some time ago Buddha gave me my instructions. He presented me with a pellet for calming the wind and a flying dragon staff. With the staff I have already subdued the wind demon, but I have not yet had a chance to use the pellet, and so I shall give it to you. With this in your possession, that woman can wave her fan at you as much as she wants, but she will not succeed in moving you an inch. You will take her fan and put out the fire. Then you will surely reach your destination."

Monkey bowed from the waist and gave thanks to the god, who took a brocade pouch from his sleeve and withdrew from it the pellet for calming the wind. Putting it inside Monkey's collar, he sewed it up securely. Then he accompanied Monkey to the door, saying: "I must not keep you any longer. The Yaksha's mountain lies to the south west of here."

Monkey took leave of the god, mounted a cloud, and in a twinkling arrived back on the Mountain of Cypress Clouds. Knocking on the door of the cave with his cudgel, he called out: "Open the door! Open the

door! Sun Wu-k'ung has come to collect the fan."

The servant-girl ran, terrified, from the door to announce: "Mistress, Sun Wu-k'ung is back again, asking for the fan!"

The Yaksha's heart froze with fear.

"That wretched Monkey can wriggle his way out of every difficulty. When I wave my fan, people are carried eighty-four thousand miles away. How can he have got back so quickly after I blew him away? But you wait, this time I'll wave my fan several times, and that'll keep him from coming back."

She jumped up, picked up both her swords, and rushed out of the door.

"Are you so fearless, Sun Wu-k'ung, that you dare to come here again, courting death?"

"Now, now, my dear sister-in-law," replied Monkey with a laugh, "you really must not be so mean. Lend me that fan of yours and I promise to return it as soon as I have got Tripitaka across the mountain. I am a man of my word."

"Accursed Monkey, are you quite without reason?" the Yaksha shouted. "I haven't yet revenged myself for being deprived of my son and you want me to agree to your whims and lend you my fan. Here, I'll give you a taste of my sword instead."

Monkey wasn't in the least frightened. He swung his cudgel in the air and struck at her sword. They closed with each other several times. The Yaksha's hands grew numb and she could hardly hold her sword, yet Monkey's strength was undiminished. Seeing that victory was favouring him, the Yaksha brought out her fan and waved it in front of the Monkey King. But

he stood as if he were rooted to the spot. He put away his cudgel and laughed mockingly in her face.

"This is not like last time! Wave it about as much as you like — it won't help you a bit. If I move so much as half an inch, I am nothing but a contemptible weakling."

The Yaksha waved her fan two more times, but all in vain. Frightened out of her wits, she quickly hid the fan and ran back to the cave, firmly shutting the door behind her. Monkey watched her go and then had an idea: ripping his collar, he took out the pellet for calming the wind, changed himself into a clothes-moth, and flew in through a chink in the door.

"I am thirsty," cried the Yaksha. "Bring me some tea, quick!"

Her chamber-maid quickly brought a pot of fragrant tea, pouring it out so fast that the tea splashed and made a froth at the top of the cup. This suited Monkey very well — he fluttered his wings and buzz! he hid under the froth. The Yaksha was very thirsty so she seized the cup and drained it in two gulps. When he found himself in her stomach, Monkey again took on his proper form and shouted in a loud, awe-inspiring voice: "Sister-in-law, lend me that fan!"

The Yaksha went quite pale with shock.

"Girls, have you closed the door properly?" she asked her maids.

"Yes, yes, we have," they answered.

"But if you have closed the door, how is it possible that I can hear Monkey shouting somewhere inside?" the Yaksha went on, badly frightened.

One of the servant-girls said that it seemed as if Monkey were hiding somewhere about the Yaksha's own person.

"Sun Wu-k'ung, what tricks are you playing on me?" the Yaksha demanded.

"Never in my life have I resorted to tricks, I perform genuine magic, my dear sister-in-law. At the moment I, Sun Wu-k'ung, am paying a visit to your worthy stomach and taking a look at your lungs and liver."

Lifting his leg, Monkey stamped hard. Yaksha writhed with pain, dropping to the floor and moaning.

"Mercy, brother-in-law, mercy!" she shouted.

Monkey stopped threshing about with his arms and legs.

"Ah, so you recognise me for your brother-in-law now, do you? All right,

I shall let you go, but I only do it for the sake of my friendship with brother Strong Buffalo. First of all, however, you must bring the fan."

"Yes, yes, you can have it at once. Come out and you can take it."

"You must show it to me first. Only then will I come out."

The Yaksha ordered one of her maids to fetch the banana-leaf fan and lay it down next to her. Monkey stuck his head out between her lips and, seeing the fan, said kindly: "I have decided not to take your life. I shall not therefore drill a hole in your stomach, but shall come out at the top. Kindly open your mouth wide."

The Yaksha did as Monkey instructed her. He changed into a clothes-moth again and flew out, sitting down on the fan. The Yaksha of course suspected nothing. When she thought he was taking a long time about it, she again asked him to come out. Monkey took on his proper form again, picked up the fan, and said: "But I have been out for some time now. Thank you for lending me the fan."

With a dignified step he made for the door, which was quickly thrown open by the servant-girls.

Monkey now turned his cloud round and flew towards the east. In a little while he lowered it next to the red brick wall of the farmhouse. Pigsy at once caught sight of him and cried: "Master, Master, brother Sun is back!"

Accompanied by the old man from the farm and by Sandy, Tripitaka came running out to meet him, and together they all returned inside. Monkey showed them the banana-leaf fan and asked the old man whether it was the right one.

"Yes, it is," said the old man.

"My worthy disciple merits our thanks," Tripitaka praised Monkey. "I am sure it must have cost him a great deal of effort to gain this treasure."

Then he and his three disciples bade farewell to the old man and resumed their journey to the west. When they had gone some forty miles, the heat grew so intense that they felt as if they had been boiled in steam. The scorching earth made the little white horse lift his legs in a rapid canter. Sandy wailed that his feet were scorched, while Pigsy moaned that his hooves were sure to melt at any moment. The ground was so hot that they could not stop, yet to go on was next to impossible.

Monkey asked Tripitaka to dismount

and all of them to wait while he went forward alone to put out the flames and summon the wind and the rain; when the ground had grown cool, they would be able to cross the mountain.

He picked up the fan and, approaching the vast fire, waved it with all his might. But this only made the fire rage even more fiercely. He waved the fan again, and the tongues of flame shot up a hundred times higher. He waved it a third time, and the flames rose a thousand fathoms in the air, licking at Monkey's body. He turned round and hurried back, the hair on his bottom completely scorched. Running towards Tripitaka he called out: "Turn back, quick! The fire is spreading."

The monk jumped on his horse, Pigsy and Sandy ran as fast as they could, not stopping until they had gone some twenty miles to the east.

"What went wrong?" they asked Monkey as soon as they had recovered their breath a little.

Monkey flung the fan to the ground and spat in disgust.

"Would you believe it! That deceiving Yaksha has tricked me. It's not the right fan."

"But why did you make us go back like this?" asked Pigsy.

"When I waved the fan the first time," Monkey explained, "the fire grew more intense, when I waved it a second time, the flames shot up, and when I waved it a third time, they rose high in the air. Had I not run away at once, all my hairs would have been scorched."

"You always used to say that neither lightning nor fire could harm you. How is it that you're afraid of fire all of a sudden?" Pigsy taunted him.

"You don't understand a thing, you blockhead," Monkey retorted. "Nothing can happen to me provided I am ready for the danger. Today I only went to quench the flames with the fan and did not recite a spell against fire, nor did I first protect myself, and that's why the fire scorched me. But never mind, I know what to do!"

"What do you suggest?" Tripitaka enquired.

"The Yaksha's husband is the demon king Strong Buffalo who became my pledge-brother five hundred years ago. He now lives on the Thunder Mountain. I'll go and see him."

Monkey instructed Sandy and Pigsy to look after Tripitaka and was gone in a flash.

The Monkey King Fights with Strong Buffalo

Monkey mounted a cloud and within half an hour had reached the Thunder Mountain. He lowered his cloud and landed on the summit. Taking a look round he found that it was an impressive mountain with a jutting summit, steep slopes and deep valleys full of fragrant flowers, trees heavy with fruit, red wisterias, speckled bamboo, blue pines and green willows. The years go by unnoticed here, without leaving any trace, the centuries make not the slightest change to all this rare beauty.

When Monkey had admired the landscape to his heart's content he came down from the mountain top and made his way through the dense undergrowth in search of a path that would take him to the demon's cave. Soon he reached a pine forest and, passing through it, found himself facing the Cloud Seat Cave. All round it there was nothing but woods and rock cliffs. The cave itself was at the bottom of a valley where countless magnificent flowers and herbs were growing as if in some garden paradise.

Monkey stopped in front of the cave and called out: "Brother Buffalo, open the door!"

The door creaked and out came an imp.

"Kindly go back and tell your highly esteemed king that Sun Wu-k'ung has come to pay his respects."

The imp nodded and disappeared inside, closing the door behind him.

The king Strong Buffalo was whiling away the time in the library, reading books on alchemy. The imp interrupted him, saying: "Your Majesty, there is a hairy monk outside who says his name is Sun Wu-k'ung and wants to pay his respects to you."

A dark cloud spread over the demon's face when he heard Monkey's name, and he blazed up as if someone had poured oil into a fire. He strode purposefully out of the library, seizing his armour in the hall and putting it on. Then he armed himself with an iron cudgel and went out.

"Who is the intruder who dares to disturb the peace here?" he shouted in a mighty voice.

Monkey tidied his clothes, stepped forward and bowed low.

"Do you still know me, brother?" he asked.

"Are you Sun Wu-k'ung, the Great Sage, Equal to Heaven?"

"Yes, that's me. It's been a long time since we last saw each other. My brother seems to be in the best of health, I am glad to see. Congratulations."

"You can keep your flatteries!" Strong Buffalo shouted. "I have heard that you played havoc in Heaven and the Supreme Buddha imprisoned you under the Mountain of the Five Elements. Then I am told you managed to escape and became monk Tripitaka's companion on his journey to the Western Paradise to fetch the scriptures. Why did you harm my son, the Red Boy? I have a bone to pick with you, and here you come crawling into the trap yourself."

"My elder brother is unjustly prejudiced against me," said Monkey slyly. "Your worthy son is now Assistant Keeper of the Treasury and is more highly placed than my worthy brother himself, enjoying endless bliss, freedom and eternal life. What is wrong with that? Why does my brother then accuse me of harming his son when I made all that possible for him?"

"Be quiet, you cheeky ape!" shouted Strong Buffalo once more. "And take

yourself away from here — I only let you go on account of our ancient friendship."

"A thousand thanks for your boundless mercy," said Monkey. "However, I have one more request to make of my worthy brother. I beseech you ten thousand times to help me."

"Are there no limits to your insolence?" the demon cried angrily. "I have shown great mercy in letting you go — why don't you go then, instead of bothering me? What is it you want me to do?"

"I do not wish to keep anything from you, brother," said Monkey. "On our journey to the west we were halted by the Fire Mountain and cannot go any farther. On questioning the natives I found that your esteemed wife, the Yaksha, owns a banana-leaf fan, and I wanted her to lend it to me. I called on her yesterday, but she refused and would not let me have the fan at any price. That is why I have come to ask you for help. You have a heart that is as generous as Heaven and Earth put together, and I am convinced you will not let me down but will accompany me while I pay a second visit to my sister-in-law. Once I have put out the flames and helped Tripitaka cross the mountain I shall not fail to return the fan, whole and undamaged."

Hearing this, Strong Buffalo seethed with anger. Gritting his steely teeth, he scolded Monkey, saying: "This is absolutely unheard of! So you've come on account of the fan. No doubt you first tried to trick

my poor wife but could make no headway with her, and that's why you've turned to me. Come here and I'll give you a taste of my cudgel."

"Don't think you can frighten me by talking about cudgels, brother," replied Monkey briskly. "I have come to you with the best intentions in the world. I hope you will see your way to helping me after all."

"If you succeed in defeating me three times in succession, I shall go with you to the Yaksha and ask her to lend you her fan. That will at least give me a chance of getting even with you."

"Quite right, brother, that's more like it! I'm afraid I have been somewhat neglectful of late and haven't visited you to find out what progress you have made in the arts of war. Now we can match our forces."

Strong Buffalo did not need to be told twice. Seizing his iron cudgel, he swung it at Monkey's head. Monkey parried the blow with his own weapon. They fought some hundred rounds without either gaining an advantage. Just as their contest reached the decisive moment, a voice could be heard calling from the mountain top: "Your Majesty Strong Buffalo, our noble king sends his greetings and asks you to join him in a banquet at your earliest convenience."

The demon held up his iron cudgel to ward off Monkey's magic one, and shouted: "Monkey, stop a while! I have to go and attend a friend's banquet. I'll be back as soon as I can."

With this he lowered his cloud and disappeared inside his cave. Taking off his armour, he put on a jacket of soft felt and eiderdown. Then he ran out of the door and mounting his steed, Golden Eye, ordered the imps to keep guard. Golden Eye carried him up into the clouds and they flew towards the north west.

Monkey, standing on the summit, watched Strong Buffalo go.

"Who can this friend of his be who has invited him to a banquet?" he wondered. "I'll follow him."

He shook himself, changed into a light breeze, and soon caught up with the demon. They flew on to a mountain, where Strong Buffalo suddenly vanished from sight. Monkey assumed his proper form, lowered his cloud, and looked round him. Below he saw a deep valley filled with clear water and next to it a stone tablet with the engraved inscription, "Pool of Green Waves on the Stone Mountain".

"Ah, Strong Buffalo must have gone under the water," said Monkey to himself. "At the bottom of the pool there will be some water spirit, dragon, fish or turtle. I'll go down and investigate."

He folded his hands, recited a spell, and changed into a crab, neither large nor small. Then he plunged into the pool, diving down to the bottom. As he went, he came across a number of delicately carved pillars, to one of which was tethered the demon's steed, Golden Eye. On the other side of the pillars there was no more water. Monkey crawled carefully forward, looking round him as he did so. Behind a kind of screen there was a palace made of gold bricks, with columns of white jade. Music came from the main hall, where the tables had been laid for a banquet. In the place of honour sat Strong Buffalo, surrounded by three or four fish demons. Opposite him was a dragon with a she-dragon and their offspring. They had just raised their cups and were toasting each other. Monkey crept right up to them, and the old dragon noticed him.

"Seize that crab!" he shouted.

The young dragons caught hold of Monkey, who called out in a human voice: "Mercy! Mercy!"

"How did you get here, crab?" the dragon interrogated him. "How could you dare to enter my banquet hall? How do you dare to crawl about here in front of my guests? I'll have your head cut off."

Monkey was ready with a convincing lie.

"I live in ponds and lakes, making my home in holes in the banks," he said, bowing to every side. "I am old and my body is all squashed. They call me the Wobbling Bachelor. I crawl over water weeds, and therefore my legs are covered with mud. Having never been taught the rules of etiquette I have now unwittingly trespassed in your palace and offended Your Majesty. I hope that Your Majesty will forgive me my error."

Hearing these humble words, all the guests pleaded on the crab's behalf, bowing in front of the old dragon: "The Bachelor has never been in the jade palace before and he doesn't know what is right and proper here. Let him go on his way, Your Majesty."

The old dragon agreed. The water spirits then ordered Monkey to leave and to remember never to do anything like it again if he wished to escape a hiding. Monkey nodded his head eagerly and scuttled off as fast as his ten feet would carry him, not stopping before he had got to the other side of the pillars. Then an idea occurred to him:

"Strong Buffalo is feasting here, and he expects me to wait for him all this time. And when the banquet ends, he will not want to lend me the fan anyway. I'll take his steed, assume his form, and go and trick that Yaksha of his. I'll surely get the fan from her and then see Tripitaka safely over the mountain."

Monkey changed back to his proper form, untied Golden Eye, jumped up into the jewelled saddle and rose to the surface of the pool. As soon as he was out of the water he changed into Strong Buffalo and, spurring Golden Eye, flew up into the clouds. Before long he was standing outside the Banana Tree Cave on the Mountain of Cypress Clouds.

"Open the door!" he shouted.

Two fairies were guarding the door, and they opened it at once. Seeing Strong Buffalo, they ran inside to report: "Madam, your husband is here and wants to see you."

The Yaksha tidied her hair and hurried out to meet her husband. In the meantime Monkey had dismounted and, leading Golden Eye by the bridle, he came up to her. Summoning all his courage, he managed to fool the lady quite easily. She was a very simple soul and suspected nothing. They held hands and went inside, where the Yaksha ordered a maid to bring tea and something to eat. All the fairies and servant-girls bowed before their master, vying with one another in making him feel at home.

Monkey and the Yaksha began to tell each other what had happened during their separation.

"You're looking very well, my dear," said Monkey finally.

"I can't tell you how pleased I am that you are here, my lord," said the Yaksha. "What good wind has brought you this way?"

"I have heard that that scoundrel, Sun Wu-k'ung, got as far as the Fire Mountain on his expedition with Tripitaka. It occurred to me that he might come here to borrow your fan. I regret very much that so far I have not had the chance of getting even with him for what he did to our son. I wanted to ask you, my dear, to be sure to send word to me if he should happen to turn up. I'll come over straightaway and cut him into a thousand pieces, thus taking revenge both on your behalf and mine."

"Oh, my lord," said the Yaksha with tears in her eyes, "that wretched Monkey almost took my life."

Monkey pretended to be very angry.

"What's that?" he cried. "When was the rascal here?"

"He may still be about somewhere. He came yesterday to borrow my fan. Mindful of what he did to our son, I put on my armour and, sword in hand, ran outside to fight him. He took no notice of my blows and even called me his sister-in-law, saying he had become your brother years ago."

"Yes, that's right, five hundred years

ago we became pledge-brothers," said Monkey.

"He made no reply when I cursed and abused him," the Yaksha went on, "and he did not dare to lift his hand against me when I showered him with blows. In the end I blew him away with the fan. In some mysterious way he must have found some spell to stop the wind, because this morning he was again shouting on my doorstep. Again I tried to blow him away, but he wouldn't budge. I used my sword, but he was not to be defeated. Becoming afraid of his cursed cudgel, I retired to the cave and closed the door in his face. I cannot imagine how he did it, but he succeeded in getting inside my stomach and all but killed me. To appease him I called him brother-in-law and gave him the fan."

"Oh, what a pity!" cried Monkey, beating his breast in pretended anguish. "What a pity! You shouldn't have done that, my dear. To think that the wretched Monkey should have got the fan! This will be the death of me."

"Calm yourself, my lord," said the Yaksha, smiling. "In order to get rid of him I gave him a false fan."

"And where is the genuine one?" Monkey wanted to know.

"Don't worry. I have it on me," was the reply.

"Where have you hidden it, my dear?"

Monkey asked. "You must be very careful with it. That scoundrel is terribly clever and might deprive us of our treasure."

The Yaksha giggled and spat the fan out of her mouth. It was no larger than an apricot leaf. She handed it to her supposed husband, saying: "Look, isn't this our real treasure?"

Monkey took the fan and examined it. He could not believe that this was the genuine fan. "Such a tiny thing," he thought. "How could it put out flames?"

"Can this tiny fan really put out a fire within a radius of eight hundred miles?" he asked.

"My lord, it's not two years yet since we parted and have you already forgotten how to use the family heirloom?" said the Yaksha in surprise. "You have to pass the thumb of your left hand over the seventh red thread of the handle and say, 'Grow!' and the fan will become a foot and two inches long," she told him. "This little treasure of ours is capable of so many changes. Even if the fire were raging over an area of eighty thousand miles, a single wave of this fan would put it out."

Monkey committed all he heard to memory, put the fan inside his mouth, rubbed his cheek with one hand, and assumed his proper form, saying: "Look who I am!"

The Yaksha was so startled that she overturned the table, staggered and fell to the ground.

"This will be the end of me!" she wailed. "This is the end!"

Not waiting to find out whether the Yaksha was alive or had died of shock, Monkey sprang across the room and ran out of the cave. He shook himself and mounted his magic cloud, floating up to the top of a high mountain. Spitting out the fan, he decided to test it. With the thumb of his left hand he brushed the seventh red thread of the handle, cried "Grow!" and the fan really grew until it was a foot and two inches long. Turning it round in his hand he examined it carefully and found that it was quite different to the false one. When he waved it, the fan gleamed with a golden sheen, giving off a strange glow. At the top there were thirty-six red threads, the warp and weft were closely interwoven, and the front and the back were exactly alike. Monkey realised that he had only learned how to make the fan grow larger but could not make it smaller again — thus he had to carry it as it was. Shrugging his shoulders, he put the fan under his arm and set off to find Tripitaka.

Meanwhile the banquet in the Pool of Green Waves had come to an end, and the guests were departing. Strong Buffalo passed among the pillars, looked all round him, but nowhere could he find his steed, Golden Eye. The old dragon had all his guests called back and asked them if they knew who had stolen Strong Buffalo's steed. All the spirits knelt on the ground.

"We should never dare to steal Golden Eye. We all ate and drank at the banquet, listening to music, and no stranger came among us."

"I shouldn't think any of my guests would dare to do such a thing," said the old dragon. "Has there really been no one else here?"

"That crab crawled in while we were at table," said the little dragons.

"That's it!" cried Strong Buffalo, on whom the truth had dawned like a sudden ray of light. "Just before my worthy friend invited me to his banquet, I had a visit from Sun Wu-k'ung, who is on his way with the monk Tripitaka to fetch the scriptures. They cannot cross the Fire Mountain and Monkey came to me, wanting to borrow the banana-leaf fan. I didn't wish to lend it to him, so we fought, without either one of us gaining the victory. I then left him to come to the banquet. That Monkey is a very cunning fellow — no doubt he disguised himself as a crab and came here to see what was going on. Then he stole my steed and rode off to my wife's cave to get the fan from her."

"Is that the same Sun Wu-k'ung who turned Heaven upside down?"

"The very same," said Strong Buffalo. "Noble lords, if any of you happen to live along his route to the West, I strongly advise you to give him a wide berth, for he is not to be trifled with."

"That being so, what about your steed, Your Majesty?" asked the old dragon.

"Don't let it worry you," said Strong Buffalo, smiling. "All of you go home with easy minds — I'll catch up with him yet."

He parted the waves and emerged on the surface of the pool. Mounting a yellow cloud, he rushed to the Banana Tree Cave. From afar he could hear the Yaksha screaming, stamping her feet and beating her breast. Strong Buffalo threw the door open; Golden Eye was standing tethered to one of the pillars in the hall.

"Where is Sun Wu-k'ung?" the demon shouted.

Seeing their master, all the servant-girls knelt in front of him.

"Where have you come from, Your Majesty?" they enquired in astonishment.

The Yaksha ran to him, flinging herself on the ground and beating her forehead on it so vigorously that she hurt her head.

"Curse it!" she screamed. "How could you be so careless and let Monkey steal Golden Eye from you? He put on your form and came here to trick me."

"Where is the ruffian now?" asked Strong Buffalo, grinding his teeth.

"That villain stole my fan, showed me his true form, and ran away," yelled the Yaksha, continually thumping her chest. "It's a wonder I haven't died."

"Now quieten yourself, my dear, this won't do your health any good," Strong Buffalo said calmly. "I'll catch up with him and take our treasure back again. As a punishment I'll skin him alive, crumble his bones and pluck out his heart. Then you will be avenged."

He turned round and shouted at the servant-girls: "Bring me my arms!"

"Oh, but Your Majesty, you have no arms here with us," they told him.

"Then bring the arms of your mistress," Strong Buffalo commanded them.

The servant-girls brought two jewelled swords with blades of tempered steel. The demon took off his party jacket of felt and eiderdown, tidied his long robe and, brandishing the two swords, rushed out of the Banana Tree Cave in pursuit of Monkey.

The Monkey King Wins the Magic Fan Again

The demon king Strong Buffalo soon caught up with Monkey. He was still some distance away when he saw the fan jutting out under Monkey's arm. Sun Wu-k'ung was hurrying forward, looking very pleased with himself.

"This wretched Monkey has no doubt found out how to use the fan," Strong Buffalo said to himself in some anxiety. "If I ask him for the fan straight out, he'll not want to give it to me; if he were to wave it in the air, I'd be blown a hundred and eight thousand miles away, and that would suit him fine. He said that Tripitaka was waiting for him somewhere. I know those two disciples of his, Pigsy and Sandy — I met them when I was still an ordinary demon. I'll change myself into Pigsy and return the compliment by swindling Monkey. I am sure he is so full of his triumph that I can easily catch him off guard."

The demon was also master of seventy-two magic changes and in no way lagged behind Monkey in the arts of war; the only difference between them was that he lacked something of Sun Wu-k'ung's quick wit, being a little clumsy. Now he hid his two swords, recited a spell, shook himself and grew a snout just like Pigsy's. Taking a short cut, he turned in the opposite direction, and before long met Monkey.

"Look who's here, brother!" he called out to him.

Monkey was quite pleased to see his fellow disciple. As an old proverb says, "Having caught its mouse, the cat thinks it is a tiger". Seeing Pigsy coming towards him, Monkey began to question him merrily as to where he was bound for. Strong Buffalo was prepared for this and had a lie ready to hand: "Since you were gone so long, the reverend Master grew afraid that you had been unable to overcome Strong Buffalo, who knows much magic. He has therefore sent me to give you a hand and help you to get that fan."

"He needn't have worried," said Monkey, laughing. "I've got the fan, all right."

"How did you manage it?"

Monkey now told him the whole story of his combat with Strong Buffalo, describing how he had followed the demon king to the banquet, changed into a crab, stolen Golden Eye and tricked the Yaksha.

"Splendid!" said the false Pigsy. "You must be very tired, brother. Perhaps you had better let me carry the fan for a bit."

It did not occur to Monkey for a moment that this might be a trap, so he willingly handed over the fan. Strong Buffalo, of course, knew how to make the fan smaller or larger according to need. Taking it in his hand he mumbled something, and the fan at once dwindled so that it was no larger than an apricot leaf. Then the demon assumed his true form and cried: "Do you know me, cursed Monkey?"

"How foolish of me!" thought Monkey bitterly, and he spat on the ground and stamped his foot in great anger.

"'So often will the hunter go in pursuit of eagles until the eagle gouges out his eye'," he told himself furiously. His rage spurred him on to action, and he began to flail the demon king with his cudgel. Strong Buffalo answered by waving his fan. He did not know that before entering the Yaksha's stomach in the form of a clothes-moth, Monkey had acquired the pellet for calming the wind and had placed it in his mouth. Later he had forgotten its existence and swallowed it, so that all his inner organs had grown tough and his skin and bones had hardened. Thus, no matter how hard Strong Buffalo waved the fan, it had not the slightest effect on Monkey, who stood his ground. Frustrated, the demon king put the fan in his mouth and brandished his two swords, aiming vicious blows at Monkey's head. A life and death struggle broke out in the air.

But let us leave these two fighting up there among the clouds and take a look instead at Tripitaka, who was sitting by the roadside, half-baked with the heat, his tongue parched and his heart thumping inside his chest.

"Sun Wu-k'ung is a fast walker who can cover two thousand miles in a flash. He's always back so quickly — how is it possible that this time he has been gone a whole day?" he asked himself. It occurred to him that Monkey had probably come into conflict with Strong Buffalo, and he told his disciples: "Which of you

wants to go and see what your brother is doing? If you happen to run into the enemy, do your best to help Monkey and bring back the fan, so that I need not suffer here any longer and we can cross the mountain soon. We have lost a great deal of time as it is."

"I'll go," volunteered Pigsy.

Pigsy tidied his black embroidered tunic, plucked up his courage and, his rake over his shoulder, he mounted a misty cloud and made off towards the east. Suddenly he heard the noise of a battle, like the raging of a mighty storm. He stopped his cloud and looked round. There he saw Monkey fighting with Strong Buffalo. He held out his rake and shouted at the top of his voice: "Here I come, brother, to help you!"

"You scamp, it's all been messed up because of you!" Monkey scolded him.

"Our Master has asked me to look for you. I can't find my way in these mountains and so I spent a long time wandering about until a god of the earth told me where to find you. That's why I am so late. How has it all been messed up because of me?"

"I'm not annoyed at your being late," Monkey explained, "but Strong Buffalo is such a cheeky fellow. You see, I managed to do the Yaksha out of her fan, and this scoundrel took on your appearance and pretended he had been sent to look for me.

I was very pleased to see him and gave him the fan, whereupon he assumed his proper form. We are now fighting to see who is the stronger. That's why I said it was messed up because of you."

Pigsy was white with rage when he heard this. He waved his rake menacingly in Strong Buffalo's direction, crying: "You wait, you blackguard, you foul abscess! How do you dare to impersonate me and trick and provoke my worthy brother?"

Wielding his rake, Pigsy beat Strong Buffalo mercilessly. The demon king was weary and exhausted after his all-day struggle with Sun Wu-k'ung, and Pigsy's rake dealt him some heavy blows; he decided he had had enough and took to his heels.

"Just a moment, you rogue!" Pigsy shouted as he ran after him. "Let me have the fan and I'll spare your miserable life."

Strong Buffalo turned round and once more attacked Pigsy with his two swords. Monkey assisted his fellow disciple, dealing the demon king mighty blows with his cudgel. Strong Buffalo showed his courage and, using his last reserves of strength, held them at bay while he retreated. The fight went on all night, yet neither side was victorious. By this time they had drawn near to the demon's Cave of Clouds on the Thunder Mountain, still hitting each other furiously and giving ear-splitting cries. This had the effect of bringing out all the imps and their chieftains, large and small, who seized their spears and swords and rushed out of the cave to help Strong Buffalo. Altogether there were over a hundred

of them. They encouraged one another, brandishing their spears, waving their swords, and shouting: "Your Majesty, our king, we come to aid you."

"You have come in the nick of time," said Strong Buffalo.

The imps surrounded Monkey and Pigsy and set upon them. Pigsy was unable to resist and fled, dragging his rake behind him. Monkey also escaped, mounting a cloud and withdrawing from the battle. Having got rid of his opponents, Strong Buffalo returned to his cave with all the imps and shut the door firmly behind him.

"That scoundrel has a lot of stamina," said Monkey. "We fought all day yesterday since early morning without either of us gaining a victory. Then you came to help me and we fought all night long, yet he still wasn't tired. As for that horde of imps, they are pretty fierce too. Now they have shut themselves up in the cave and you can be sure they won't come out in a hurry. What shall we do about it?"

"We'll hardly be able to get hold of that fan of his," said Pigsy. "How then shall we cross the mountain with Tripitaka? Perhaps we'd better go back and try another route."

"How very clever!" Monkey exclaimed. "Stop talking such rot! I must fight him one more time and take the fan from him. Then we'll lead Tripitaka to the other side of the mountain."

His words put new hope in Pigsy. They both started out again, one wielding his rake and the other his cudgel. Bang! bang! bang! they hammered on the door of the Cave of Clouds until they had smashed it to smithereens. The terrified doorkeepers

rushed trembling inside to report that Monkey Sun Wu-k'ung had returned with a large host and had battered down their door. Strong Buffalo flew into a great rage, put on his armour, grasped his iron cudgel and ran outside.

"Accursed Monkey!" he shouted. "Who do you think you are, that you come here banging at my door and breaking it down!"

"You old rascal!" Pigsy retorted. "Who do you think you are that you give yourself the right to judge others? Come here and let me give you a taste of my rake!"

"You good-for-nothing windbag!" cried Strong Buffalo. "What are you doing here? Call that Monkey of yours, and be quick about it!"

"You miserable beast!" Monkey joined in the argument. "Only yesterday I still called you brother, but now you are my greatest enemy. Come and let me give you a taste of my cudgel!"

This angered Strong Buffalo to the point of madness, and he flung himself upon Sun Wu-k'ung. An even more cruel battle than before took place. All three rolled in a heap on the ground. They clashed some hundred times, beating each other madly, determined to win or die. Pigsy now gave full play to his violent nature and thrashed about him with his rake, not in the least afraid, since he knew that Monkey with his magic arts was at his side. They were more than a match for Strong Buffalo, who was forced to turn round and run for his life. Monkey, however, outpaced him as the demon was about to enter his cave.

"Where are you off to, strong king?" he mocked him. "You wouldn't keep me waiting, would you?"

Seeing that he could not get inside, Strong Buffalo swung round, but behind him was Pigsy with his rake. The demon took off his armour and threw away the cudgel, changing himself into a wild goose and winging his way up into the clouds.

"Look, Pigsy," chuckled Monkey, "the demon has given us the slip."

Foolish Pigsy had seen nothing. He ran about frantically, searching all round the Cave of Clouds.

"Over there, up in the clouds," said Monkey, pointing.

"But that's a wild goose," said Pigsy.

"Quite right — Strong Buffalo changed himself and there he goes."

"What shall we do now?"

"You go inside the cave and finish off all the imps, plunder this robbers' den and prevent Strong Buffalo from going back there. In the meantime I'll fly up after him, and we shall go on competing in changes until one of us defeats the other."

Pigsy did as Monkey told him, rushing inside the cave. Monkey hid his cudgel, recited a spell, shook himself, changed into a hawk and soared off into the air. When he saw the wild goose beneath him he plunged down and sunk his claws in its neck, pecking at its eyes with his beak. Strong Buffalo knew it was Sun Wu-k'ung attacking him, and he quickly changed into an eagle. Then he, in turn, attacked the hawk. Meanwhile Monkey had assumed the form of a black phoenix and gave chase to the eagle. Strong Buffalo, of course, recognised him and changed into a white stork, uttered a long-drawn cry and flew off to the south. Monkey landed on the ground, ruffling his feathers and changing into a red phoenix, whereupon he warbled in a high-pitched voice. Strong Buffalo, in his disguise as a white stork, knew only too well that the red phoenix is the king of birds and that no bird would dare to disobey him. He therefore waved his wings and came down on a mountain slope, where he changed himself into a doe. He stared around him as he grazed on the grass. Monkey recognised him at once and followed him down to the ground, changing into a hungry tiger. He swished his tail, stamped with his paws and threw himself on the doe. Badly frightened, the demon quickly changed into a striped panther and prepared to maul the tiger. Monkey was ready for him, however. He turned to face the wind, shook his head and changed into a golden-eyed unicorn. He had an iron brow and a head of copper and his roar was like thunder. Twisting round quickly, he attacked the panther. Strong Buffalo was almost exhausted by now. He changed into a bear, planted his legs wide apart and drove off the unicorn. Monkey made a somersault on the ground, changing himself into a huge elephant. Swinging his trunk from side to side he lunged forward to seize the bear.

Strong Buffalo laughed and showed his true form — that of a huge white buffalo with a head the size of a mountain peak and eyes like red-hot embers. He had horns like two iron pagodas and teeth as sharp as sword-blades.

"Wretched Monkey!" he called out in a mighty voice. "What will you do now?"

Sun Wu-k'ung now also assumed his proper form and, taking his gold cudgel from behind his ear, he leaned forward and cried: "Grow!" At once he grew immensely tall; his head was as large as Mount T'ai, his eyes were like the Sun and the Moon, his mouth like a pool of blood, his teeth like the posts of a door. He held his cudgel in his hand and struck out at Strong Buffalo. The demon had a hard head, however, and he charged forward in an attempt to gore his opponent. A fierce struggle followed, rocking the very mountains and making even Heaven and Earth tremble. Both of them used all their skill and strength. They clashed on the mountainside again and again, until at length Strong Buffalo grew faint and could no longer withstand Monkey. Feeling unsure of himself, he dropped to the ground, took on his demon form and fled in the direction of the Banana Tree Cave. Monkey followed his example by stopping his magic and running in his footsteps. Strong Buffalo rushed into the cave and closed the door firmly behind him.

Monkey had just started thumping on the door when he heard Pigsy approaching with much noise.

"What are things like in the Cave of Clouds?" Monkey asked.

"All those imps," laughed Pigsy, "were nothing but mules, donkeys, calves, pigs, foxes, does, sheep, tigers, fallow-deer and stags. I have polished them all off. I also set fire to the main passageway. Now I have heard that the demon's family lives somewhere near here, and that's why I have hurried over to see what I can find out about them."

"You have done well, wise brother," Monkey praised him. "Congratulations. As for me, all my changes were just so much wasted effort. I still have not succeeded in defeating Strong Buffalo. He changed into a huge white buffalo, while I made myself grow in size until I almost reached up to the sky. We fought long and hard, but in the end he again put on his demon form and hid himself in the cave."

"In which cave? This one, the Banana Tree Cave?" Pigsy demanded eagerly.

"Yes, that's right," Monkey agreed. "The Yaksha is there as well."

"Why don't we break in and take them to task?" Pigsy wanted to know. "We'll make them hand over the fan, and then they can do as they like. They can stay there and talk of their love for each other."

Foolish Pigsy swelled out his chest to give himself courage. Then he lifted his rake and, exerting all his strength, smashed the door so that it crashed to the ground, taking a piece of the rock with it. The servant-girls ran inside, frightened out of their wits, and reported that someone had broken down the door. Strong Buffalo had just arrived, gasping for breath, and had hardly finished telling the Yaksha how he had fought Monkey for possession of the fan, when he heard this annoying piece of news. He spat out the fan and handed it to the Yaksha, whose tears showered down upon it.

"My lord," she cried, "let us give the fan to that ape and be rid of him."

"It's no longer a question of whether we'll give him the fan or not," Strong Buffalo replied. "The fan itself is unimportant where I am concerned, but my hatred has

grown too strong. Wait here while I go and match forces with him once more."

He tidied his clothes, selected two fresh swords and made for the door. Pigsy was standing there with his rake. The demon did not say a word but struck out at Pigsy's head. Pigsy parried the blow with his rake and retreated several paces to where Monkey was waiting, waving his cudgel in the air. The buffalo king mounted a whirlwind and flew away from them, both fellow disciples at his heels. Thus yet another battle started on the slopes of the Mountain of Cypress Clouds. Taking his life in his hands Strong Buffalo fought fifty rounds, but then he felt his strength fading and fled the field of battle in a northerly direction.

His way, however, was suddenly barred by the Heavenly King Li and Crown Prince Natha with the Heavenly Generals Great Spirit and Fish Belly, who were waiting in the air.

"Not so fast!" they called out to him from a distance. "We have orders from the Jade Emperor to take you prisoner and punish you."

Strong Buffalo was terrified, and he again changed into a huge white buffalo, charging towards the Heavenly King with lowered horns. King Li brandished his dagger. At that moment Monkey arrived on the scene.

"Great Sage," cried Natha in a mighty voice, "I am clad in full armour and cannot therefore greet you in the proper manner. My father has spoken with the Supreme Buddha, who has sent a message to the Jade Emperor saying that the reverend monk Tripitaka is prevented from continuing his pilgrimage because of the Fire Mountain and that the Great Sage Sun is unable to defeat the king of demons Strong Buffalo. The Jade Emperor has given orders to my heavenly father to bring his army to your aid."

"The scoundrel truly knows a great deal of magic," declared Monkey. "What are we to do with him, now he has changed like this?"

"Don't worry, Great Sage," said Natha, smiling. "Look how I shall bring him to heel."

The Crown Prince cried "Change!" and at once he had grown three heads and three pairs of arms. Soaring up, he jumped on Strong Buffalo's back and, using his demon-slaying sword, cut off his head. A new head immediately grew in place of the old one, a dark cloud came from his nostrils and a gold flame from his eyes. Natha again swung his sword, and again Strong Buffalo's head flew off, yet a new one immediately grew in its place. Ten times more the Crown Prince wielded his demon-slaying sword, and ten more heads grew on Strong Buffalo's neck. Then Natha hung a fire-wheel on Strong Buffalo's horns and fanned the flames so that they leapt high in the air, giving off a shower of sparks. Strong Buffalo was in great pain, shouting loudly, shaking his head to and fro, and swishing his tail. He was about to take on his demon form again, but the Heavenly King Li aimed his magic mirror at him, making Strong Buffalo unable to move, much less escape.

"Spare my life!" he moaned. "I shall obey you in everything from now on."

"If you value your life, give up the fan immediately!" cried Natha.

"My wife has the fan," Strong Buffalo whispered.

Thereupon Natha took out his rope for the binding of demons, threw a noose round his neck and, taking him by the nose, drew the rope through his nostrils, leading him away as if at the end of a chain. Meanwhile Monkey, accompanied by the Heavenly King Li, General Great Spirit and Pigsy, formed up behind them, following them to the Banana Tree Cave.

"My dear, bring the fan and save my life!" Strong Buffalo called out in a sad voice.

The Yaksha came out of the door, holding out the fan in the palms of her outstretched hands. Seeing so many Immortals, as well as the Heavenly King and his son, she went down on her knees, bowing and beating her forehead on the ground.

"Great Immortals, forgive us our errors. I shall gladly give this fan to my brother-in-law, Sun, and wish him every success."

Monkey stepped forward and accepted the fan from her. Together with the celestial spirits he then mounted a magic cloud and departed towards the east.

Meanwhile Tripitaka and Sandy were still waiting for Monkey to return, alternately sitting down and pacing about. He had been gone so long that they were gripped by anxiety. Suddenly the sky filled with bright clouds, a magic glow surrounded the Earth, and then a heavenly host appeared above their heads. Tripitaka was overcome with awe.

"Look, Sandy, what heavenly host is that?" he asked.

"Reverend father, that's Crown Prince Natha leading the Buffalo," replied Sandy, who was quick to recognise them. "The one with the mirror is Heavenly King Li. Our brother Sun Wu-k'ung is holding the banana-leaf fan in his hand, our second brother is just behind him, and the others are all members of the Heavenly Defence Corps."

Hearing these words, Tripitaka at once exchanged his old monk's cap for a new one, put on his ceremonial robes and, together with Sandy, bowed to welcome the Immortals.

"What an honour for an unworthy monk like myself," he said, bowing respectfully, "to have these most reverend celestial spirits descend to Earth on my account."

"Rejoice, holy monk," Heavenly King Li told him. "Our task has been successfully accomplished. Upon the orders of the Supreme Buddha we have hastened to your assistance and, helped by your disciple, have fulfilled our mission."

The Monkey King advanced towards the mountain, fan in hand, and waved vigorously: the flames on the Fire Mountain at once grew small and began to die down. Only here and there a small tongue of flame still flickered. He waved the fan a second time — a soft rustle was heard and a light breeze sprang up. He waved it a third time, and the sky grew dark and it began to rain. Tripitaka had by this time completely recovered from his gloom and he looked on with a clear brow. The pilgrims then gave thanks to the celestial spirits and prepared to climb the mountain. The Yaksha was still standing a little way off, as if waiting for something.

"Why don't you go your way?" Monkey turned to her in surprise. "What are you doing, standing here like this?"

"Great Sage, I appeal to your generosity — please return the fan to me," the Yaksha pleaded, kneeling in front of him.

"Wretched woman, don't you know what's right and proper?" Pigsy scolded her. "We have spared your life — that must be enough for you. How can you be so impudent as to ask for the fan? When we cross the mountain, we'll exchange it for something good to eat. We have spent so much effort in getting it, and now you expect us to give it up again. Go home or you'll get wet, for it is raining."

"The Great Sage promised me he would return the fan once he had put out the fire," said the Yaksha, bowing once more. "I intend to use it in future only for good deeds."

"I am told by the peasants that even when they have put out the fire, it starts again once they have brought in the harvest. Can it not be put out once and for all?" asked Monkey.

"The fan must be waved forty-nine times in succession, then the fire will be put out for good."

Monkey took the fan once more and waved it as hard as he could forty-nine times in the direction of the Fire Mountain.

It began to rain heavily.

The fan did absolute marvels. Where there had been fire, the rain was particularly heavy and persistent, where there had been no fire, no rain fell and the sky was blue and clear.

Tripitaka and his disciples retired to

a spot where there had been no fire and avoided getting drenched.

They waited the whole night through, and only in the morning did they gather their packs together, saddle the little white horse and return the fan to the Yaksha.

"If I failed to return it to you, people would say I cannot keep my word," Monkey told her. "Here you are then, but mind you don't use it for any wickedness. You may go now."

The Yaksha accepted the fan, shrinking it to the size of a leaf and hiding it quickly in her mouth. Then she thanked the Monkey King and vanished. Later she changed her name and began to do good deeds.

Monkey, Pigsy and Sandy surrounded Tripitaka and started on their journey. They felt refreshed, the ground under their feet was cool. Early in the morning they crossed the Fire Mountain and set off towards the west.

In the Western Paradise

Tripitaka and his disciples went on and on until one day they finally arrived in India. This was truly a blessed land, quite different from all the others they had seen. Rare flowers and magic grasses grew everywhere, as well as ancient cypresses and silvery pines. Wherever they went, they came across kind, generous people, every family giving food to the passing monks. On every mountain there were many hermits; the prayers of worshipping pilgrims came from every wood.

Our pilgrims retired early every evening and started out again at break of dawn to continue their journey. After about a week they saw in front of them towers with high battlements. Pointing ahead with his whip, Tripitaka said: "What a fine place is this, Sun Wu-k'ung!"

"Why do you not dismount, Master?" answered Monkey. "We have reached our destination. This is the Supreme Buddha's citadel."

Full of wonder, Tripitaka got off his horse and stood in front of the palace gates. A young priest was waiting there, leaning against the gateway.

"Are you by any chance the pilgrims from the east, come to fetch the scriptures?" he called out to them.

Tripitaka tidied his clothes and looked up. Sun Wu-k'ung recognised the speaker at once and informed Tripitaka that it was the great Immortal of the Golden Halo from the Jade Truth Temple at the foot of the Providence Mountain, who had come out to meet them. At last Tripitaka realised that they were really in the Western Paradise. He stepped forward and made the Immortal a deep bow.

"So the holy monk is here at last," said the Immortal, smiling at him. "The Goddess of Compassion has misled me. Ten years ago she received orders from the Supreme Buddha to go to China and find someone who would come and fetch the scriptures. She told me the pilgrim would be here within two or three years. I have been waiting for many years now without seeing any sign of him. Little did I suspect you would come only today."

Tripitaka folded his hands and said: "I thank you most heartily, noble Immortal, for your patience."

All four now entered the temple, dragging their horse behind them.

Early next morning Tripitaka changed

into his embroidered robe, put his ceremonial cap on his head and picked up his staff before going into the temple to say goodbye to the Immortal, who told Tripitaka he would see him off. Monkey, however, claimed this was not necessary, as he knew the way.

Monkey led Tripitaka and the others up to the top of the Providence Mountain. They walked slowly, yet soon they saw the Voice of Thunder Temple some way above them. In a forest of silvery pines they came across a party of pious nuns, and in a cypress grove they met a group of monks. Tripitaka bowed low to them all, but the nuns and the monks greeted him with folded hands, saying: "Holy monk, it is not to us that you must pay homage. Wait until you have seen the Supreme Buddha, then come and greet us in the correct way."

Monkey smiled at this, and said: "Come, let us go and bow to those at the top."

Tripitaka strode on, trembling with excitement, with Monkey leading the way, until they reached the gates of the Voice of Thunder Temple. Four guardian gods came out to meet them.

"So your Reverence has at last arrived," they said.

"Your disciple Tripitaka has come at last," the reverend father replied, bowing and then turning towards the door.

"Kindly wait a second, your Reverence," one of the guardian gods halted him. "I must first announce you and only then can you come in."

The guardian god beckoned to a porter, instructing him to go and tell the guardians at the second gate that Tripitaka had arrived. They, in turn, announced his arrival at the third gate, which was guarded by holy monks having access to Buddha himself. As soon as they heard of Tripitaka's arrival, they hurried to the Hall of Majesty where they reported to the Supreme Buddha that the holy monk from the T'ang Empire had come for the scriptures. Father Buddha was very pleased by this news. He called to him the guardian gods, three thousand guardian spirits, eleven planets and eighteen temple patrons. They lined up in two rows in front of Buddha, who gave instructions for Tripitaka to be brought in to his presence.

When the pilgrims entered the Hall of Majesty, they first bowed to the Supreme Buddha and then to all the assembled Immortals. This they repeated three times. Then they knelt in front of Buddha and presented their passes to him. Buddha inspected them carefully before handing them back to Tripitaka. The monk bowed once again and said: "I, disciple Hsüan Tsang, have come by order of the Emperor of the great T'ang Empire, making the long journey to this sacred mountain in order to ask you for the true scriptures, which are to be the salvation of all mankind. May our Holy Father Buddha show us his favour and hand the scriptures over to us, so

that we may quickly return to our native land."

Buddha showed his compassion and said: "Your country lies far to the east of here. The soil there is fertile, and the land is populous and rich. But it is also full of wickedness, greed, murder, frivolity and lust, and deceit and falsehood have become firmly established. So wicked are the sins of the people that only the torments of Hell can make up for them. However, I have in my possession three baskets of scriptures which could save mankind from its bitter fate and take away from it all suffering."

Turning to two of the Immortals, Buddha went on: "Ananda and Kashyapa, take these four pilgrims to the jewel-studded tower and give them some food. After that, open the Treasury and select several scrolls from each of the three baskets of my scriptures and give them to our guests. May they bring eternal grace to the Eastern Empire."

The two Immortals did as Buddha instructed them, taking the pilgrims up into the tower, which was so full of treasures that Tripitaka and his disciples hardly knew where to look first. The guardian gods quickly prepared a feast — of delicacies, fruits and juices unknown in the world of mortals. Tripitaka and his companions bowed once more in honour of Buddha and sat down to eat with an easy mind.

When Annanda and Kashyapa had finished feasting the four pilgrims, they led them to the Treasury. As soon as they entered, they were dazzled by the rays of a miraculous light which enveloped everything inside the room. A pale-coloured mist filled the room from floor to ceiling, entering every nook and cranny.

Ananda and Kashyapa showed Tripitaka all the scriptures, and he carefully studied their titles.

"Holy monk," said Ananda and Kashyapa, "no doubt you have brought us some fine gift from the far eastern land. Kindly show it to us now, so that we may hand over the scriptures to you."

"Your impoverished disciple has come a very long way, and for that reason has

brought nothing with him," replied Tripitaka.

"Well, would you believe it!" exclaimed Ananda and Kashyapa. "So you expect us to let you have the scriptures for nothing, and our children can go hungry as far as you are concerned!"

Seeing that they were being awkward and did not wish to hand over the scriptures, Monkey was seized with rage and cried: "Come, reverend father, let's complain to Buddha! He will give us the scriptures himself."

"What are you shouting about?" Ananda asked him crossly. "Where do you think you are, that you dare to flaunt your bad manners in our presence? Come here and take your scriptures!"

Pigsy and Sandy overcame their rage and soothed Monkey. Then they all stepped forward to receive the scriptures, which they stuffed, scroll after scroll, into one of their packs, putting it on their horse's back. They made two huge bundles of the rest of their luggage, and Pigsy and Sandy took charge of one each. They left the Treasury, bowed to Buddha and thanked him, and passed through the temple gates, bowing twice to every lesser Buddha and god they happened to meet. Finally they passed out of the main gate and bowed to the groups of monks and nuns; and, having taken leave of them all, went down the mountain as fast as they were able, to the main road.

But let us return for a moment to the

Treasury. The Buddha Torch-bearer was in the habit of looking in there occasionally. He had been present in one corner of the room while the scriptures were being handed over and, unseen by the others, had seen and heard everything. Ananda and Kashyapa, irritated at not having been given any gifts by the pilgrims, had revenged themselves by handing over empty scrolls without any writing on them. The Buddha Torch-bearer mounted a whirlwind and flew out over the gates of the Voice of Thunder Temple, going as fast as the magic forces could carry him.

The pilgrims were walking along when they suddenly felt the strong blow of a gust of wind. It hit them so fast they were unable to get out of the way. A roll of thunder followed, and then a hand reached down from the sky and snatched the scriptures from the horse's back. Tripitaka was overcome with horror, and he wailed and beat his chest in despair. Pigsy tried to grip the mysterious hand but missed and fell. Sandy clung to their luggage, but Monkey soared up into the air in pursuit of the thief. Seeing him coming up behind him, the Buddha Torch-bearer grew afraid that Monkey would not wait for any explanation and would hurt him with his cudgel. He therefore ripped open the pack and threw the scriptures to the ground.

When Monkey saw the pack opening and the wind carrying the scrolls down to earth, he abandoned the chase and lowered his cloud to look for the scriptures. He was quickly joined by Pigsy and together they collected all the scrolls and took them back to Tripitaka.

"Dear disciples," Tripitaka said with tears in his eyes, "who would have thought that even here, in this paradise, evil demons would lie in wait for us."

Sandy began to roll up the unravelled scrolls. Looking more closely at one of them he discovered to his amazement that it was quite blank, without anything written on it. Horrified, he handed it to Tripitaka, saying: "Look, Master, there's not a word on this scroll!"

Monkey quickly examined another scroll, only to find that it too had no writing. The same was the case with a third one which Pigsy looked at.

"Examine every one of them!" said Tripitaka.

None of the scrolls contained any scriptures — they were just blank paper.

"What a catastrophe for our people!" sighed Tripitaka. "What use are these scriptures to anyone?"

Monkey now knew exactly what had happened.

"I know who is behind this, reverend father," he said. "Those two scoundrels, Ananda and Kashyapa, gave these empty scrolls to us because we brought them no gifts. We must go back at once and lay charges against them for fraud and blackmail."

"Yes, yes, serve them right!" cried Pigsy. "Let's go and charge them!"

The pilgrims hurried back up the mountain, going straight to the temple. All the Immortals bowed to them with folded hands.

"Have you come to exchange your scriptures, holy monk?"

Tripitaka nodded and returned the greetings. The guardians at the gates did not stop them, and they were shown into the Hall of Majesty.

"Buddha!" cried Monkey. "In spite of all the traps laid for us by demons and the other hardships we had to put up with on the way, we came from the Eastern Empire to pay homage to you. You gave orders for the scriptures to be handed over to us, but Ananda and Kashyapa, angry at not receiving any bribe, worked together to cheat us and gave us nothing but empty scrolls. I ask you: what use are such scriptures to anyone? I hope that Buddha will punish them."

"There is really no need to shout," said Buddha, smiling. "I have already been told that they demanded bribes. However, true scriptures are not given away just like that, you know. You came here with empty hands and were accordingly given empty scrolls."

Nevertheless, he ordered Ananda and Kashyapa to go to the Treasury once more and bring the real scriptures. This was to be the pilgrims' reward for having undertaken so long and hazardous a journey.

Ananda and Kashyapa took the pilgrims to the Treasury a second time, again asking for some gift.

Though Tripitaka had nothing of any value, it suddenly occurred to him that he might perhaps give them his golden alms

bowl. Telling Sandy to bring it, he held it out to the two Immortals in both of his hands.

"I am but a poor monk and have undertaken this long pilgrimage without thinking to bring gifts. This bowl was a personal gift to me from the Chinese Emperor, who told me to use it when begging for alms on the way. Please accept it as a token of my great esteem and respect. When I get back home and report to the Emperor, he will send you many rich gifts. Therefore I beseech you not to scorn this humble offering and give me the true scriptures in exchange, so that I may not disappoint the expectations of His Majesty the Chinese Emperor and that my pilgrimage should not have been in vain."

Ananda took the bowl with a contemptuous grin. All the servants and guardians right down to the last kitchen-boy doubled over with laughter, slapping each other's backs, pointing with their fingers and turning up their noses.

"The shameless, grasping frauds!" they cried. "They'll squeeze even a poor monk like this one."

The two Immortals reddened to the roots of their hair, but they did not give back the bowl. Kashyapa picked up the scrolls and handed them to Tripitaka.

"Look at them very carefully, disciples, so that we are not taken in once more," Tripitaka said.

They looked at one scroll after the other, and found they were all covered with writing. All told, there were five thousand and forty-eight of them, making one basketful. They rolled them up carefully and put them on the little horse's back. Those that were left over they tied in a bundle which was given to Pigsy to carry. Sandy saw to the rest of their luggage. Monkey took the horse by the bridle, Tripitaka picked up his staff, put his embroidered cap on his head and tidied his robe. Happy and light at heart, they took their leave of the Supreme Buddha and started out on their return journey to China.